The Killer Coin

by

Doc Macomber

PublishAmerica
Baltimore

First printing

ISBN: 1-4137-0045-4
PUBLISHED BY PUBLISHAMERICA, LLLP
www.publishamerica.com
Baltimore

Printed in the United States of America

DEDICATION

For Wade and Ada Lee Weekly,
who would have been proud...

ACKNOWLEDGMENTS

In the course of any writer's life, there are a number of people who, whether they know it or not, often influence or articulate a writer's quest. To those individuals or organizations who contributed to my growth as a writer, I thank you. I hope that you will find pleasure in knowing that despite specific mentioning, you too were responsible for my success.

In addition, I wish to express my deepest gratitude to the following: Columbia Motorcycle for giving me the time off to write; Tsgt Mike Vu who shared his personal story with me; former Marine Capt. Bill Montgomery who introduced me to the treasure hunt; to those tireless readers: Glynis, Laury, Bill, Karen, Lenny, Joni, Jimmy and Suzanne, who gave all, and asked little in return, and whose comments and suggestions helped this book greatly; Karl Gillepsie of Diversity Design Studio for designing the book jacket. And lastly, to Birdie – my sweetheart – a smart, funny, talented tattooist and painter, whose editing skills, and numerous suggestions and loving support, ultimately made this book possible.

"There are strange things done in the midnight sun
by the men who moil for gold..."
~ Robert Service

CHAPTER 1

The withering heat of Bourbon Street pressed him deeper into the narrow alley. His sanguine demeanor belied his frustration and rage. Sweat trickled. His lips parted and heat burned down his throat. Finally, she arrived and worked her way through the milling crowd outside the Hotel Montelanne. He leaned forward as she moved toward the entrance and displayed her badge. His world flashed white as his pupils narrowed. An arrow of light from the gold shield had found him. When his vision cleared, she was gone....

* * *

The French Quarter housed many elegant turn-of-the-century hotels like the Montelanne. The lobby of marble, woven lavender, and blue twill seemed to covet the sweet floral scent of bougainvillea. The gilded walls arched toward a gaggle of chandeliers and sparkling lights. Detective Gates figured the rooms started around two bills and went up from there. Smiling, she remembered an old beau explaining the art of seduction: "The better the hotel, the better the sex."

Across the lobby she saw a uniformed officer step into the elevator and hold the door.

"Hello Dorene." It was Reese from the 83rd. "Where's the new partner?" Reese needed a shave and stunk of cheap cigars. Gates stepped up to the control panel and punched the 14 button, though it was already lit. Her silence echoed in the slowly ascending elevator.

The activity centered around the west wing where several firemen were calling it quits. The uniform assigned to watch the victim's door yawned, folded up a newspaper, and told Gates the details. His name was Franklin, from the 36th Precinct. It had been a false alarm. No real flames, just a smoldering single white female dead on the floor. The maid had been in the vicinity and responded to the alarm. He had called it in. Forensics had been notified.

Gates pulled on a pair of rubber gloves. Where the hell was Hill anyway?

"I hear it's pretty grizzly in there," Franklin warned as he swapped places with Reese at the door.

Gates raised her finger to her lips. “Don’t spoil it for me, Franklin.”

Gates switched on her flashlight and tried the wall switch. Nothing. Apparently the fire department had killed power to the main breaker. She shined her beam of light along the plaster wall. No electrical panel here. Moving toward the tunnel of yellow light, she stepped into the foyer and froze as the curl of pungent smoke hit her.

“What’s cookin’?” The voice from behind startled her.

Gates glared over her shoulder at her partner, Bruce Hill. He was out of breath and panting like an excited Pekingese. *Only a rookie would take the stairs*, thought Gates.

“See if you can find the breaker box,” Gates instructed. Hill patted down the wall. Gates was no epicurean, but she knew the odor wasn’t right. Now she became aware of a strange crackling sound – like the sound of cicadas droning? *Nah, too early.* The hiss was low, indecipherable and insistent. “You hear that?”

The lights switched on. They waited while their eyes adjusted.

“Holy Jesus!”

CHAPTER 2

She was naked except for what remained of a melted negligee coiled like a snake around her mid-section. A hot iron had sizzled through tissue and bone, leaking a darkening pool of fluid onto the smoking carpet.

Gates snapped out of it. "Unplug it." She pointed to the cord. She took out a handkerchief, covered her nose and mouth, and stepped back, the rancid smoke causing her eyes to water.

Hill yanked the cord from the wall.

A clouded blue eye stared out accusingly from the twisted face. The stench of burnt and decaying tissue hung like death's cruel veil concealing the image of the iron still branding its deep imprint into the fleshy part of the woman's abdomen. Gates swallowed hard.

Hill opened a window, allowing a fresh breeze to blow in. "I think I'm gonna puke." Hill moaned.

This was Hill's first homicide.

Gates instructed, "Check the other rooms. See if you can find some ID."

How many scenes had she been in where an innocent victim had taken their last breath? Each death different, but similar in its effect. It incised a piece of your soul.

Standing by the open window, Gates breathed in the cool night air. Distant lights from the Spanish Plaza shined through the sky heavy with smog – a rare glimmer of remote hope that someday things would change.

Gates dug out her notepad and began the slow, calculated inventory of the room's personal effects. With the exception of the overturned ironing board, and a nearby glass lying on its side next to a small wet stain on the carpet, the room looked intact. No obvious signs of a struggle.

Gates figured the woman had been facing the ironing board when the accident occurred. She fell backwards, pulling the hot iron with her. The body showed no obvious cuts, scratches, bite marks, abrasions, or bruising; evidence often associated with rape cases. She stooped over and smelled the damp stain beside the overturned glass. Scotch. Single malt and expensive.

Gates slid a gloved finger beneath the melted slip, searching for possible traces of semen.

Hill walked up packing an eel-skin wallet. He glanced down at the woman's raw, contorted face and then diverted his gaze, examining the picture on the airline's identification card.

"She wasn't bad looking," Hill commented.

Gates guessed the victim was in her late twenties, maybe earlier thirties. It was difficult to get a feel of how the woman looked under normal circumstances. Now, most of the tissue had been damaged, pulled taut under the intense heat like latex under a heat lamp. Gates noted the nails, manicured and painted by skilled hands. The skin around the nails and toenails had lost its pinkish color; common during the early stages of rigor mortis.

Gates picked up the victim's right hand.

"Shouldn't we wait for Forensics?" Hill asked.

Gates ignored the comment and inspected beneath the nails, looking for any traces of epidermis. Even through rubber gloves, Gates could feel the victim's contouring in the cold hand. As if the hand was Gates's window into the deceased's soul – a subjective history carved in skin. That had once been just a lot of metaphysical horseshit, but that was before logging ten years in Homicide in the Voodoo Queen's city.

Hill, busying himself in the closet, broke the silence. He pulled out a freshly pressed airline's uniform.

"My bet, she was getting ready for work," gesturing as he went along. "She irons her uniform and hangs it back up. Goes over to the ironing board. Maybe picks up her drink, takes a sip or two, sets the glass down and feels light-headed. Maybe she passes out and strikes her head on the floor. The iron goes with her, topples over onto her. She's either unconscious or too out of it to know what's happened. I had an uncle once that had low blood sugar. When he drank alcohol he'd pass out colder than a cucumber."

Hill returned the uniform to the closet. "You don't buy it, do you? Well, maybe she had a heart attack? Or maybe someone knocked her over, made it look like she fell? Or, maybe someone else ironed her uniform so we'd think she did it? You know how weird these sons-of-bitches can be."

Gates ignored the fact Hill was inexperienced and quick to form opinions. She needed quiet. She knew the evidence was in front of her.

"She doesn't fit the profile of a cardiac arrest," Gates reasoned. "It's possible she fainted...or had a mild seizure. I don't see any evidence of an overdose. You brought up a good point though. Maybe she's diabetic. Check for a medical tag."

Gates leaned toward the victim, ignoring the overpowering odor.

Something shiny and gold glistened on her neck. "I see something."

She lifted the victim's hair back from her neck. A tiny metallic face beckoned. Pulling a pair of well-worn tweezers from her personal tool kit, she attempted to lift the metal from the neck, but it held fast.

"There's marked indentations in the skin," Gates noted, staring down at where the skin had folded around the coin like a orchid enclosing on a dew drop. Maybe the heat from the iron...she risked damaging crucial evidence if she continued. Then she noticed a smudge – a possible fingerprint on the patina of the coin.

Gates put her tweezers away. "I don't think she fainted," Gates added. "See beneath the ligature, where the chain goes around the neck? There's bruising and discoloration. Let's look at the eyes. Pull back the lids." Hill hesitated, all thumbs, like a reluctant schoolboy conducting his first dissection. Losing patience, Gates pushed him aside. She pulled back the left eyelid. "See the small spotty hemorrhages? It's presumptive evidence of death by asphyxia. This was no accident."

CHAPTER 3

Andrews Air Force Base is located in Maryland about ten miles southeast of Washington, D.C. The 4300 acre installation first opened during WWII. During its 60 years it had grown like many small towns across America to include two eighteen-hole golf courses, a skeet range, a twenty-four lane bowling alley, tennis courts and three outdoor swimming pools. It is the home of Air Force One. It is also where 27,000 active-duty personnel and their families live and work. And like many closed communities, it has its rules and its secrets.

Special Investigator, Staff Sergeant Jack Vu, rode his canary yellow PX 200E Vespa past the 33rd Field Investigations Squadron Building, Headquarters AFOSI, and figured he'd take the shortcut along a dirt trail that lead directly to the fairway. The path was wide enough for his motorbike and an occasional wary squirrel. He had spent his youth weaving in and out of chaotic traffic in Saigon on a bike just like this.

The brilliant blue sky stung his eyes and his close-cropped dark hair caught the warm autumn air. A few fat robins chirped in the treetops lining the trail. Even now, twenty years later, he had the urge to hunker down in the grass and aim his slingshot at the wild birds.

For all the negatives of reporting to work on a Saturday, in some sick recess of Vu's brain, he was very curious. Why had he been picked for this assignment? Was it his Vietnamese background? His linguistic skills? Or something else?

As he neared the fairway, pockets of dust kicked up under his chrome wheels and he shuddered at the thought at having to clean the bike again.

He'd started off the morning bright and early giving the scooter a good washing, even though it didn't need it. He'd entertained the notion of washing the neighbor's Australian sheepdog. The dog was starting to emit a pungent odor which aggravated his allergies. Some of his countrymen would have simply put the dog on a spit.

Vu parked his scooter alongside the fairway and pulled out a small pair of binoculars. His slight five foot three stature belied his agility and strength. He had common Vietnamese features: broad cheekbones, large fleshy lips, dark eyes. With the exception of his ears, which stuck out from his small head like little flapjacks, Vu looked like any other guy you would see in China Town.

A few minutes later, looming over the hill from the second hole and kicking up a pollen cloud the size of a hot air balloon, careened a golf cart. Branch Chief Wheylicke sat behind the wheel wearing a neon yellow knit shirt and baggy pants. A sun visor squeezed his stubby gray flattop. Beside him sat a fit, slender man, wearing an embroidered cotton shirt, plaid golfer's pants, and cleated shoes. Vu barely recognized the Branch Chief out of uniform, or his companion, the former Commander of the AFOSI 52nd Field Investigation Squadron in Ankara, Turkey.

Vu repressed his surprise in seeing his old mentor and wondered what he was doing in Maryland.

"Hello, sirs," Vu announced, as the two men climbed out of the cart and gathered up their clubs. Both his superiors were out of uniform, but he nevertheless felt it was his duty to salute.

"Hello, Vu," his former commanding officer said, dropping the formality. "How goes the battle?"

"Adequately, sir." The colonel stared at Vu's Italian cycle.

"Yours, Sergeant?"

"All one-hundred sixteen kilos, sir."

"I'm a Harley nut, myself," he said and faced the major. "You ride, Major?"

The Branch Chief scratched himself. "Never owned one."

"Well, I can't say I'd buy the new V-Rod. Little wild for my taste. Looks like a mock version of Boeing's X-plane."

Vu looked at the two men. Sweat rolled off the Branch Chief's brow as flies buzzed overhead. Vu removed his leather jacket.

Turning toward Morgan, Vu extended his hand. "What brings you to Maryland, Colonel?"

Morgan boasted a million dollar smile that could win over a constipated judge at the Westminster Kennel Club.

"I've been transferred to Maxwell War College, so I stopped by for a friendly game of golf."

It was the old cat and mouse game. Give nothing away. Take what you can. Vu was adept at the game – so was the colonel.

"Come by the campus and pay a visit sometime."

"I will, sir."

"Now gentlemen, I do believe I hear the beckoning call of the third hole."

As the colonel snatched his favorite driver, he discreetly nodded to Vu. Something passed between the men to which Branch Chief Wheylicke hadn't been privy. The Branch Chief, absorbed in deciding which iron to select for his next shot, dropped his clubs back into his bag and approached Vu. There was business to discuss, and Vu assumed his former commander knew about it. Morgan was giving Wheylicke the professional courtesy to inform his soldier in private.

Vu sensed Wheylicke disliked him on sight. Many men of Wheylicke's age had developed an inbred distrust of the Vietnamese after Vietnam. It was well disguised at times, but always lurking under the surface. A lion's jaw waiting to snap closed. Vu knew the ideology traveled in both directions.

"I'll cut to the chase, Sergeant. You ever hear of a Special Ops man named Lyman?"

"Lyman?"

"Staff Sergeant, Jim D. Lyman?" Branch Chief echoed.

Everybody had heard a version of the story: Two years ago, a secret team of Special Ops dropped down inside Beirut – a classified mission kept from the American public. The whole thing turned to shit. In the heat of the conflict, one man got left behind. Jim Lyman. Vu knew the story had been a cover. But this early in the game he wasn't letting on.

"He's MIA, sir," Vu replied.

"For twenty-four months. He's also a former kick-ass Navy Seal who transferred to the 42nd Air Force Special Ops squadron, earned a Distinguished Cross, and was twice recommended for a silver star. He's not a man to mess with."

"Has Lyman's status changed, sir?"

"In a manner of speaking, Sergeant."

"Sir?"

"It's mere speculation at this juncture. But the man may have reappeared in the U.S."

"AWOL?"

"Speculation, Sergeant. That's the key word. AWOL or not, it's all fuckin' speculation."

It was the spy game again. "Okay, sir," Vu said, "I will just speculate."

Branch Chief glanced over his shoulder. Vu assumed he didn't want others hearing what was coming next. "Yesterday, I received a call from the New Orleans Police Department. A Detective Gates informed me a print matching that of Sergeant Lyman was discovered by their forensic's unit at a crime scene."

"A thumb print, sir? No other prints?"

"Not a one, according to the detective."

"Unusual. What was the nature of the crime?"

"Murder."

"Did Lyman kill the victim with his thumb?"

"No, Sergeant. His print was found on a coin."

Vu scratched his head. "He killed someone with a coin?"

Branch Chief nodded. "Sergeant, I want you on the next available flight to New Orleans. We've got to nip this thing in the bud before the press gets wind of it."

Vu pulled from his pocket a small clear bottle containing green tablets. A Chinese herb mixture. He popped a few tablets into his mouth and closed the bottle.

"You okay?"

"Parasites, sir."

Branch Chief studied him. "When you get back, you should get that checked out."

"Yes, sir. Anything else, sir?"

"See Detective Gates with the City of New Orleans Police Department, Homicide Division ASAP. It's all in the file."

"Do I relay my findings to the Judge Advocate's Office or to you?"

"To me, Sergeant. Everything runs through my office. I'll see that it finds the proper channel." The Branch Chief looked Vu hard in the eye. Vu bowed his head.

"The colonel recommended you for this assignment. He indicated that you're our kind of man. That you know how to be discreet with whatever information you discover."

Vu paled as the connections lined up in his mind.

"I will do my best, sir," Vu said. Vu cleared his throat. "Sir, I apologize in advance if I'm about to be impertinent. Why would Sergeant Lyman – a decorated war hero – fail to report to his old command?"

"His health could have deteriorated. He's been MIA for quite a while. It may have affected his mental faculties. At any rate, I'm not convinced they've found his thumb print. Mixups have occurred. God knows, the government has made its share of blunders."

"Yes, sir."

"Sergeant, at this point, we know dick. But the whole matter could blow up in our face and be an embarrassment to the military. Don’t let that happen. Understand?”

Vu’s stomach growled.

“Betas has your orders.”

CHAPTER 4

The door to Betas' office was open. Vu entered and observed the major's chair had not been moved since the janitor had mopped the floor the previous evening. Across the room, a half-pot of coffee smoldered on a tarnished hotpad. The room also smelled of something sweet. Perfume?

Vu sneezed. He pulled out a handkerchief, blew his nose, dried his eyes. Then he heard it – a barely audible grunting coming from an adjoining office.

"Betas!" he called out. "It's Sgt. Vu." The noise stopped. Vu waited, listened, and then heard a cry.

Vu hurried into the next room. Airman Julie Betas, a.k.a "War Dog", aka the Branch Chief's personal assistant, was down on all fours doing pushups. Beads of sweat glistened on her bushy brunette eyebrows.

Struggling to pump out one last rep, she dropped to the floor, panting. She rolled over and lifted her flushed face. "Hello, Jack," she uttered between breaths. Her eyes were as big as sand-dollars. "I finally did it."

Vu helped the young recruit to her feet.

"Did what?" he asked.

"I'm scheduled for my annual fitness evaluation next week."

"Has the Aikido helped?"

"Very much. You were right. I should've started years ago."

"Take it easy, Betas. There's plenty of time. Passing the yearly fitness test is one thing, mastering the art of Aikido is another."

Betas' eyes lit up. "Let me show you something..."

Vu lowered his eyes. "I need my orders."

"It can wait," Betas barked.

Betas moved to the center of the room. "C'mere, Jack," she said between breaths, motioning for him to join her. Vu watched Betas drop down into a low martial arts stance, plant her feet, and raise her fists like an amateur boxer. Betas looked a bit awkward, Vu thought. But she had the basics down. What she lacked in technique she made up for in enthusiasm.

"C'mon!" Betas goaded him, her eyes eager and alert. "Come at me!"

Vu sighed. "As you wish." Effortlessly, Vu, like a sullen Cobra with deadly intentions, slid forward, penetrated Betas' guard, and struck the kidney.

However, lucky for her, Vu had only brushed an open palm across her side. More as a wake up call, than a desire to inflict pain. Nonetheless, Betas stood her ground. Vu figured he'd give Betas another shot.

Frustrated, Betas parried – locking Vu's arm with a clumsy Judo-like maneuver, thrusting her knotty hip out, and flipping him in the air. Vu landed on the floor, stunned. His eyes rolled back in his head.

Betas leaned down. "Are you okay, Jack?"

A stupid grin appeared.

"Your style lacks grace but it's effective." He beamed.

Betas proudly puffed out her chest. "You've created a monster, Jack. Don't give up on me now. Let's go again..."

Vu declined. "No time. Now may I have my orders?"

"I'm in my moment of glory and you wanna talk business?"

"I'm afraid so."

Betas looked disappointed. She helped Vu to his feet and reached down and brushed his pants. Vu quickly stepped out of her reach. Betas huffed across the room, removed the manilla envelope holding Vu's orders from her desk, and flung them toward him. Vu caught the package before it struck the floor.

"You win merits for your delivery," Vu said.

"I don't trust our new CO. What's your hit?"

"He's our Commander."

"How ethical of you."

Vu ignored the comment and examined his orders. He knew he was dodging the subject but discretion had become his way of life. Betas knew this about him. But she was pushy. A typical Jersey brat. Vu didn't mind it, really. He enjoyed Betas. She was a hard worker and his friend. Vu looked upon Betas with the affection of a sister. But even though they both worked for OSI, shared an occasional movie, their beliefs and backgrounds were worlds apart.

Betas snapped, "Your flight leaves tonight at six-thirty-five. You're booked direct to New Orleans. Window seat, near the restroom, as you prefer. I didn't book a return. The commander thinks you'll be gone at least a week, maybe more..."

"Could you do me a favor?" Vu asked.

Betas pressed on. "If you're going to request preliminaries on Lyman, it's already done. The major requested a complete dossier from DIS and MAJCOM. I've included these documents with your orders. You'll find the information attached to your travel voucher. Try not to lose your receipts this time, please."

"You're exceptional, not to mention, deadly," Vu teased.

"And you're full of crap."

Vu bowed his head in a mock show of respect. "It is my duty."

"You'll like New Orleans." Betas smirked. "It resembles your neck of the woods. It's crowded like Saigon, humid as hell, and the streets smell like rotting Kim Chee."

Behind the smile, Vu noted the seriousness in Betas' eyes, but let it go. Betas stretched out her back. "Vu – why do I like you?"

"Because I'm humble. Or, perhaps it's that I allow you to water my bamboo while I'm away?"

"Shit!" Betas exclaimed. "I gotta go into that greenhouse you call an apartment?"

Vu casually pointed toward the window. Beyond the clean glass, parked in the lot behind the building, stood Vu's shiny new scooter. Betas beamed at the imagine of freedom on two wheels....

"Deal," Betas uttered. "Oh, I spoke with Detective Gates in New Orleans. She's expecting you, but she doesn't sound too thrilled about it. She was either having a very bad day. Or she's a royal bitch."

"You're filling me with such anticipation."

"How often do I water your weeds?"

"Two gallons per plant, every other day. The palms will be fine for a week. If I'm not back—"

Betas interrupted, "You have palms now? Where the hell do you sleep?"

"In the arms of Buddha!"

"Right, Jack." Betas held out her hand. "Keys?"

Absently, he dropped them on her desk. His mind was already moving back in time to another war and the soldier left behind.

CHAPTER 5

The 8mm projector was twenty-five years old and made a squeak, squeak, squeak sound that reminded Gates she needed to take her Cadillac into the garage and have the brakes checked.

Gates threaded the next strip of film in behind the lens, following the directions and the illustrated diagram on the projector cover. Through her sexual affiliation with a certain former Air Force Reserve Recruiter, Gates had managed to obtain several outdated recruitment films taken during Vietnam. Old footage of the USAF's Special Ops Group in action. Her friend had assured her that despite the film's age, the footage was authentic and would have educational value. And he would be happy to supply her with any number of films on a regular basis. Gates wasn't certain the sex had been that good.

While window shopping on Dauphine Street that morning she spotted the old projector in a pawn shop and persuaded the owner to rent her the machine for an afternoon. She lugged the heavy projector back to the precinct, up flights of narrow stairs, and was panting like a chronic smoker when one of her co-workers, Sergeant Packwood, the duty desk officer, offered a hand.

"Haven't seen one of these pieces of shit in a long time." Sgt. Packwood said, kicking open Gates' office door.

"Thanks, Dicky," Gates said, and dumped the projector onto her cluttered desk. "I've got it now."

"If you're goin' to watch porn, Dorene dear, you ought to invite the rest of us." Sgt. Packwood grinned and headed out the door.

Funny. The whole business of watching old war footage made her feel kind of horny. She didn't like to admit it, but even recruitment films made her wet. Same buzz she got watching those old black and white X-rated films she used to sit through when she worked Vice. There was one particular theater, a sleazy one down in the French Quarter, where she busted that psycho for jerking off in a public telephone booth...what was that perv's name again?

Her thinking drifted to more mundane matters. Like the knowledge the feds would show up eventually regarding the Marken Case, and she needed to remain one step ahead of them. When she had found out Lyman was with

Air Force Special Ops, she started to do her homework. Being unprepared before had been her nemesis.

She turned on the projector and stared at the fuzzy-edged, flickering images displayed on the wall. She threw back some cold, nasty coffee and watched the film. A husky soldier rappelled from a hovering helicopter under heavy gunfire and made his way into the thick wet jungle. *Damn...* Gates closed her eyes and played it back a second time. Then a third. *Damn...*

Then her own dark version materialized. The film and her past merged. Her counselor would have been pissed had she known what Gates was doing – soliciting dangerous, sexual imagery – a big throbbing, thrusting hunk of rotating steel slipping into the big deep blue. Flesh sliding down, down, down into the warm murky bed of moist grass. Body piercing armament cracking open the earth.

She wiped a spot of perspiration from her forehead. She sat up in her chair panting, shut down the film, leaned forward and put her head between her legs. *Control your breathing*, she recited, *control your thoughts...*

After a few minutes she turned the projector back on and was thankful the action footage was over and focused now on basic entry requirements of the Special Ops Squadron. She listened as the narrator explained:

"Selection is limited and begins at Basic Training. New recruits undergo three tortuous, grueling hours of physical abilities and stamina testing at Lackland Air Force Base, which eliminates roughly 70 percent of all enlistees. Only the exceptionally fit and toughest survive. Then, the real training begins. A twelve week journey into hell..."

Gates had done some pretty dangerous things in her life. But she didn't think she was cut out to jump from a perfectly good airplane into the belly of exploding shrapnel and enemy gunfire. Plucked from the sky like a Mallard during hunting season. No, this was not her idea of fun.

It looked dangerous. It was dangerous goddammit. You'd need testicles as big as cantaloupes. And God had passed over her.

The film rattled to a stop. Gates got up and turned on the overhead light. She felt a little queasy. Here she thought she had been watching a recruitment film, then a porno film, but in the end she had found herself drawn back into the war of her own life. Tears pooled.

Gates grabbed a handful of Kleenex, blew her nose two or three times, straightened her fucking bra for the fourth time. Her black knit sweater had bunched up. She pulled it down below her beltline. She slipped on her cowboy boots. It had been more comfortable watching the films in stocking feet.

And with the exception of a loose eyelash floating on her cheek, she was ready to re-enter the world.

About then the door to her private office flung open. And in walked a short, fat cop named Riley from Vice. Riley was an inconsiderate son-of-a-bitch and a lousy cop. Her counselor had warned she'd have to work on not being so judgmental. That would be tough where that fat fuck Riley was concerned.

Standing behind Riley was a dwarf. Well, not actually a dwarf. He was a short Asian man wearing a conservative dark gray suit, white shirt, and black tie. Gates didn't recognize him. Just another little beady-eyed bastard who'd immigrated to the U.S. and was sucking up all the good positions within the ranks.

"Gates, you got a visitor."

Riley departed in the same tactless manner with which he arrived. Gates tossed her used Kleenex in the trash can and stepped out from behind her desk. The stranger held out his hand, a small hand with long straight fingers.

"Hello Detective," he said, "I'm Sgt. Jack Vu. I work with the Maryland Office of Special Investigations. I believe you are expecting me?"

Gates hated the bastard already. But since she had just handled her stinky feet, it seemed appropriate she shake hands with the man. He hooked her hand like it was a baseball glove and gave it a tug.

"I spoke with your Branch Chief yesterday," Gates commented, pulling on a black leather jacket. At least his handshake was not weak or clammy like she'd anticipated.

"Yes, I am under Major Wheylicke's command. Did I interrupt something important?" Vu glanced down at her messy desk. Documents spread out everywhere. Film cases. Books.

Gates glanced down too. *Shit!*

"I was conducting research," Gates acknowledged and discreetly slid the film canister lid beneath a stack of loose papers and rearranged a few secondary items. She did not want Vu to know she was versed on the USAF.

Vu's eye swept the certificates on the wall. His orbs turned to coal. "This case is a priority for us," he said. "When can we get started?"

Gates figured the Air Force would send some snot-nosed 2nd Lieutenant fresh out of college who couldn't hold his liquor, but would at least have a cute ass. She was unprepared for this midget. She just hoped he would stay the hell out of her way and not eat Kim Chee around her.

"Let's get a few things straight first. I won't hesitate to use my authority here. This is local jurisdiction and your office has no legal standing. Cooperate and I'll see that you are provided with the necessary documents and information to keep the government off both our backs. Fuck me, and you'll be on your way to Maryland with your dick in a splint. That clear?"

Vu didn't blink an eye. "You have a unique way of expressing yourself, Detective Gates. It is a weakness of mine to always start from the end and work forward. Did I say you may call me, Jack? It would be better if you viewed me as one of your peers."

"That's not going to happen, sweetcakes," Gates replied. "I've been burned by every federal agent that ever walked through that door. I've been laughed at, demoted, rejected, and downright beaten to the punch one too many times to go limp dick now. The only reason I'm cooperating is because of a certain captain who signs my paycheck. Understand? So if you want to tag along and make your nice little inquiries, be my guest. But don't get in my way. We can either butt heads or find a way to get through the next couple of days without incident. It doesn't really matter to me either way."

Vu reached into his front pocket and removed his small vial of tiny green pills. He counted out eight into his hand and dropped them into his mouth. Dry swallowing, one caught in his throat. Gagging, he circled the desk like a pigeon looking for a place to poop. He took hold of the mug of cold coffee and drank. His eyes were watering. He swallowed hard, gagging.

Gates stepped back behind her desk. "You OK?" she asked, amused by the little man's suffering.

The flush faded from Vu's face. He stared into the cup. "I'm fine. Continue, please."

"Hell, now I lost my train of thought." It took her a moment to collect herself.

"As I see it these are the facts: One, you want to review the evidence and lab results from our forensics unit. Two, you want to revisit the crime scene and gather your own opinions of what happened that night. Three, you want to determine the method and manner with which Lyman picked his target. And four, you want to know if our office has established a sound motive for the crime. That about it?"

Vu twitched his nose, thinking. His eyes were still watering. This cluttered office had aggravated his allergies.

"If you don't mind, I'd like some tea now, and then I'd like to review the forensic evidence."

"The department has not been able to get a copy of Sgt. Lyman's military records. A subpoena would help. But it's not forthcoming."

"I would assume his records would be public domain."

"Our criminalist doesn't agree."

"Then I will make an inquiry for you."

"In that case I'll allow you to examine the evidence."

Gates stomped out of her office. Vu followed. Gates shouted across the room. "Hill!"

From a small cubicle by the window, Hill raised his head and rubbed his eyes.

"Show our little friend, Sgt. Vu, to the lunch room. And afterwards, dump him at Forensics. He'll want to see the Marken file."

Hill rolled out from behind his desk, banging his knee on a filing cabinet. "C'mon, Sergeant. This way," he said, limping. Gates imagined a stripper would show more enthusiasm receiving a smile as a tip.

Vu frowned. "You are leaving, Detective?"

"Relax," she said. "New Orleans doesn't come alive until after happy hour. You may be hot to trot now but I need some lunch."

Vu offered, "I'm on an expense account."

"How nice."

Vu gave her his best innocent smile but it failed to fracture the stone-cold face glaring at him. He stood in the center of the room and watched the formidable iron maiden leave.

Hill said, "You can lead that horse to water but you can't make her piss."

Vu used a lobby drinking fountain. Hill stood over his shoulder waiting on the little man. "Don't let Gates get to you. I think she's got a woody between her legs."

Vu poured a cup of hot water from the coffee machine in the break room and pulled a green tea bag from his inside pocket. He pulled out a small complementary packet of honey he'd taken from the plane and squeezed it into his porcelain mug. Hill stuck a few quarters into a Coke machine and hit the button. A plastic bottle of Coke popped out the bottom. Hill unscrewed the top and soda geysered out onto his shirt.

"Shit!" Hill uttered. "How do you figure they can send a man to the moon but they can't design a pop that don't piss on ya?"

"You could drink tea."

"I'd rather drink from a toilet."

Vu studied Hill's face. "Stick out your tongue."

"What?"

"Let me see your tongue."

Vu remembered a time when he had been obligated to drink toilet water to stay alive. The thought haunted him every time he went to the bathroom. Because of that bleak memory he was going to punish Sgt. Hill.

Shrugging, Hill stuck out his tongue. It was pasty around the edges and very red, dry and cracked on the surface. Vu studied it for a few moments and then resumed stirring his tea.

"Well?" Sgt. Hill asked.

"Your chi is blocked. You have poor circulation. Your sex drive would be improved if you drank tea."

"Really?" Sgt. Hill stuck out his tongue and looked at it in the mirror over the sink. Vu walked up from behind and stuck his tongue out too.

"See mine," Vu said. "It is not so fiery in the center. The sides are moist and coated white. This indicates good digestion imparted from the juices of the tea leaves I have been drinking."

As the two men were examining their tongues together, Betty Caan, a young, attractive lab assistant walked in and stopped beside the two men. She too stuck out her tongue and looked in the mirror.

"What are we looking at?"

Hill who had a mild crush on Ms. Caan, snapped his jaw closed, clipping the edge of his pinkish flesh.

"Vu, this is Betty Caan," Hill mumbled. "She works downstairs in the medical examiner's office. She's working the Marken case with Detective Gates."

Vu was more interested in observing the girl's tongue. "Hello, Ms. Caan. You have very pink tongue. Your chi is flowing very nicely. Would it be okay if I followed you downstairs and reviewed the Marken file?"

Ms. Caan closed her mouth. She had full red lips that caught the light and sparkled. Vu studied them, admiring the glitter.

"You may follow me as long as you don't stick your tongue out at my cadavers."

"Vu's from the AFOSI office in Maryland," Hill added, as if by doing so he rode on the coattails of the Great Hunter.

CHAPTER 6

Hill spoke to Caan in the corner while Vu reviewed a number of official documents, lab tests, toxicology, blood analysis, x-rays, and color photographs of the crime scene and close-ups of the victim's body. At one point Ms. Caan walked by Vu carrying a vial of clear liquid.

"Careful, Sergeant," she said, "or you'll be wearing vitreous humor."

Vu sighed. "Ocular fluid might stain my tie..."

"I like a man who appreciates the dead."

Sgt. Hill seemed jealous by the way Ms. Caan started hovering around the government investigator.

"Is that Ms. Marken's?" Vu inquired.

"No. It's from a local parishioner who had his retina dislodged by a candelabra." Ms. Caan pulled out a legal-size file folder and swapped items with Vu and commented on his dull, sallow coloring. Vu removed the vial from his jacket.

Ms. Caan asked, "Bacteria or parasites?"

"Parasites. I contracted the condition from a polluted water supply in Southeast Asia."

Smiling, Ms. Caan continued "So, tell me Sergeant, are you married?"

Hill curled up his lip in disgust and hung his head outside the pathologist's door, as if he couldn't take the heavy odor of formaldehyde. He shouted to Vu from the doorway. "You might want to get that gut of yours checked out..."

Vu excused himself and found a quiet place to spread out and review the additional documents. It took Vu twenty-seven minutes to review the remaining evidence. It was pretty much cut and dry. Her name was Leslie Ann Marken, 28, an airline stewardess for Delta Airlines. No priors, no outstanding warrants. Born in Dallas, Texas. Nothing that hadn't been included in a hundred other cases like it. The thing that struck him as being unusual was the murder weapon, and the lack of fingerprints at the scene. Of course lack of fingerprints would not be the problem. There were hundreds of fingerprints – nearly every object in the room was covered. Common sense dictated that hotel rooms collected fingerprints.

Vu stood up and looked at Ms. Caan. "Did you run a Methylumbelliferyl Phosphate test on the bed spread?"

"Yes, we ran a MUP. The UV went crazy. You can imagine how many cum stains are on a hotel comforter."

"The evidence doesn't indicate that Ms. Marken was sexually assaulted."

"That's correct. We did find traces of semen in both the vagina and the rectum. But the areas were 'consistent with history.' The comforter had been exposed to various partners. Ms. Marken's fluids were only one of several dozen we found."

Ms. Caan's reply registered loud and clear in Vu's eyes. "Are you indicating that Ms. Marken had multiple partners?"

"Possibly. We ran DNA testing on both samples and were able to obtain two cold hits. The vaginal deposit belonged to a Mr. Long. John D. Long. An airline pilot. A co-worker of Ms. Marken's. Detective Gates followed up and discovered that Long was on an international flight at the time of death. Since PA is only detectable up to about twenty-four hours, Mr. Long's statement that he saw the victim the night prior to the murder runs consistent with our tests. The other sample removed from the rectum appears to have occurred during that same time period, which means either Ms. Marken had sex with two partners simultaneously, or one partner came before or after Mr. Long. No pun intended..."

Vu scratched a small bump on his upper lip and recorded the name in his notebook. "Do you have DNA results for the second donor?"

"Still waiting for the test results to come back."

"Was it common for Ms. Marken to have a layover in New Orleans?"

"Beats me. Check with Gates on that."

"Did you find anything abnormal in your procedures?"

"Nope. But it's possible Ms. Marken had a miscarriage. We found scarring in the uterus."

Vu reflected. "What is your theory on the murder, Ms. Caan?"

"That it's a homicide."

"That is not helpful."

"Ask me again after a few drinks."

Vu changed the subject. "Something's askew."

Perhaps a closer view of the murder weapon...

The photographs had shown a gold medallion necklace. He concentrated on the photographs.

Ms. Caan was looking under a stereoscope when he looked up from the documents. It came as a surprise to Vu when she stopped, glanced over at him, and in a calm assertive voice offered: "It's been booked into evidence. Property Room. Upstairs, third floor. See Sergeant Packwood."

"That was remarkable," Vu said. "Sometime, you must explain how you were able to do that."

Ms. Caan remained deadpan and continued on with her work.

"You found only the one thumb print on the necklace?"

"That's correct."

"No lifts were removed from the chain?"

"Smudges, only. If I had a hand for comparison, I might be able to get a match."

Following Hill upstairs, Vu thanked Ms. Caan and left the folder on the desk. Upstairs he spoke with a Sergeant Packwood, your typical desk sergeant. Big and burly with a sour face, he begrudgingly pulled out the evidence box and slapped it down on the counter.

"Sign for it."

Vu nodded and removed the yellow evidence envelope from the box. He started to sign his name on the back of the envelope, but his pen sputtered out of ink. He turned toward Sergeant Hill.

"May I borrow a pen? Mine has run out of fluid."

Hill stood up straight and pulled a pen out of his shirt pocket.

Vu pushed up his glasses and asked Hill, "Have you slept with Ms. Caan?"

Hill stopped dead and seemed to forget about the pen. "What the hell does that have to do with tea in China?"

Vu shrugged and took the pen from Hill. After signing his name he stuck the pen in his pocket and moved to a table nearby to view the physical evidence.

"Do you think Ms. Marken felt affection toward her murderer?"

Hill stepped back, thinking. "How would I know? The guy offed her. You can ask him when we find his sorry ass."

"Were you ever in the service, Sergeant?"

"You jump around a lot."

"If I make you uncomfortable..."

Hill interrupted, "Two years – Army. Recon. 82nd Airborne. And it makes me sick to think we're lookin' for a former Special Ops guy. Know what I mean? Bad blood."

Vu waited until Detective Hill had left the area before he opened the final piece of evidence, a small envelope containing the purported murder weapon.

Pulling on gloves, he held the necklace up to the fluorescent light.

The chain was 14 carat gold of good quality and skilled workmanship. Each loop of the chain had been soldered. Certainly durable enough to crush someone's larynx and block the trachea, preventing the victim from breathing. While he examined the gold coin he noticed skin particles embedded in the outer ridges and in the roasted brown patina. The necklace had been pulled so tightly that the coin had cut into the flesh. He felt sickened by the image. So he focused on the obvious: the date, the lettering, the insignia. He was not a numismatist, but it looked to be a British Sovereign. He looked for a mint mark but could not find one.

He turned his attention toward the watchful sergeant who had returned to his station and was staring at him across the counter.

Vu made conversation. "Unlikely murder weapon, don't you think, Sergeant?"

The officer shrugged and watched Vu coil up the necklace and return it to the envelope.

CHAPTER 7

Midnight in Jackson Square in the belly of the French Quarter. Amidst the hectic nightlife, street musicians, and drunken tourists, Emily Douchet got lucky. She met a man. His name was Jim Lyman.

Earlier that evening, she had been with a group of girls from the convention – the Society of Cosmetic Professionals. Emily was attending the five-day conference held in the main ballroom of the Clare Monte Hotel. Some of the girls had asked her along on a wild night on the town. It sounded exciting to the Midwesterner. Why not have a little fun for a change?

One of the girls suggested they get their palms read in Jackson Square. Emily laughed at the idea. But why not?

Jackson Square was bustling with activity. Emily stood by the fountain and took it all in. The crowds, the flashing lights, and sweet smell of chicory coffee mixed with the loud clanging tambourines and drums spilling out into the streets from the busy clubs. Any number of amusements could be had for a small price.

The girls split up. Emily wandered over to the palm reading tables and sat down in front of an old Russian woman who called herself Madame Blanchet.

Madame Blanchet wore a gauze dress draped with an assortment of silk shawls and leather knee-high boots. She had long hands with knuckles like a knot in a tree and crooked little fingers choked with gaudy rings. Her old wrinkled face softened when Emily smiled into her eyes. She fluttered her long dark lashes with a young girl's enthusiasm when she looked at Emily.

She picked up Emily's hand and held it tightly. Emily could feel the woman's warmth radiating through her flesh.

"My girl, I see passion in your life. You have been alone too long. You are creative and need a release. You are troubled by your smoking. You go through life living each day as if the phone will ring and take you away from your current surroundings."

Madame Blanchet looked deep into Emily's hazel eyes. "Shhh...don't speak. You must go forward with your life, my dear. Do not let the past keep you from experiencing the present. There is a man in your future. A tall man, a strong man, a good man. But he has many secrets. Do not pry. For if you do, he will not bring you the fruit of love."

Emily knew Madame Blanchet was not a mystic. Her encouraging words were repeated to each person who visited her little table. But she didn't care. They struck a cord in her heart. She happily placed a twenty-dollar bill into the crystal jar and left.

From that moment on, Emily drifted. She strolled through the busy sidewalks. Madame Blanchet had breathed life into her step. She caught her reflection in a shop window and admired her long blonde hair and golden skin. The weeks spent in the tanning beds had paid off. She looked radiant. Not bad, for forty-three.

Sure, she needed to firm her tummy and maybe lose a few inches around her mid-section. Maybe tighten up her butt here and there – what woman her age didn't? She wasn't Britney Spears. Women were expected to have a few minor imperfections when they worked as hard as she did.

Jim Lyman spent the afternoon in Jackson Square planning. His only surviving relative was a sister in Salt Lake City, who didn't know he was alive. His parents were long dead. Buried a year apart, long before he was sent to Southeast Asia, then on to Spain. The sister had sold the farm and paid off the back taxes and several liens against the property. After all debt was paid off, he and his sister split nine thousand and change. After a long weekend in Monte Carlo, his inheritance was gone. He was broke again. He reasoned, he just wasn't a farmer at heart.

His sister wrote telling him how she had found a neighbor lady willing to take the three Maine Coons, but the heifer, Penelope, was doomed to a meat packing plant in Nebraska.

Lyman figured the last news his sister had from the State Department was that he was MIA somewhere overseas. Lyman knew he couldn't contact her. The Feds would be looking for him.

He had shaved off his mustache and had dyed his hair black and the last eighteen months had taken a toll on his body. His nightmares had ceased. The latent memory of beatings had subsided. Beneath the veneer of slacks and a knit shirt, his body was firm – but scarred. He had always been in exceptional shape, mentally and physically. Special Ops men had to be.

He was down to his last buck. He had two thousand miles to cover. He made a few notes on a cocktail napkin and shoved it inside his leather jacket, polishing off his beer.

A smiling blonde sat down beside him and ordered a peach margarita from the bartender. She sipped and made eye contact. Then she pulled out a pack of Ultra Lights and lit one.

She turned her barstool toward him and asked, "This isn't bothering you, is it? I can put it out."

Lyman looked her straight in the eye. He knew what he had to do. "Don't...My name's Jim." He held out a hand. The woman smiled, put her cigarette down, and shook his hand.

"I'm Emily. Pleased to meet you, Jim."

Her hotel was within walking distance. It had been built in the late eighteenth century and decorated with antiques. A parking garage in the basement was made available to all guests free of charge. Emily was pleased about that. It meant she didn't have to pay for parking her rental car, a white, four door, Toyota Camry.

She had trouble getting her key card into the lock on her hotel room door. Lyman offered assistance. She'd left the bar feeling tipsy and the walk in the cool night air had not sobered her. Lyman, on the other hand, was sober.

He sank down in an overstuffed chair and waited. Emily slipped off her black heels, pulled something out of the closet, and giggled off into the bathroom. The last bed Lyman had slept in was a hard cot, smelly but free, courtesy of the Salvation Army. The king sized brass bed across the room seemed decadent. Everything about the room made him feel awkward and out of place, even the designer handbag resting on the dresser. It had been over two years since he had been with a woman. The last had been in Morocco, a local girl, half his age, and very eager.

The door to the bathroom creaked open and Emily appeared in the dim light. She had on a see-through silk slip and her hair was pulled back from her face. She had sprayed Opium perfume on her chest and had removed her jewelry. Lyman stood up, smiled at her, and unbuttoned his shirt.

CHAPTER 8

Vu woke up to the harsh sounds of a woman's fist pounding on his hotel room door.

"Sergeant Vu! It's Detective Gates! Sergeant Vu!"

Vu had been dreaming about his new scooter. Ms. Caan was with him in his fantasy, her hard, naked body lewdly spread across the seat. Long sexy legs calling to him...

"I'm coming! I'm coming!" Vu called out, not knowing if he was answering the door or the desires of his dream girl. And, at that precise moment, he was aware that the detective was beginning to irritate him.

Vu opened the door and Gates marched in. She stopped dead in her tracks and broke down laughing. Vu stepped back away from the door.

Vu thought that perhaps his fly was open. He was wearing silk boxers beneath his black kimono and wood sandals on his feet. After checking to see if his fly was open, he realized his kimono was inside out. That's what happens when you jump out of bed discombobulated.

He turned his back toward the detective and removed his kimono. Detective Gates spun around and watched him undress.

"Why are you here so early, Ms. Gates?"

Gates smiled and looked him over. Vu fumbled with his sash and faced her. "You are not abashed, are you Detective?"

"I was curious about what kind of package you had. That's all. Looks like they grow 'em as big in China as they do the good ole' U.S.A."

"I am not Chinese," Vu snapped. "I am third generation Vietnamese."

"Proud, are you? Your people killed my dad."

Vu's eyes locked onto the detective's.

"Skip it. Just get dressed."

Ignoring him, Gates inspected Vu's room with the same careful eye used during a homicide investigation. Nothing was out a place. Vu's closet was arranged neatly and according to color. His polished shoes were beside the bed. "We're in kind of a hurry, Sergeant." Gates mentioned, noticing Vu had not made an effort to move.

"Are we going to Ms. Marken's hotel room?"

Gates ran her hand over the back of one of the room's mahogany chairs. "We have a stop to make before I take you over to Ms. Marken's hotel. You want to find Lyman, right?"

Vu's eyes brightened.

Vu didn't like riding in police cars. He felt trapped and claustrophobic. It was one reason he owned a motorbike. A girlfriend once told him he felt the way he did because he had grown up in a large family, all sharing a tiny two-room apartment in South Vietnam. It was a dangerous and squalid environment for a child. She was also not surprised he disliked airplanes.

But Vu disagreed. He knew his phobias had not started at home. His discomfort of small places stemmed from the days when he was a prisoner of the North Vietnamese soldiers. After the U.S. had pulled out of Vietnam, Vu's family had fled their home and were forced to live in the swamps and jungle like animals. Later when Vu was thrown into a work camp, he was made to dig miles of canal through the jungle from sunrise to sunset with one bowl of rice a day. At night, they were crammed into a fenced area to sleep. Many of the workers died from suffocation, disease, and starvation. Vu survived the work camp because of one reason – he escaped.

Vu rolled down the passenger window and took a deep breath. The air smelled like disinfectant and vomit.

"Where is Sergeant Hill?" Vu asked, removing his vial of pills from his pocket. He popped a handful into his dry mouth, and swallowed hard.

"I sent him on ahead. He'll meet us at the hotel."

From the outside, the hotel reminded Vu of a brothel he once visited in Amsterdam. The view from the inside, however, was different. The furniture was elegant and clean. Vu was pleased about this. It meant he might make it through the day without another sneezing attack.

They got off the elevator on the fifth floor and followed a narrow carpeted corridor to the end. Gates knocked on the door and it opened. Sergeant Hill greeted them. He wore a blue blazer over a white shirt and tie. Vu thought he needed a shave.

"Morning Vu, I had room service deliver some breakfast. Hungry?" Gates pushed by Hill and went inside. "Where's the victim?" Gates inquired over her shoulder.

"Bathroom..."

Vu noticed a shiny room service cart blocking the center of the room. The crime scene was a mess, clothes thrown everywhere, furniture overturned, broken glass next to the bed where a lamp shade had hit the floor and shattered, magazines and newspaper scattered about.

Gates ignored it all and snooped through the plates on the food cart. Before long she came up with a croissant. She bit off the end, disregarding the shower of powdery flakes floating toward the floor. Vu found the conduct unprofessional. How could they conduct an investigation like this? Now he knew his friend had been right: "Things are different down South, Vu. Watch yourself."

"Want tea, Vu?" Hill lifted a silver pot from the cart. Vu declined. Hill poured a small amount of tea in a cup and tasted it, crinkled up his nose, and filled the remains with coffee. "Well, Sergeant, what do you think of New Orleans?"

"What are you drinking?" Gates asked from across the room, shoveling the remaining pastry into her large mouth.

"I'm not sure," Sergeant Hill replied and stared inside his cup. Little specs of tea leaves floated up to the surface. "Coffee mostly."

"You should drink tea, Sergeant." Vu snapped. "Coffee, it is not good for you."

"Yeah, right. It'll block my chi?"

"That is correct," Vu said.

Gates frowned. "Your what?"

"His chi, Ms. Gates," Vu added. "One's inner strength."

"All a man needs is his dick, Sergeant. If it works he's happy. If it doesn't, he's not."

Hill pinched off a laugh and bit his lower lip. Gates crossed the room like a mean cat and began rifling through the contents of Emily Douchet's waste basket. Vu watched, grumbling to himself.

Gates dipped the end of her ballpoint pen into the receptacle and pulled out a used condom. She studied it under the light.

"Somebody got lucky..." she mused, then dropped the condom back into the trash. Next she pulled out an empty bottle of "Love Potion" – body lotion typically found in public restroom dispensers.

"Yes, I see our 'vic' had her some fun last night," Gates said. "How 'bout you, Vu? You get lucky last night?"

Vu was very disgusted at how they were handling the investigation scene. How disrespectful they were being toward the dead. He shook with anger.

"How can I assist?" Vu snapped at Hill. Then glared at Gates.

"Chill, man. Pop a few pills. It'll just be a minute. I think maybe your chi is backed up."

Vu could take it no longer. He stared at first one and then the other. They were idiots. He put on a pair of rubber gloves and stomped toward the bathroom door. The two detectives standing across the room smirked at each other.

"I'm going in."

Gates smiled. "Suit yourself."

Vu twisted the handle and marched inside the bathroom and came to a dead halt. He expected to see a gruesome homicide scene. Blood, guts, horror. Instead, seated on the toilet before him with her dress down around her knees and very much alive, was a middle-aged blonde with bright red lipstick, big hair, and bloodshot eyes the size of hamburgers. Vu took several apologetic steps backward and eased the door closed behind him.

Gates and Hill broke into laughter. Vu's face was flushed. He peeled off his gloves, tucked them back inside his pocket, replaying Gates' words back through his head, wondering how he could have made such a silly assumption as this.

In a calm, controlled voice, Vu asked the detectives: "Where's Lyman?"

"What are you talking about?" Gates voice had a tone to it.

"Hasn't Lyman reappeared?"

Hill looked across the room at his partner. "Lyman? The woman's name is Emily Douchet. She reported her car stolen out of the hotel parking garage. That's it. How'd Lyman get into this?"

Vu chewed on it for a few minutes then let it go.

Emily Douchet introduced herself. She had already explained her story to Sergeant Hill but Gates managed to pry it out of her again.

"Would you care for something to drink, Ms. Douchet?" Gates asked. Vu was in the corner cooling off, still unable to look Emily in the eye.

"Some coffee, please."

Vu's hand was still shaking as he pulled out a file from his briefcase and began reading. He had prepared himself for a dead body, not a live one, and it would take him a few minutes to recover.

"As I was explaining to Sergeant Hill before you arrived, I don't usually go out at night. Not alone at least. And I don't bring strangers back to my hotel..."

"You've made your point, Ms. Douchet," Gates said. "Just tell us what happened."

Ms Douchet blushed and glanced at Vu. "Well...we had sex. Several times, I believe..."

"Consider yourself fortunate," Gates encouraged. "Is that what happened to your room?"

Emily nodded, with a faint smile rising to her lips.

"What else, ma'am?"

"Well, when I went downstairs this morning, I found my car stolen."

"And you think the man you brought back to your hotel room is involved?"

Her head bobbed.

Hill pulled out his notebook. His partner's brash comments had no affect on him. Vu once again disagreed with Gate's tactics.

"Okay, Ms. Douchet. Just run down a description for us and any pertinent facts that might help us recover your stolen car. Then the three of us will be on our way."

"It's not my car," she said. "It's a rental. A...a blue or was it gray?" she uttered. "Now isn't that funny, I can't remember the color. You see I just drove it once. From the airport to my hotel and that was several days ago."

Vu closed the file and offered help. "If it is a rental, do you have the paperwork with you? Perhaps it is in the room somewhere?"

Ms. Douchet paused. "I'm afraid it is in the car's glovebox. I didn't remove it."

"Do you remember the rental agency?"

Gates interrupted and stared at Vu. "Sergeant, you're doing such a fine job, would you care to handle this?"

Hill flashed an angry look to his partner. Vu said nothing and sat down. He removed Lyman's file from his briefcase, opened it, and began reading.

Hill looked at Ms. Douchet. "It'll be just a moment, ma'am." Hill and Gates went across the room to discuss something in private. Vu glanced up to see what the detectives were doing and then resumed his own business. Ms. Douchet scooted her chair over closer to him.

"That was real nice of the detective to order room service. How long have you been working for the department, Sergeant?"

Vu did not want to entangle himself in formalities nor did he want to retrace his adventures at the New Orleans Precinct. It would be better for both of them if he just followed directions, kept Hill on his good side. Gates was going to be a problem.

"I'm new," Vu replied.

"As I was telling the other sergeant," she continued, rambling, "I don't know his last name. We met at a night club off Jackson Square last night and I guess you could say, I was taken by the man. He was different. He was handsome and had strong hands. He was six one or six two. Dark hair and dark brown eyes. Very tan. And the scars..."

Vu looked up. "What type of scars, Ms. Douchet?"

Ms. Douchet blushed. She loosened one button on her dress collar. Talking about it, inspired something powerful in her eyes and in her voice. Vu had seen the transformation occur two other times in his life. Both cases involved young women smitten with bad boys. One of them, a colonel's daughter, even robbed a convenience store and said she'd do it again out of love.

"I didn't study them."

"Gunshots? Knife wounds? Birthmarks?"

"It was dark, Sergeant, and I was a little tipsy."

"I see."

"Our hearts are what matter, aren't they, Sergeant?" Emily drifted.

Vu waited patiently for her to continue.

"I suspect he stole my rental car and a gas credit card and some cash. He left me with twenty dollars and he didn't steal my other credit cards. Just the gas credit card. I believe he's in some kind of trouble."

"How much cash did he take from you?"

"A couple hundred. I don't have an exact amount. I just wish he would have asked me for help." Leaning closer, Emily whispered, "I don't care that he stole, you understand? I just want him back."

Ms. Douchet started sniffling. Vu removed his handkerchief and offered it as a small token to lost love. He allowed Ms. Douchet a moment with herself and opened Lyman's file again. A small passport photograph taken before Lyman was reported MIA was paper clipped to the inside cover. Ms. Douchet blew her nose and wiped it dry and looked down at the sergeant's open file. Ms. Douchet's eyes snapped open.

"That's him!"

Vu slammed the file closed. Hill and Gates were having a heated moment, lost in their own troubled world across the room.

Ms. Douchet reached for the file. Vu took a firm hold of her wrist and placed it back onto her lap. Then he opened the file for a second time and asked in a very clear, firm voice. "Look, closely, Ms. Douchet. You're certain this is him?"

She nodded adamantly. Vu's lips curled into a smile. He returned the file to his briefcase and secured the lid.

"Wait!" Ms. Douchet uttered. "Please, one more look."

Vu motioned for her to be quiet. "I will see what I can do for you, Ms.

Douchet. I cannot make promises. I guarantee if the two officers across the room hear us, you will never see him again. Do you understand?"

Ms. Douchet's eyes watered. Vu reached into his pocket and took out a business card and handed it to her. "If he contacts you, call this number."

Ms. Douchet scribbled down some numbers on the backside of her business card and gave it to him. Across the room, Gates belted out, "Ma'am, Sergeant Hill's going to wind up here. You coming, Vu?"

Vu tucked the card inside his jacket. "Thank you, Emily."

CHAPTER 9

They picked up the tail after stopping off at Marken's hotel room. Gates was unaware they were being followed. It wouldn't be until much later she would learn Vu had known all the time, but had kept quiet about it.

Gates drove in silence. Vu gazed out the window as if he was in some kind of trance. His mood had plunged right after entering Marken's room. *Very morose*, Gates mused.

She had kept her mouth shut while he took his sweet ass time examining the crime scene. He stood in the spot where Marken had been killed, crossed his arms, closed his eyes and took several deep breaths. Afraid he'd begin chanting, Gates went outside and waited.

Finally, Vu joined her on the balcony. His eyes looked hollow, vacant, his shoulders hunched over like a man who had undergone a caning.

Gates tossed her spent Juicy Fruit over the ornamental railing. "Ya hungry?"

Vu stared out into the busy street below, his eyes gazing off into nothingness. "No," he muttered.

"Suit yourself," she said, surprised at how the rejection felt.

The drive was uneventful. Vu occasionally glanced in his sideview mirror while Gates drove him to his hotel. He climbed out of the car without saying goodbye, watched the detective drive away, and then ducked into the doorway and peeked out the lobby window.

The sedan pulled to the curb and killed its engine. It was a newer unmarked, two-door Plymouth, with Florida plates. There were three Arabs in the car. The men remained in the car and stared out the window toward the hotel. Vu made a mental note of the vehicle's license plate and headed upstairs.

He entered his room and locked the deadbolt behind him. Across the room the red light on his phone blinked. He looked out his window into the street below. The men were still watching the hotel. Two messages had come in while he was away. He listened to each, jotted down a few notes on a hotel pad, and then erased them. Next he placed a call to Hertz Rental Agency. He provided his governmental credit card number to the agent and agreed to pay the extra fee to have the car delivered to his hotel garage.

"I want a full-size American made car, please," Vu told the agent on the other end of the telephone line.

"I'm sorry, sir. All we have available are compacts. I can set you up with a very nice Hyundai Elantra." Vu figured there were always tradeoffs in life.

Vu put down his wallet and then arranged for some Chinese takeout to be delivered to his room. While he was in the shower, the phone rang. He ran across the carpet wet and naked and answered on the sixth ring. An AFOSI affiliate in Baltimore. Yes, they could run a trace on the credit card ... no, he did not want them to notify the State Police ... yes, he had a positive identification ... yes, he would wait for their call... yes, he would keep them informed. And, by the way, could they run a DMV check on a Florida plate...

He barely had time to dry off before a knock on his door announced his food's arrival.

He ate slowly and drank his tea in solitude. Who were these guys tailing him? State Department? He doubted it. Too thuggish. Mercenaries? More probable. But why? Maybe it was all in his mind. He'd been edgy lately. The photographs of the dead stewardess were grotesque and struck a deep cord. Death was something he couldn't share with another. He looked out his hotel window again. But the car was gone. Afterward, he turned on the clock radio. A local station was broadcasting Christian music. He took off his clothes, lit a stick of Nag Champa incense, and meditated. Then, he watched a rerun of *Jag* in the buff, and turned in early. At seven-forty-five the next morning, the call he had been waiting for arrived.

CHAPTER 10

Gates pressed down into the bench and wrapped her sweaty fingers around the nickel-plated bar. Hill spotted from behind, staring down into her bloodshot eyes.

"Where do you think the weasel is?" Gates asked her partner.

"His name is Vu."

"I was referring to Riley."

"Riley'll check in."

"Riley's an ass."

"Gates. Everyone's an ass to you."

"And your point is?"

Hill had never looked down into the eyes of a woman like Gates before. The view was kind of intimidating. She had a nice face, although not very feminine. And as for her body, well, her spandex top was bulging beneath layers of rippled pecs like one of those chicks in *Muscle*. She had a silver hoop piercing in her belly button, which Hill knew Headquarters didn't authorize, because the department's policy on tattoos and piercing was clear. Don't show, don't tell.

Maybe if he stuck with Gates long enough he could flatten his stomach like hers. Harden up his thighs and buttocks. Girls were always interested in nice tushes.

"Anytime, hotshot!" Gates barked.

Hill snapped out of it. "Eight reps, right?" Hill asked.

"That's right."

Gates arched upward and a small puddle of glistening sweat rolled into her belly button. Hill wanted to lick it out with his tongue but he knew it'd never happen. Gates wanted to let on like she was a tough, raunchy bitch who fucked around. But he figured the truth was different.

"Ughhhhh! Ughhhhh!" Gates' face was puffy and the veins in her neck stuck out.

"That's enough, Dorene," Hill uttered. "Christ's sake, you'll tear a tit."

Dorene dropped the barbell, sat upright on the bench, and swiped a hand towel across her sweaty face. Hill removed one of the two forty-five pound plates from the barbell she had been lifting and slid on a twenty-five pound plate in its place.

"Spot me," he said.

Dorene smiled, "Did you say I'd bust a tit?"

Hill took the bench. "Just spot me."

The two cops were on the way to the locker room when a cop from Robbery stuck his head out his office door.

"Hey, Gates. That was Riley," the cop said. "He told me to tell you he lost Vu. Whose Vu?"

Gates eyes ignited. She slapped a wall locker. "Fuck! Didn't I tell you?"

The cop repeated the question. "Who's Vu?"

"Did he specify where he lost the guy?" Gates asked.

"About five miles South of I-10. Guess Riley had a little accident, too. He phoned from the hospital."

"Great. Thanks for making my morning, Jimmy."

"Any time, sweetcakes."

She looked Hill in the eye. Hill wondered if his partner was taking steroids or something. Her eyes were on fire.

"Don't start with me, Dorene."

CHAPTER 11

Across the street from Vu's hotel the Arabs were up to no good. The leader, Nigel, sat at an outdoor cafe picking crusted ketchup from the table top. Nigel wouldn't admit it, but the old ketchup reminded him of a Serb he'd killed.

The other two Arabs were across the street snooping around the entrance of Vu's hotel, getting a feel for the fat cop who sat in an unmarked, dirty sedan, watching the front door. The Arabs were hip to shithead cops. They would have enjoyed pouring Turkish coffee in this one's eyes. But they needed him. The detective was the perfect decoy.

So the New Orleans Police Department didn't trust the Vietnamese investigator any more than they did? Interesting... Nigel motioned toward his men and flicked his cigarette butt out into the street.

* * *

Vu was aware of the tail. But it wasn't the Arabs this time. He smiled in his rearview mirror and had to give Gates credit for sending the fat cop, Riley, from the station to do her dirty work. Vu didn't care one way or the other if she knew his immediate whereabouts. He was heading about sixty-five miles south to Houma, Louisiana, off Highway 90, in the heart of gator country. Miles from her jurisdiction.

Freeway traffic was heavy. Vu waited until the moment was right. He saw an exit ahead. He pressed on the accelerator and moved into the fast lane. In his rearview mirror he saw the green sedan change lanes and follow him.

Riley was feeling pompous. He had the little shit in his sights now – maybe he should call it in. Nah he'd wait. Gates was a bitch anyhow.

Riley lit a fat cigar and puffed away. So the Gook was changing lanes. Well, fine. He'd change lanes too. Riley thought he saw the sedan in his mirror again. Arab fucks. Probably nothin'. Fucking job was an incestuous pit for paranoia.

Suddenly all hell broke loose ahead – a cacophony of screeching brakes and blaring horns. "What the fuck!"

The last thing Riley remembered seeing was the big shit-eating grin of a little kid's face plastered on the ass end of a Franz's bread truck...

Vu continued south out of the city on Highway 90. He eased back into the seat and stretched his toes and wondered what Riley was thinking about now. Being a cop was dirty business.

Despite his knee-high rubber boots being a half-size too small, circulation was still flowing to his feet. He loosened the waist around his Levis and removed a plastic barcode tag from the collar of his new flannel shirt. He picked up a Yankee baseball cap off the seat and tried it on for size. Large, but it would do.

The four-lane highway turned into a two-lane road outside of Des Allemades and Vu began to enjoy the view. Miles of marshland and scraggily trees stretched out into the milky horizon as far as the eye cared to follow, like an endless passage of time, weathering itself into cypress fields and aged-wood structures whose roofs sparkled like stones in the morning sun. Mile upon mile of farmland and cattle and old houses with vines hanging from eaves blowing in the breeze and shingle-less barns, lean-tos, and outbuildings, and families whose very survival depended on the severity of the next economic tide or next passing storm. A world similar to the one Vu had known as a child.

Vu eased up on the accelerator and changed lanes and kept his eye peeled for the next road marker. A rumbling eighteen-wheeler hauling livestock passed him on the left, turned off the main highway, and kept going. Vu wasn't aware of the sedan hanging back in the traffic following from a safe distance.

Up ahead, over a tiny knoll, a small restaurant and gas station appeared. Vu sat up straight. This was the place. He slowed, pulled off the highway and parked in a gravel lot. To the right of his car was a big, bold, hand-painted road sign: "Home of Alligator Swamp Tours."

* * *

The sedan with the three Arabs passed by the restaurant and continued down the highway for several miles before it pulled off to the side of the road and killed its engine.

Nigel said: "He does not know as much as we thought. This will give us time..."

CHAPTER 12

The restaurant was an old single-story building with gray siding and a white roof. A cedar planked deck had been recently built in back. Vu thought he'd get a good look at the place before he went inside. The back door was propped open onto the Chatalogue River – a narrow, stagnant, dirt colored swamp water that the locals fished in from time to time when the gators weren't around.

Vu figured the back door was as good as any door, especially if Lyman was inside. Emily Douchet's rental car did not appear to be parked in the lot. But Vu had been stung before. And it nearly cost him his life – but that's another story...

Vu checked to make sure he had his 9mm with him and then went inside. The restaurant was empty with the exception of a cranky old waitress with a face like cracked leather. She had on a pink waitress uniform and fuzzy slippers. She was busy peeling back the skin on a ripe banana.

"You missed 'em, sonny!" she said, and tossed the dark limp peel into the trash. "They all left twenty minutes ago."

"You are referring to the swamp tour?" Vu asked.

"If you want lunch, you gotta wait," she said firmly. "We open at eleven-thirty."

The waitress flashed a jack o' lantern smile. Some of the banana mush seeped from between her missing teeth. She looked the sergeant up and down, licked her lips, and offered him a hunk of banana. It was true what they said about the South, you sure couldn't knock 'em for their hospitality.

"So whatcha want?"

"I'm looking for somebody," Vu said.

"Just me, Carl and Rufus now," she said. "Looks like the tour sold out again. Who you lookin' for?"

Vu bent his head in an attempt to read the waitress's nametag which was upside down. The letters appeared to be "EINNA" – "ANNIE" spelled backwards. Annie mimicked his behavior.

"Your name's Annie?"

"It is indeed," she replied. "Now, who you lookin' for?"

"I am looking for a man," Vu told her.

Annie alarmed, stood up straight. "You better not say that too loud. Carl's got a thing against homosexuals."

"I did not mean—"

"Look, sonny," Annie interrupted, "I don't care if you like sheep, just keep your voice low around Carl if you're going to have lunch with us later. That's all. No tellin' what he might do to your food."

Vu looked over Annie's shoulder and on the bar he saw a skinned pig on a cutting block. "That's tomorrow's special, dear," Annie said. "Today's is liver and onions."

Just the mentioning of cow's guts made him queasy. He suddenly lost color in his face and bent forward at the knees, holding his stomach, like a bloody boxer in the tenth round.

His pills...

He dug into his pocket and started sweating. The waitress polished off the banana, amused by the little man's antics.

She grabbed Vu a glass of water and waited while he chased down his medicine. Slowly his color returned. He removed a handkerchief and blew his nose. Annie reached up and slapped a neon Budweiser sign making an annoying humming sound above their heads.

"You feel better, sonny?"

"Yes... I need to use the restroom, please."

"If you need t.p. just give us a shout. Just head back the way you came in... You'll see the door."

Annie pulled out a tray of silverware from beneath the counter and dropped it on the bar. "Oh, one other thing. Careful of Rufus. He's kind of cranky this morning. I think somebody from the tour group spooked him."

Still lightheaded, Vu followed the drawn arrows on the wall, remembering that before he nearly lost his breakfast on the floor, he had been looking for Lyman. Lyman certainly didn't appear to be here. Who the hell was Rufus?

Vu took off his glasses and holster and laid them on the counter and washed his face and hands. The paper dispenser was empty so he used his shirttail to dry off. He then stepped up to the urinal. Somewhere to his right, in one of the stalls, he heard something move along the floor. Down South it could be most anything, he reasoned. Probably a leaky pipe making that gurgling sound. But being the curious type he rocked back on his heels and peered under the stall door. Without his glasses, all he could make out were shadows and fuzzy images. But something moved back there. He was certain of that.

Instead of worrying about it, Vu focused on peeing. Nothing like a good flow of urine to put a smile on a guy's face. Especially after drinking three double-sized cups of green tea.

He felt something offensive and prickly brush up against his leg. With his fly open and his penis lodged in his hand, he turned. Staring up at him was the most horrific creature he could have imagined.

A six-foot alligator with one missing eye smacked his knotty jaws up and down against Vu's leg. Its big lonely yellow eye rolled back and forth in its socket and his chomping razor sharp teeth zeroed in on Vu's flesh.

"Ahhh!" Vu's voice box garbled out. "Hel-lep! Hel-lep!" In that instant, Vu knew he couldn't reach his 9mm and so the urinal seemed like the next best thing. He jump up and grabbed the wall for balance. His boxers and baggy pants came tumbling down around his ankles, pinning his feet.

Annie burst through the doors wielding a broom handle and a stern face. She faced Rufus bravely and rapped the gator's snout. "Rufus! Stop that!" Annie yelled. "Right this minute!" She repeatedly struck the amorous gator on the head and then snatched the short heavy chain hanging off Rufus's collar and tugged hard. Rufus dropped to his belly and snapped his jaws closed. Annie beat Rufus back into his corner.

Vu's eyes were the size of gourds. He seemed oblivious to the fact that his penis was hanging out.

"Don't worry there, sonny. His bark's mightier than his bite."

Shaking, but using a calm voice, he pontificated, "But a bite is mightier than a bark, is it not?"

Annie pointed at his penis. "You selling hot dogs?"

Vu reached down and jerked his pants up.

Annie laughed and went about chaining Rufus to the toilet.

"You can get down now. It's safe."

A new form of rigor mortis had penetrated Vu's body. And much like his ancestral cousin had done moments earlier down at his feet, the sergeant trembled and grunted but just couldn't get hold of himself. Thinking the pills would help, he pulled them out only to watch the vial plop into the urinal.

Vu stared at the tiny clear vial as if it was a diamond dunked in manure.

Thinking the little man probably needed help, Annie mercilessly whacked Vu's shoulder. It seemed to snap him out of his daze. He slowly crawled down off the urinal and fetched his gun and glasses.

Annie tapped him on the shoulder and pointed to the small bottle lying in the urinal drain. "You want 'em?" Vu looked her straight in the eye.

"No, ma'am."

"Might back up the system? Better fish 'em out."

"Yes, ma'am."

Annie had a tone. Vu was now scared of her. He pulled his sleeve up and fished out the wet vial.

"Was that a gun I seen there?"

"Yes, ma'am."

"You'll need one bigger than that if you plan on staying around these parts long."

Back outside the men's room, Vu pulled out a photograph of Jim Lyman and handed it to Annie.

CHAPTER 13

Lyman breathed in air scented with wet grass and okra and stared up at the hazy humid sky sprinkled with cumulus clouds, promising rain soon. He crouched down in the marshy swamp water and crept forward. Five, five-and-a-half, hours of daylight remaining. Plenty of time...

Lyman waded up to his waist in deep muck. A few feet ahead, a snake poked its head out of the tall swamp grass and glided effortlessly through the gray murky water. Overhead, a spindly-legged osprey flapped its powerful wings and screeched through the dense cypress. A frightened nutria ducked back into its dark hole. Lyman swatted blood-sucking mosquitoes and continued plowing through the wet grass. Near the shoreline a feral hog devoured the rotting remains of a half-eaten carp, floating in a pool of stagnant water. Lyman stopped, catching his breath. Up ahead he could hear a diesel generator running. Not much farther.

This was the remote bayou of the soul. Heartland of gator country. Only the wild survive in a place like this. Nestled between towering cypress and marshland and miles from civilization, Lyman found him. His former colleague, a Special Ops man, who had deserted him.

Lyman crept closer, keeping a watch for Ray Kano. Kano's place was surrounded by swampland, a single-level house built on eight-foot by two-foot cedar planking sunk in deep Louisiana soil. The structure was built on stilts to provide a safe haven from black bears, alligators, and other wildlife. Detached from the house was a small lean-to. A skiff with a fresh coat of paint rested on rickety sawhorses. Nearest Lyman was an outbuilding with what looked like an old float plane inside. Various equipment and tools, and generators were scattered about the property. Lyman scanned the sky for power lines. There were none.

Earlier, Lyman learned the place once belonged to a federal game warden named Lon Hunter. Hunter and Kano had been good friends. One day Hunter's body was found floating face up in federally protected waters, a place called Eagle's Peak. Cause of death, a single .357 shot to the head. The official version of the story indicated Hunter had been killed by poachers. But some of the locals were skeptical. A State Ranger with eighteen years experience should know better...

The man who had put him onto Kano was Carl Stone, a longtime resident of Houma, a former buck sergeant in the Army, who was now practicing his culinary talents as a civilian. He said Kano made frequent trips to the West Coast. That Kano had a girlfriend who worked for the airlines. But he couldn't remember which one. No one for certain knew how Kano had come up with the cash to buy the estate outright. Or, why a man of Kano's apparent means, would choose to live in such a hellhole.

But Lyman knew.

Lyman had been in the tepid water for an hour before he heard the sound of a swamp boat drawing near. He re-checked the long tree limbs he had used to camouflage the wooden skiff, and slipped back into the tall grass and waited.

The jet boat killed its motor and glided up to the small dock. It was Kano all right. He could recognize the man nicknamed: "John Wayne" anywhere. Kano had gained a few pounds around the middle, and had shaved off his hair. There was a nasty scar on his bald head. He had a strong, square jaw and a graying goatee. His arms and legs rippled beneath the tanktop and faded jeans. A large bowie knife was strapped to his right leg. He was wearing a revolver strapped around his waist like some fictitious cowboy. Kano was the same rough looking bastard he had known in the service.

Kano secured the mooring lines and strode up to the house. Lyman waited for a few minutes and then climbed to his feet.

He took three steps through the dense trees and stopped. Down at knee-height was a taut, camouflage colored, trip wire strung between two Cypress trees.

Kano was expecting company....

CHAPTER 14

Three years earlier, it had been a booby trap similar to this that had nearly taken the life of an airline stewardess named Leslie Ann Marken.

Lyman was leaving the Lebanon embassy when he bumped into Ms. Marken on the steps. She had on a sleek fitting, black airlines uniform. Her shiny hair was pulled back from her face. He remembered the sparkling eyes, the deep, blue diamond pools, and the beautiful almond-shaped lips.

"Excuse me," Lyman said, and straightened his sunglasses. He was thinking how delicious this stewardess looked standing with her hands on her curvaceous hips there on the embassy steps, when four blocks away an explosion rocked their world. The sound was deafening. Para-military maneuvers, Lyman figured, gunshots and explosions were a common occurrence in Beirut. Ms. Marken fell into Lyman's arms, visibly shaken. She watched the funnel-shaped smoke cloud dissipate into the gray sky over the city. Ten minutes earlier, she had walked by the very spot where the explosion had occurred...

Lyman later heard the details. A Jewish boy chasing a soccer ball ran into homemade explosives made from fertilizer and diesel oil. The bomb had been trip-wired to the undercarriage of a government-owned vehicle. Planted by Pro-Islamic Fundamentalists. Two others had been injured in the explosion.

Ms. Marken slipped out of Lyman's arms as gracefully as she had fallen into them. She stepped back and brushed the front of her dress. Then she looked Lyman in the eye, as if she recognized the face, but couldn't place it.

"You always that calm, Sergeant?" she said. Lyman's face was solid as stone.

"Are you all right?"

"I believe so, yes."

"You're sure?"

"Yes, quite. Thank you."

"Have we meet before?" he inquired curiously. "You look familiar..."

"I don't mean to stare." She explained. "It must be the haircut. I have a brother who works for the State Department. You guys all must use the same barber."

Lyman was not allowed off base in his uniform. No soldier was. Potential targets for terrorists. And Lyman was always on guard.

"You're very perceptive, Ms?"

"Marken," she added quickly. "Leslie Marken, pleased to meet you." She offered to shake hands.

"Well, Leslie Marken, it was a pleasure running into you. Maybe we'll have a chance to do it again. Under better circumstances."

"Don't count on it." She smiled, and left.

Lyman watched the elegant young woman saunter up the dusty steps and enter the brick building. The lady had class.

Later that night, Lyman had the unexpected pleasure of meeting her for a second time that day. It was at a small Italian restaurant a few blocks from the embassy. Ms. Marken and her brother Gerry joined them at their table.

Ray Kano couldn't take his eyes off the lovely airline stewardess. Lyman held back his surprise.

Kano introduced the new guests. "Gerry," Kano said, "who's your lovely date?"

"Leslie, meet a couple friends of mine. Ray Kano and Jim Lyman. Special Ops guys. They're here with the 82nd Airborne."

Both men stood up from the table. Ms. Marken smiled at Kano and shook his hand. Ms. Marken turned to Lyman.

"Mr. Lyman and I have already had the pleasure of meeting." Lyman enjoyed the raw warmth of her hand in his.

The proprietor came up to the table holding a bottle of his best red wine. Leslie sat next to Lyman, Gerry next to Kano, indicating he had some business to discuss with Kano. The cheerful owner filled their glasses and left. Lyman turned to Leslie.

"How long have you worked for the airlines?"

"About two years now—" And then realizing she had been wearing her uniform earlier in the day, said: "You have a good eye for detail, Mr. Lyman. Are you here on official or unofficial business, Mr. Lyman?"

"It's Sergeant Lyman."

"Very well, Sergeant. Well, what is it?"

Lyman changed the subject. "A little dangerous, isn't it? Dealing with the threat of terrorism on the airlines these days..."

"The airlines look out for us. And having a brother in the State Department doesn't hurt. I don't like the way Arab men treat their women, but I mind my own business, and try not to get involved. I leave the hard work for Gerry. So

– do you enjoy the enlisted ranks, Sergeant?"

"Staff Sergeant." Lyman smiled. "You're not one of those girls that just dates officers, are you?"

"Actually, I prefer a man with soiled hands. And you, Sergeant? Do you always seek out the prettiest girl in a room? Or do you go for the sleazy type?"

"Hey you two – let's have a toast!" Gerry announced, holding his glass of wine up. The others joined in. "To us and the merry millions that await us. God help us if they catch us."

The group toasted. Lyman's face grew concerned.

"What's wrong?" Leslie asked, "is it the wine?"

"Excuse me for a minute."

Lyman and Kano left the table for a few minutes. There was a moment of heated discussion in the back of the restaurant during which Kano angrily handed a small device to Lyman. The two men then returned to the table.

Leslie said playfully, "What was that about?"

"Old business." Lyman pulled out a small tape recorder. "I'm trying to break his habit of tape recording everything, especially our private conversations." Lyman returned the recorder to his pocket and opened his menu.

"What has my brother gotten you all into this time?"

"My lips are sealed."

Leslie rolled her eyes. "You military types are all alike."

"OK, it's a minor security detail."

"I don't believe you. Especially if it involves my brother. You're surely not as devious as he?"

Lyman sat back and studied the girl. He was not willing to discuss business around her. But he did find her attractive.

"How long are you here for, Leslie?" he asked finally.

"Two days," she said.

"I have tomorrow off."

Leslie frowned. "I'm busy, I'm afraid." Her tone was pleasant, but final.

"Too bad." Lyman was surprised by how the rejection hurt. But he shrugged his shoulders and smiled. "Shot down again. And this time, no parachute."

Leslie laughed. "Perhaps another time. Leave your information with Gerry. I'll call you the next time I'm in town."

After dinner, Gerry and Kano had some business to conclude and Gerry asked if Lyman would walk his sister back to her hotel. Lyman would have preferred to iron things out with Kano before Leslie's brother left, but it would have to wait. He agreed to see Leslie back to her hotel. And it was during their evening stroll that Lyman began to fall in love with the former 25-year-old cheerleader from Texas.

CHAPTER 15

Detective Gates and her partner walked out onto the windy tarmac at Barksdale Air Force Base squinting into the sun. Hill put on his sunglasses and gawked at various military aircraft, lagging behind. The detectives were looking for Captain John D. Long, aka JD, a pilot and member of the 939th Air Force Reserves. Instead they bumped into a group of young servicemen boarding a C-130.

Gates took a few moments to enjoy the scenery. The soldiers aroused an interest in the detective. Afterwards, up near the front of the aircraft, Gates spotted Long assisting with preflight preparations and hydraulic checks under the starboard wing.

Long was a tall, handsome guy with dark hair and intelligent eyes. Gates was surprised to see Long was older than she had expected. Yet he still had a boyish charm she imagined attracted plenty of attention from the opposite sex. Long put down his clipboard and shook hands with both detectives.

"Thank you for seeing us," Gates said. "We are sorry about your friend, Leslie."

Long forced a smile. "Thank you, Detective." Long glanced down at his clipboard.

"Hell of an aircraft," Hill said, "I was with the 82nd Recon out of Fort Bragg."

"Good unit," Long said. "Active or Reserve?"

"Active. Got out in ninety-eight."

"Detective Gates," Long said, changing the subject, "didn't I already speak with you about Leslie?"

"Yes," Gates said. "But I have a few more questions to clear up."

"Fire away."

"You say you last saw Ms. Marken on the night of the 6th. Is that correct?"

"I had a shuttle flight from Minneapolis. Both Ms. Marken and I were scheduled on an international flight the following evening. We were excited about it. It had been several months since we've worked the same flight."

"You stated earlier that your relationship with Ms. Marken was strictly work-related. You both work for Delta, correct?"

"I've flown with them for about twelve years now. I think Leslie had been with them for just under four. Administration can supply you with specific dates."

"And how long have you been in the Reserves?"

"I'll be eligible for retirement next month."

Gates made several scribbles into her notebook.

"Were you and Ms. Marken dating?"

"No. Not really."

"Could you be more specific, sir?" Gates said and waited while Long scribbled something on his clipboard.

"We were friends."

Gates inquired firmly. "So you didn't sleep with her?"

"Let me correct that. We were slightly more than friends... I assume you got the DNA match from my military history? I would prefer you did not pass that piece of information on to my wife. We're in the middle of divorce proceedings." Long took a break from the conversation and checked out the running gear. Gates followed him. She noticed Long's left hand, specifically where a wedding band would be worn. The finger held no ring – just white skin exposing its recent departure.

"Did your affair with Ms. Marken come before or after your wife left?"

Two soldiers dressed in BDU's, or Battle Dress Uniforms, walked by. Long waited until the men were out of range and toyed with his pen. Hill seemed fascinated by the large barn-size aircraft doors where the soldiers entered. He walked up and pounded the fuselage. His limited attention span aggravated Gates.

John frowned. "What was the question again?"

"Did Ms. Marken have anything to do with the breakup of your marriage?"

"No. We slept together only that one time." Gates knew the man was lying.

Hill stepped forward. "Why only once, Captain?" he said curtly. "Good lookin' girl like Ms. Marken. Hell, I'd be bangin' her every chance I got."

Long stepped back. "As I said earlier, Leslie and I were mostly just friends."

"You always sleep with your friends?" Gates pressed. Long's jaw tightened. He moved away, fiddling with the aircraft.

Gates let it go. "Let's move on, shall we?" she said tactfully. "What can you tell us about Ms. Marken's personal life? We know she traveled frequently. Any money problems? Personal problems? Did she mention any other men?

Any other relationships she might have had?"

"I don't think there was anyone specific? And no, she did not appear to have money problems."

"Did she ever mention Jim Lyman?"

Long fidgeted with his clipboard. Lyman's name made him nervous. "Not for a long time."

"What can you tell us about him?"

"They had a thing for each other."

"When was this?"

"Several years ago. Lyman was in the service."

"So you comforted her after a breakup?" Hill prodded.

"I became her friend and confidant, Detective," Long said and glared at Hill. "We've known each other for a number of years. I encouraged her to apply with the airlines. She and my daughter went to the same high school.

"How many children do you have, Mr. Long?" Gates asked, making a note in her notebook.

"One. Angie will be twenty-five next month. Why are you interested in Jim Lyman?"

Gates ignored the question. "You didn't have contact with Lyman? You're both in the Air Force. Sometimes paths cross?"

"I don't recall anything specific right now."

"Let's back up," Gates said. "Tell us more about Ms. Marken's relationship with Lyman."

"They were engaged. Lyman was on an overseas assignment – Lebanon, I think. They saw each other off and on for several months, whenever she had a layover in the area. Lyman was scheduled to get discharged and they were going to be married on the East Coast. But Lyman disappeared."

Gates studied the pilot's eyes. "How did she take the news?"

"How would you take it, Detective?"

"Soon after, we heard Lyman's unit was ambushed. Leslie's brother worked for the State Department. He notified her. Lyman was reported MIA. That was the last anyone heard of him."

"I'm asking you again. How did she take it?"

"It devastated her," Long said.

"How did you take the news?" Hill asked.

"I didn't know Lyman. But as you can imagine, I felt for Leslie. As I said, she loved the man."

"You never met, Lyman?"

"No!" Long snapped. "You asked that already."

"When did she start dating again?" Gates asked.

Long swallowed, gazed out over the tarmac. "I don't know. If I had to guess I'd say, seven, eight months later. I'm guessing here. She didn't discuss it. I was out-of-state attending pilot refresher courses in Arizona."

Hill jumped in. "When you came back from Arizona, did she mention other men in her life? Or, women for that matter. Anyone who might have had a motive to kill her?"

"No one specific," Long replied.

"What about Ray Kano?"

Long stopped making notes and looked up. "Who's Ray Kano?"

"We checked her voice mail at the hotel. He made several calls to Ms. Marken's room, leaving his name each time. Your voice is also on the machine," Gates rattled off. Long was visibly shaken.

"She mentioned Kano's name in passing. I don't remember the details. I think Kano and Lyman were in the same unit. You'll have to speak with him."

"Any idea where Kano lives?"

"No."

"The hotel has no credit card receipt for the room. Why do you think Ms. Marken would pay for an executive suite with cash?"

"Sorry, Detectives. I can't help you."

"But you said you were her confidant?" Hill reminded.

Long snapped, "And part of her mystique was that she didn't tell me everything."

Gates jotted something down in her book. "Was Ms. Marken taking any antipsychotic drugs that you know of?"

Long cringed. "After her brother died, she saw a therapist for a few months. I don't believe he put her on medication."

"How do you explain the recent mood swings then?"

The comment surprised Long. "You've spoken to her co-workers?"

"Just doing our job, Mr. Long," Gates said. "Please answer the question."

"She seemed in good spirits the night we had dinner together. However, I was aware of the rumors."

"What rumors?" Hill prodded.

"That she was considering a job change."

"Why?"

"She was tired of the schedule."

Gates said, “Were you aware that Ms. Marken had a miscarriage?”

Long tightened his fist. “No.”

“Tell us about your last evening together.”

“I took her to her favorite restaurant in the French Quarter. Acme Oyster Company. We sat at the bar. She drank a little more than usual. But then so did I. Then we went back to her hotel. We ordered dessert from room service and then I left several hours later.”

“What did you talk about at dinner?”

“Nothing special. My separation mostly.”

“Did Ms. Marken mention if anything was bothering her?”

“No.”

“But you discussed your wife with her?”

“I might have mentioned her.”

“How did Ms. Marken react?” Gates asked.

“She was sympathetic.”

“I bet,” Hill said sarcastically. Long glared at him.

“Did your wife know about Ms. Marken and your relationship?”

“Yes. My wife knows everything.”

“Is your wife capable of murder?”

Long paused. “My indiscretion with Leslie would hardly be motive for murder.”

“Why does she want a divorce?” Hill asked.

Long got in Hill’s face. “As I said, Ms. Marken and I were not lovers. Our relationship was purely platonic until a few days ago. My wife left me because she found someone that doesn’t spend seventy percent of his time away from home. Does that satisfy your morbid curiosity, Detective?”

Gates remembered something. “Did you give Ms. Marken a gold necklace?

“If you mean the one with the gold coin – that was a gift from Lyman. She hasn’t worn it in years.”

“Let’s back up.” Gates yawned. “Tell us about Ms. Marken’s brother?”

Long’s throat was dry. He swallowed and continued. “He worked for the State Department. He died in a plane crash two years ago. You probably read about it in the paper. A number of people were killed. Fifty-three, I believe.”

“What’s his full name?” Gates asked.

“Gerry Marken. I don’t know his middle name.”

“Did Lyman give Ms. Marken the necklace overseas?” Hill asked, making notes of his own.

“She returned from Lebanon wearing it.”

Detective Gates stared off across the tarmac like something had just struck her dumbfounded. "Does Ms. Marken have any other siblings that you know of?"

"No. Her mother and father are both dead. They died when she was a senior in high school. Car accident."

"Unlucky family," Hill noted.

Long remained quiet.

Gates closed her notebook. "Did Ms. Marken move in with another relative after her parents' death?"

"No. There was a small insurance settlement. She used the money to rent an apartment. Gerry was already in college at the time."

"Thank you, Mr. Long. If we have any further questions, we'll be in touch."

CHAPTER 16

Lyman waited. He was good at it. Two years of confinement teaches you nothing, if it doesn't teach you how to wait. Patience was the key. Ray Kano was dangerous. And this was his turf. His hacienda. Lyman would wait until the time was right.

He needed sleep. He had been up for days. His hiatus with Emily Douchet was exhausting. Enjoyable, but exhausting. The woman had been insatiable. He would repay the money, somehow.

He took a closer look at the trip wire. It was a poor version of a treadle spring snare. For wildlife or for humans? Kano still remembered the survival skills taught during the ground phase of pararescue school – affectionately called, "The Pipeline."

Lyman reached into his pocket and broke off a chunk of jerky and chewed as he studied the snare. The salty juices restored his energy. The milligrams of protein sawed a hole in his fatigue. He was going to need every ounce of strength he had to kill this son-of-a-bitch. *Chew damnit, chew.*

* * *

The sun was starting its slow descent, bright as a golden beach ball in a lavender pool. The jetboat zipped and glided and tossed side to side in the shallow water, carving a path through the grassy marshland. Vu closed his terrified eyes as a flock of squawking osprey took flight. Even with protective ear muffs on, deafening the roar of the 427 turbo engine and large powerful prop, Vu could hear the bird's cry. It was like a warning from the swampland – a warning to all who dare cross waters here – danger lies ahead.

Dunkin, a gangly kid, freshly flunked out of high school, and raised in the outbacks of the Segnette Bayou, rapped Vu's shoulder and pointed ahead.

"See it? To your right!" the kid shouted.

Vu dried his glasses on his shirttail and tried to focus through the streaked lenses. He could see miles of marshland.

Vu had confabulated a story at the restaurant about why he had needed to locate Jim Lyman. Something to do with national security. Dunkin's older brother had grown up more north in the Atchafalaya Basin area, the nation's largest swamp. "Young Dunkin's the kid for the job. That guy was askin' about Hunter's ole' place." Carl blinked and swatted at a fly buzzing their heads. "Dunkin can find it. He's young, cocky and mean as a junkyard rat. He'll find 'em." Then Carl held out his enormous hand. "Now let me see the money."

Dunkin didn't seem to care about all the government hype or the cash Vu had given his big brother Carl in advance. If it kept Carl from makin' him go back to school, so be it.

Vu cinched his seatbelt tighter as if the last thousand yards would be the most treacherous. Dunkin's driving scared the hell out of the little Vietnamese man.

"Do you have a gun?" Vu shouted above the loud engine noise.

"What?"

"A gun. Do you have a gun?"

Dunkin pulled out a 30-06.

"Does a duck have a dick?"

Vu sank back in the high-backed seat and warily watched Dunkin's thick hand yank the throttle stick and steer the boat toward a very narrow opening in the trees. They were going to die, Vu was sure of it. Gun or no gun. The canopy of trees was too narrow for the boat to pass through and the cypress stumps were like spears popping up everywhere.

Why Vu suddenly thought of Rufus, the one-eyed alligator, was beyond comprehension and poorly timed. How he hated alligators now. Even the harsh scent of turtle poop could not snap Vu out of it. Trembling with fear, he kept his eyes wide open.

What was that? Vu swatted a dead low-hanging branch, thinking perhaps it was a poisonous snake or a creepy swamp thing swinging down out of the trees to sink its venomous teeth into his flesh.

"Can't you slow down?"

"You're not scared are you, faggot?"

The powerful V-8 descended into the heart of the Bayou.

* * *

Lyman snapped his eyes open. He heard a door squeak open. Kano appeared on the deck, carrying an armload of chicken skins and lard. He walked down the steps, whistling to the wildlife. Lyman watched. Kano scattered the meat around the perimeter of the stairs and then stepped back, three stairs up, waiting and staring into the woods. He clapped his hands loudly three times, and searched the deep swamp.

Lyman sank back into the dense brush. Something was moving through the tall grass. It stunk. He could hear them coming. Four, maybe five small gators, snapping their knotty jaws open and closed, excitedly scrambling toward the piles of raw meat.

Kano smiled.

Damnit. Lyman was pissed. The son-of-a-bitch had alligators surrounding his steps. How in the hell was he going to get around them? Food? He reached into his pocket. No more jerky. *It was a stupid idea anyway*, Lyman thought.

The baby gators devoured the chicken meat and lay down to nap in the grass. Kano himself yawned. He removed his buck knife and stretched out in a hammock strung out on the deck. Closed his eyes. Before long, Kano was snoring.

Lyman was a former Navy Seal. He could do this. With a small cuticle knife he had lifted from Emily's cosmetic bag, he peeled the bark off several long, spindly willow branches, braided the branches together into a long piece of wet rope. Earlier he had found a long branch, maybe six feet long, and stout. He carved it smooth on both ends, cut a small groove at the head and looped the braided strands around several times and made a noosing wand. He slipped one hand in between the noose and yanked. The noose pulled down tight and held. Slow, but worked. He needed a lubricant. It would help where the strand was knotted. He looked around in the grass. He found a slug stuck to the base of a cypress trunk. He rubbed the slug's belly up and down along the strands. The slippery slug juice worked.

Time was wasting.

He crossed the wet grass, the long stick out in front of him like a fly pole, and crept through the area where the gators slept. One opportunity was all he had if the gators awoke.

Then he heard the sound.

CHAPTER 17

Kano snapped open his eyes and jumped up as Nigel stepped out of the dense foliage and into the light. The Arab stopped a few feet away from the gators and kept his distance.

"You will do something with these?" Nigel shouted to Kano.

Kano veiled his surprise. He hesitated, scanning the area thoroughly, felt for his buck knife and realized it was gone. He clapped his hands and watched the gators scurry for the protective cover of the swamp.

"Where's the cavalry?" Kano asked.

"I came alone."

"Sure you did."

"Come, my friend, we are not going to bicker at one another. We have much to talk about." Nigel smiled, and a gold tooth glistened in the sunlight. "Shall we discuss our shipment?"

Kano backed toward the door. "Long has it."

"I do not believe you."

"Have a look around then."

"I think I would like that very much. But I have more questions for you first. That was very messy, what you did in New Orleans."

"It was an accident."

"I think she knew too much," Nigel said. "That is what I think."

"Think what you want."

"I also think you're planning to keep all the gold. And not repay your Arab friends for their generosity."

While Nigel and Kano gazed at each other, Lyman, who had crawled along the dense marsh until he was within view of the deck area, peered out and caught his breath. He recognized Nigel almost immediately. It was the shiny gold tooth that brought it all back to him. His heart raced.

Nigel moved closer toward the house. Kano put up his hand for him to stop.

Kano said, "Damnit Nigel – you let Lyman live."

"Of course, Ray." Nigel grinned. "How do you think I found you?"

"You were instructed to kill him."

"Of course, that was the agreement. But then, you were to deliver our gold to us once it was in the United States. Neither one of us has kept our promise."

As Kano made for the door, the two Arab thugs lunged from the shadowy interior of the house and struck Kano on the head with a .45. The big man swayed backwards and crashed to the floor.

Nigel stood on the deck looking down at Kano's still body. He seemed pleased with himself. "Sorry, Ray – it was an accident."

CHAPTER 18

The guttural cry pierced the dense swamp land.

"What was that?" Vu asked nervously.

"Blue Heron. They're thick in these parts."

Vu pushed the wet willowy branch aside and watched the long-winged bird fly away through the trees. Dunkin killed the engine. The boat glided soundlessly through the narrow tunnel of dense foliage.

Dunkin pointed out over the bow. Vu turned. Ahead was Kano's house, slipping into shadows as the sun worked its way west. When the time was right he casually stepped off the bow onto the small dock and tied off the mooring lines and helped the little shaking Vietnamese man onto terra firma.

Dunkin watched as Vu pulled from his pocket a small vial of green pills. "Hey, Vu'y! Those get you high?" Dunkin asked, holding out his hand. Vu cringed at the mispronunciation of his name.

"What?"

"Those pills. They get you loaded, Vu'y?"

"Please stop calling me that."

He watched Vu gobble the pills.

"Just don't do anything weird. I got a rifle."

Vu walked on Dunkin's heels up to where the ground beneath his feet finally felt solid. The area near the lean-to smelled like diesel. The generator wasn't running. He touched the motor. Still warm. He pulled out his 9mm.

Dunkin yelled: "Anyone home? Hey Drano you in there!" Dunkin chuckled at his own joke.

Vu frowned, motioned with his finger to remain quiet.

Dunkin checked the shop. He poked his head out of the wood doors and shouted: "Just a bunch of junk!" Dunkin hustled across the grass, packing his 30-06 with its hand carved stock.

Vu told Dunkin to wait down below while he checked out the inside of the house.

The interior was gloomy. The shades were drawn down to keep out the sunlight. There were two rooms and a kitchen. Furnishings were handmade. Bed, sofa, kitchen table, chairs. Basics. One wall in the kitchen was stocked with canned meats and vegetables. The refrigerator stocked with beer, milk, eggs, butter, bread, and chickens. Whole chickens. An ashtray by the sofa had several cigar butts in it. Vu held one of the butts to his nose and sniffed. Old. He checked the bedroom. Five or six changes of men's clothing. A big man. Six three, six four. Size 12 shoe. Fit the profile. Two unopened cases of Off insect repellent behind the door. Vu went outside and looked around on the deck. Hammock strung. An empty Budweiser can. He raised it up, sniffed. Fresh. A noose snare leaned against the window sill. He inspected the handiwork. Ran his hand over the wet strands. Primitive but functional. Felt slick. Interesting...

Dunkin shouted up to him. "See anything, chief?"

Vu shook his head. He placed the snare back where he found it and walked down the stairs.

In some weeds near the water, Dunkin spotted something shiny sticking up. He stooped down and picked up the piece of jewelry. It was a man's military ring. He quickly dropped it into his pocket. Vu reappeared and Dunkin pointed out fresh alligator tracks, and what looked like chicken bones scattered about. Probably where Kano threw out his nightly scraps.

Down on the ground near the waterline, Vu spotted some fresh tracks in the wet grass. Deep grooves in the grass. The tracks ended at the waterline. He stooped over and felt the impressions. Something wet and dark caught his eye. Reddish liquid. Pool about the size of a softball. He dipped his finger into the substance, held the tip of his finger toward the light. Blood. Fresh blood.

"Look!" Dunkin shouted from the bush. He pointed out toward the water. He waded out a few feet out and pulled some long tree branches back. Beneath the camouflage covering was a wooden boat. "Never mind. It's just a junky old boat."

Vu snooped around the track marks. Something floated just beneath the surface of the murky water. He rolled up his pant legs and cautiously waded into the water. It was a leather wallet. He opened it.

"What'd ya find?" Dunkin trotted up.

"A wallet."

Vu pulled out a Louisiana State Driver's License. Dunkin got excited, jumped into the water, and fished around beneath the surface. Something solid grabbed his attention. "Hey, Vu'y" he called out. "Think I found somethin'..."

Dunkin pulled the object from the water. "Fuck!" He tossed the object into the grass.

Vu walked over to it and stared. Dunkin picked up his rifle. Spinning around, he fired off six rounds into the water.

"Fucking gators!"

After Dunkin was finished firing a deadly quiet fell. Vu silently squatted down and examined the hunk of flesh.

It was a man's left hand.

Dunkin began babbling. "Fuckin' gators! Fuckin' gross shit!"

Vu concentrated. A memory descended. He stepped back and took several deep breaths.

"Any more of him left?" Vu inquired. Dunkin stared down at the water. Shook his head.

"Fuckin' shot the hell out of 'em," Dunkin reflected.

"We arrived too late," Vu said, feeling like he should say something profound. But what ceremony do you give a man's hand?

"Damn square," Dunkin chimed in.

"Start the boat. I'll be right back."

Dunkin loosened the mooring lines on his boat. An hour earlier, Ray Kano's jet boat had been moored in the same spot.

Back at the main dock, Dunkin killed the engine and glided to shore. Vu reached between his feet and retrieved the brown sack containing the remains. He climbed off the boat, looked back at Dunkin.

"It would be better if you kept this to yourself," Vu said. "Here's an extra twenty dollars." Dunkin reached out and took the cash.

"Whatcha goin' to do with it?" Dunkin pointed at the brown paper bag.

"We have facilities for things like this."

"Fuckin' body parts?"

"Yes."

Dunkin reached down and hit the start button. The big V-8 fired up. "Fuckin' gators..." he grumbled.

Vu watched the swamp boat speed off, leaving behind a glistening oily sheen on the water's surface.

CHAPTER 19

Millie Lyman was baking bread when she heard the car pull into the driveway. She turned down the radio, wiped her hands on her apron, and went to the door. She pressed her good ear against the wood and listened.

She could hear what sounded like a man's footsteps on the gravel drive. Millie stepped back from the door, ran a hand over her hair and waited. Her eyes wandered. A moment later the door bell rang. Millie released the deadbolt and opened it.

The man at the door knew in advance Millie couldn't see him.

"Yes, who is it?" Millie asked pleasantly.

"Hello, Ma'am," the man said. Millie noted the deep Midwestern tone. Strangely familiar yet unrecognizable from her list of acquaintances. "I'm looking for Ms. Millie Lyman. Would that be you ma'am?"

Millie smiled. "Yes. That was my maiden name. Who are you please?"

"My name's Ray Kano, ma'am," the voice said. "I'm an old friend of your brother's. Jim and I were in the service together."

"Jim?" she exclaimed. "Do you have news?" And without waiting for an answer she turned, saying "Come in, please."

Millie trailed her hand along the wall, leading the way. Passing the small living room, she pointed to a large overstuffed sofa. "I was just about to make some coffee. Would you care for some?"

"That would be fine."

"Good. Have a seat, Mr. Kano." Millie left the room.

"Please call me Ray."

"Very well, but then you must call me Millie."

Lyman sat down. Not much had changed since his last visit. Still the family portraits and several pictures of the relatives and neighbors. Porcelain knickknacks, the old organ in the corner, the brass lamp next to the chaise lounge, the pine coffee table, and several hardbacks which he knew were done in Braille. The room still smelled like spring roses, Millie's favorite scent, and the walls still needed painting. A Merle Haggard tune played.

Millie called out from the kitchen. "Are you on leave, Ray?"

"Yes, ma'am, I mean Millie. I just finished serving my second tour of duty in Kuwait."

Millie came in carrying a platter with coffee and fresh-baked tollhouse cookies.

"What can I do to help?" Lyman rose to assist her.

"Sit down, Ray," she instructed. "I've been without sight for a number of years. It's really not that much of a handicap."

"You have a nice home here."

"It could probably use some dusting. My late husband, Steve, used to do it for me. I don't tend to be so diligent with housework these days."

Lyman sank back, shocked at this revelation. "I'm sorry about your husband. Jim didn't know."

"Steve died last year. Stroke. God rest his soul. At least he didn't suffer."

Lyman's eyes dropped to the floor. Thinking of Millie stranded helpless once again so many miles from town, opened up old emotions.

"How do you take your coffee?"

"Just sugar. No cream."

"Funny, Jimmy used to take his the same way."

Lyman snapped out of his daze. "I thought Jimmy liked his with Jack Daniels."

Millie chuckled. She took a small silver spoon and spooned in two scoops and passed the cup to Lyman. "Here you are," she said. "Just help yourself to the cookies. I'm afraid I'm fresh out of whiskey."

Millie took a dainty sip of coffee and stared toward Lyman. "So what brings you to Salt Lake City?"

"Jim asked me to deliver something to you. I'm sorry it took so long."

Lyman sat his cup down and reached into his jacket pocket. He retrieved a fat envelope and set it on Millie's lap. Kano wouldn't need it anymore. And now that Millie was alone, she could certainly use the money.

"Your brother said if I made it back in one piece, you were to have this. We served together in the 83rd Airborne Division. We were good buddies. I miss him."

Millie put her cup down. "So do I. I haven't heard a word about Jimmy in so long. Has anything changed?"

"I don't believe so, ma'am."

"It'll be two years and two months next week."

"Yes, ma'am. I held onto this package in the hope he could deliver it himself."

Millie handled it gently. "When did he give this to you?"

"About a week before he disappeared."

"Where were you?"

Lyman became aware he was tapping his foot up and down. "Just north of the Iraq border. We were on an exercise. I won't go into details, but your brother knew I was about to get transferred. At the time I thought I was coming back to the United States. But I got reassigned after the incident. This is the first opportunity I've had to deliver it."

Millie lifted the envelope to her nose. "Funny, it kind of smells like him. Jimmy always loved to wear that strong aftershave."

Lyman smiled. He'd specifically eaten garlic and had stopped by a department store and splashed on some sweet queer cologne to disguise his smell. He knew Millie's legendary radar would be up.

"Did Jimmy ever tell you how I lost my sight?"

"No, ma'am."

"It was a freak hunting accident. He blamed himself. I was only ten. For years I blamed him too. Whenever I could, I'd make him feel guilty. He started following me around, watching me. Trying to protect me. I could always smell him and his cologne. Then one day I quit feeling sorry for myself and started feeling sorry for him. I realized we were both damaged from the accident. From that point on, we've tried to take care of each other.

"But I don' think he was ever the same. We all have demons inside of us, Ray. Even Christ had to deal with his. Jimmy had a few of his own, I'm sure."

Lyman swallowed hard, tears streaming down his face. Something inside of him was cracking open. Maybe if he could draw up a happier memory...

"He told me a story about driving with you in a old truck. I've got to ask – was that just bullshit, excuse my French, ma'am, or is it true that you drove a vehicle blind?"

Millie chuckled and slapped her thigh. "The neighbors thought Jimmy was absolutely insane to let a blind girl behind the wheel. That first time we stayed on back roads and I can't tell you how much fun it was. You'd be amazed at the number of phone calls I got. Millie was that you I saw ... Millie you should know better than ... Millie this ... Millie that...."

Millie picked up a Kleenex and dabbed at her eyes. "Okay – let's see what's inside."

Millie opened the envelope. A wad of hundreds spilled out onto the floor by her feet along with a note. Lyman stooped over and picked up the money and handed it to Millie. Millie grabbed onto his hand, felt it, then reached toward his face. Lyman pulled back out of reach and gently placed her hands around the money.

Lyman studied Millie's face as she let it go and ran her hands over the stack of cash.

"Is this money?"

"Yes, and there's a note with it."

"Could you please read it for me?"

Millie's eyelids closed. She folded her hands into her lap and sat up straight.

Lyman's voice cracked. "Dear Millie," he read. "I thought I'd pass on some of my good fortune. Use this money to buy that Braille computer you were telling me about. All is well here. Plenty of sand and surf and sun. Love, your big brother."

Lyman folded up the note as Millie blew her nose.

To distract himself from wanting to hold his sister, he pretended to count the cash and then handed it back to Millie. "There's five thousand dollars here. It's all hundred dollar bills."

"Thank you, Ray. You are a good friend. This has been a truly remarkable day. Can you stay for dinner?"

"No. I'm afraid I must be moving along. I'm on my way West. Got a few service buddies in Oregon to look up next."

"Jimmy always talked about going to Oregon. Said the Northwest had great fishing. How can I thank you for keeping your word? It's a rare commodity these days."

Smiling ruefully, Lyman grunted agreement. Spying the cookies, he inquired.

"I haven't had any home baked cookies in a long time. Do you think I could have a few for the road?"

"It's the least I could do."

As Millie prepared his food, Lyman felt a door closing firmly on his vulnerable heart. As Millie handed him his cookies, he said goodbye to his old demons.

"Drive carefully." Millie stood and held her hand out. "Thank you again," she said. "If you're ever back this way, please stop by."

Lyman took one long last look. "I'd like that very much."

CHAPTER 20

Nigel utilized his illegal network of foreign informants and learned that Lyman had a sister in Utah. He assumed Lyman would contact her at some point; however, kidnaping her would be too risky. Besides, Lyman didn't have the gold. No – it would be far better to ferret out Captain John D. Long, but not on a military installation. Since 9-11, Arabs were under suspicion and it would not be prudent to try and gain access. Their passports were forged and it would not take long for authorities to discover their motives for being in the United States were questionable. Nigel had to assume since the gold was not found at Kano's that he had been telling the truth and that Long did indeed harbor the sovereigns. Kano had filled him in on all aspects of the operation – at least to a point. Oh, the wiles of the greedy heart...

There were still two other possibilities. But Nigel preferred not to think about those presently. The gold could be in the hands of the other members of the squadron or the government could have it. If it was the former, Lyman would be hot on its trail soon enough. If it was the latter, then it made no sense to send in the Vietnamese investigator unless they wanted to keep the incident quiet. Yet things were now growing more complicated.

According to Nigel's sources, Long rented a condo in Bossier Heights – more of a fuck pad than an actual residence. As it turned out, Long was a lady's man with the stewardesses. He had a wife who filed for divorce recently and he was seeing Ms Marken before her death. Busy man. Certainly in need of cash – lots of it. The sovereigns were a sure ticket to wealth, but with his high profile, he would have to be cautious. The IRS would pounce on his bank statement if it appeared lopsided suddenly and the Air Force might become suspicious. Nigel figured there was a plan. It probably involved others. Someone to fence the gold, etc... JD, Nigel figured, had been in the game long enough to know you can't just show up one day with a shipment of gold or a bank deposit of a million bucks and not draw unwanted attention.

Nigel felt a tap on his shoulder and looked out the car window. Long's silver and gray Porsche was pulling out of the garage.

"Stay with him but don't make it obvious..."

Fifteen minutes later, Long's Porsche pulled off the main highway and turned into the Bossier Municipal Airport and bypassed the passenger terminals and headed straight for the flight line. He knew he was being followed by the fuckin' ragheads. *So they made it into the United States... well, just peachy ... first Marken and now Nigel. Fuckin' Kano...* This operation was getting very complicated. He let up on the gas and had a wild thought. Hell no, he wouldn't shake them after all. *This could work to my advantage....*

The Arab's car pulled into the airport. "Where the hell does he think he's going?" Nigel shouted into the driver's ear. The driver cringed and glanced in his rearview where he could see Nigel's volcanic eyes.

He shrugged. "Shall I follow him?"

"Yes, damnit, follow him."

By the time the Arabs located the Porsche it was sandwiched between two large aircraft maintenance buildings parked beside a refueling truck and Long was nowhere in sight. Out on the tarmac, commercial as well as private aircraft whipped around in the wind, parked in tidy rows with their wings secured to the pavement with tie-downs.

"Were the fuck is he?" the driver asked.

"Pull over," Nigel instructed. "Search the building."

The two men jumped out. They disappeared inside the building. Several minutes later they reappeared frowning, raising their hands in defeat.

Nigel stood at the car and gazed toward the runway. "Try the other building."

As the men moved toward the hanger, its doors sprang open. Inside, a twin-engine Cessna fired its engines and began rolling forward. The men jumped back out of the plane's path as its powerful blades sliced at the thick humid air outside.

Long was in the pilot's seat, headsets on, steering the aircraft toward the runway. As the plane rolled past, he flipped the men off. Stupefied, they stopped in their tracks. The Cessna picked up speed and left them in a cloud of dust and exhaust.

Nigel pulled a .45, pointed it at the plane, then changed his mind.

"Get me his flight plan!"

CHAPTER 21

Warrenton is a small coastal town located south of Astoria, Oregon with a population of about seven hundred during the winter months. The small fishing community there sticks pretty close together and looks out for each other.

The Flenner brothers grew up there, went to high school in Astoria, and returned there after a stint in the military – at least the two older brothers, Alex "AJ" Flenner and Case Flenner. Bobby Flenner, the youngest, got into some trouble with local law enforcement which sent up a red flag when he went down to the recruiter's office and tried to join up. The two older brothers never held it against Bobby. He was just sixteen at the time of his petty theft charge, and in a way he did his part by keeping the family business going while they were away in Afghanistan. Bobby had also looked in on AJ's pregnant wife, Pam – the former Astoria High Homecoming Queen of 1999. And Bobby had kept Lucky Lady afloat.

But that was then. The clouds were rolling in over the marina. And Bobby was late again.

Bobby turned off the main road, hopped a ditch on his dirt-street motorcycle, and skidded to a stop at the dock. The 46 foot Lucky Lady with her twin Mercury diesels bobbed in the ebb tide. AJ was in the pilot house fidgeting with the instrument panel while Case was loading tackle aboard.

"Where the fuck you been?" Case shouted at Bobby. Bobby took off his leather jacket, threw it over the gunnel and jumped aboard.

"Sina wouldn't shut up."

"Sure, Bobby." Case spotted a broken eye on one of the salmon poles. He pulled out a pocket knife. "AJ wants to see you in the pilot house."

"What's he want?"

"How the hell would I know?"

Bobby and Case were always butting heads. Bobby hopped over a pile of nets, dodged empty jerry cans and made his way toward the pilot house. He poked his head through the steamy door.

AJ was ass to elbows in electrical wiring. The transducer on the knot meter again.

AJ leaned back and clipped a butt connector on a strand of 12 gauge wire. "Why didn't you get any oil?"

"Fuck! I forgot." Bobby exclaimed. "I'll go get it."

"There isn't time."

"I said I'd get it."

"Bobby, when are you going to start taking this operation seriously?"

"I said I was sorry. Don't fuckin' lecture me."

"Go give Case a hand with the tackle. We got four going out today."

"Not that prick from Salem?"

"Yes, the prick from Salem."

"I don't know why you had to start funneling charters. I liked it when it was just the three of us. And I'm gettin' sick of cleaning up puke."

"It pays the fuel bill, doesn't it?"

"Yeah, but?"

"Go inspect the rods. One of them is broken."

"Case is fixing it."

"Then pump the bilge."

Bobby kicked the empty jerry, frustrated with himself for forgetting to do the few things his brother had asked. He knew things were tight. Case kept saying their payday was going to come in. They just had to be patient. Keep Lucky Lady going a few more months.

The first charter arrived. A couple from Portland. The husband worked for an engineering firm called RZA. The wife was an administrative assistant for Bonneville Power Administration, BPA, they called it. They were wearing matching sweatshirts purchased in Astoria, baggy jeans and bright yellow rubber boots. Stupid. AJ always told his charterers to wear sneakers or lace boots. Last thing you wanted if you fell overboard was a pair of floppy boots that'd fill up with water and sink you to the bottom like concrete blocks.

"Hello Mr. and Mrs. Prescott," Bobby said. "Take a seat up front."

Mr. Prescott hesitated and frowned at his wife. "Go on, tell him," Mrs. Prescott said. Mr. Prescott blushed. "If you won't tell him, I will." She said gruffly. "My husband lost his Dramamine patch this morning. You have extras aboard? Your name's Case, right?"

"It's Bobby, and no ma'am we don't."

"See, Frank, I told you."

"Rita, don't start," Mr. Prescott snapped.

AJ poked his head out of the pilot house. "Good mornin'. How were the accommodations?"

Behind their backs, Bobby mimicked his brother's hobnobbing. He glanced at Case who was staring toward the marina. A taxi pulled into the parking lot. A tall, thin man got out of the back. He paid the driver and walked toward the dock carrying a small black briefcase.

Case shouted toward the pilot house, "AJ!" AJ looked up. Case pointed toward the stranger.

AJ looked surprised and hopped down from the wheelhouse. "Bobby!" he shouted. "Help the Prescotts with their life jackets. I'll be right back."

AJ climbed off the boat and headed toward Captain John D. Long.

CHAPTER 22

They were standing at the grave of the famous Voodoo queen herself, Madame Laveau, with the early evening Creole moon rising over St. Louis Cemetery. Ms. Caan placed a candle on the headstone of her great sister of the South and then stepped back from the immediate area so others from the group could pay their respects.

Vu was off to the side listening to the soft harmonic chants of the dozen or more gatherers. One by one each paraded up to the grave and spoke to the dead queen. Down at his side was a small ice chest which he had been carrying with him for nearly an hour. Inside, wrapped in brown paper, was the unidentified hand he had pulled from the swamp.

Earlier that day from the telephone in his hotel room, he had asked Betty for a favor.

"What do you want with a finger printing kit?"

"I'll explain it later."

"I don't know, Jack. Sounds mysterious."

"It is important."

There was a long silence. "Will you meet me at 1200 Royal Street, in The French Quarter, at a little restaurant in back called the Black Orchid? It's where the Voodoo Tour organizes."

"Voodoo tour?"

"Bye Jack. See you at 7."

He reasoned he needed her help at whatever the price. If stomping through a cemetery would do it, so be it. Besides, the dead did not disturb Vu. He believed the soul passed on, and that the dead did not come back to haunt the living. The soul was too pure for such trivia. Hollywood wanted you to believe otherwise.

* * *

Strolling through the historic cemetery, Vu's thoughts drifted. The tour group they had been part of went on ahead. Betty latched on to Vu's hand suddenly and drew him aside into a dark hollow between two tall concrete vaults and pressed her warm chest against his. Vu could feel her excited heartbeat. He reached back, felt the cold stone, and stared into his companion's gleaming eyes.

"Cemeteries get me hot," Betty whispered.

"I am happy for you," Vu uttered. "What exactly are we doing here?"

"Do you find me attractive, Jack?"

"Yes, but..."

"Shhh..." she hushed.

He could feel Betty's steamy breath move down along his neck and her palpating heartbeat pressing against his trembling chest. And for a moment, he believed that the spirit of the infamous Voodoo queen had invaded her soul.

"Just kiss me! Kiss me, Jack!"

Then, out of the deep dark night, another voice sounded from beyond, breaking the mysterious spell.

"Hey, you two. No breaking off from the group!" the tour guide shouted.

Betty quickly stepped back, brushed herself off. She looked coyly at Vu.

"Ms. Caan... Betty... you're a very attractive woman..."

"Yes, Jack," she said cheerfully.

After the tour group concluded at the shrine of a voodoo temple, Vu took Ms. Caan next door inside the Black Mojo Bar and bought her a double Cutty Sark on the rocks. Later, inside Ms. Caan's office, he placed the cooler on the counter, took off his jacket, and asked Betty if she wouldn't mind doing the honors.

Stroking his arm, she replied, "I thought you'd never ask" and leaned forward to kiss him.

He was losing his mind. Hadn't he explained to Betty why he was on this date? Why he had been packing this silly cooler all around the city?

Sighing, Vu reached inside the cooler, pulled out the frozen brown paper bag, and dropped it on Ms. Caan's desk.

"What's this?" she asked.

"A hand."

"Cool..."

Ms. Caan slipped on a pair of rubber gloves. "Hey, what'd you do to Riley anyway? Everybody around the office is talking about it."

Vu ignored Betty. He watched her slender hands unfold the brown paper bag. His body quivered, like the alligator that snipped off the bony appendage was slithering its jagged teeth inside his soul.

"You okay, Jack?"

"Just continue please."

Betty drew out the fleshy, frozen hand. "I'm going to have to thaw it out," she told him. "It'd be quicker if I put it in the microwave."

Betty placed the hand on a scale. "1.6 pounds," she said, and recorded it on an official document. "C'mon, let's go upstairs. There's a microwave in the break room."

"Is that a good idea?" Vu asked. "It is not standard protocol."

"That's why I like you, Jack," Betty said. "Deep down you're a bad boy at heart."

"I am?"

"Uh huh," she purred.

Vu wondered. "Could you put it back in the cooler for transporting?"

"Getting shy on me now?"

They passed several uniformed officers leaving the break room as they entered carrying the small cooler. A vice detective known as Blake was waiting for his burrito to finish cooking in the microwave. Betty went up behind him and placed the cooler at her feet. Vu crept in and sat down across the room. Blake spun around and grinned.

"Hey, you the cop that put Riley in the hospital?"

Vu muttered, "I believe I might be the one responsible."

"Well, you did us a favor. That fuckhead is worthless. He's threatening to sue the city. You believe that horseshit? He was probably playing with his dick when it happened."

The microwave bell rang. Blake popped open the door, pulled out a steaming burrito on a paper plate and flopped it down next to Vu. Vu watched the detective stuff the foot long doughy wrap into his big mouth. "Shit! Shit!" the detective blurted, spitting out parts of the burrito onto his plate. "Damn, thing's hot!"

Behind Blake's bobbing head, Betty winked at Vu as she slipped the frozen hand into the microwave and closed the door.

"Hey, Blake – how much time for a frozen hand?"

"Betty, don't fuck with me like that."

"Okay – I'll put it on defrost for two minutes. That should be enough."

Betty walked over and sat down beside Vu. They both looked at each other like they were hiding a deep secret. Blake looked at them. "You weren't serious?"

"Of course not. Jack brought me some dim sum. Want some?"

Blake stuffed the cooling burrito in his mouth and chomped away. Vu's mind wandered, watching the detective chew.

The bell chimed. Blake looked up eagerly. "Maybe I'll give it a shot. It's got to be better than this horsemeat." Blake spun his chair around and watched Betty pull the steaming hand from the microwave. Blake spat the last of his unchewed burrito onto the plate.

"Christ, Betty..."

"Yum. Yum. Sorry, Blake. Looks like there is just enough for two."

Betty waved for Vu to follow.

"Nice to meet you, Detective..." Vu said, and shuffled toward the door.

Blake sat like a stone and stared at his plate.

CHAPTER 23

Betty picked up the limp hand off the stainless counter top and held it a few moments to get the feel of it. One by one she pressed the fingers into the ink and rolled them onto the white sheet of print paper, checking her work as she went.

"I've never fingerprinted a hand without a body attached before. It's kind of awkward."

"You're still using the old system."

"We're a bit behind the times. A computer is coming."

"I very much appreciate your help."

Vu pulled out his vial of green pills and popped a few.

"You gotta stop eating raw meat, Jack."

"I don't think that will be a problem now," Vu replied, staring at the inky decomposed meat before him.

"So when are you telling Gates about this? You know she'll find out. And when she does, shit's gonna hit the ceiling."

"Will you tell her if I withhold the information for a few days?"

"Eventually, I'll have to. But not right away." She smiled conspiratorially as she pressed another finger to the paper. "She doesn't trust you."

"Obviously. She had me followed."

"You sure about that? Could have been anyone. . . even me."

Vu stared hard at Betty, his mind processing this new information.

"By the way, where's the rest of the body?"

"I can only speculate."

"Jack you're toying with me. How sexy..."

"You are a good woman, Betty."

Betty wiped the excess ink from the hand and placed it back into the paper bag. She stuck the bag into the cooler and closed the lid.

"I'm risking my position, you know."

Vu picked up the fingerprint paper and examined the quality of Betty's work.

"I will take all responsibility."

"That may not be good enough."

Betty turned, took the paper from Jack's hand and examined his own fingertips. "Okay, Jack. We'll do it your way for now."

"Thank you," Vu replied and bowed.

Betty stepped closer. Vu could feel her body heat filling up the area. She placed his hands around her waist.

"You want me to run the prints through our data base now?" she whispered in his ear.

"Not at the moment," Vu's voice softened.

Betty smiled as she removed Vu's glasses and set them on the counter. Pulling his face close to hers, she opened her lips. "Don't worry, Jack," she whispered, "this won't hurt a bit."

Vu blushed. "Okay, Betty, we'll do it your way for now."

CHAPTER 24

Gates lived in the Garden District. A shotgun house in the dark part of town. Out her livingroom window she could see the fading lights of Commander's Palace. A historic landmark in New Orleans, dating from slavery days. *A blight on Creole soil*, Gates thought.

She poured herself a Wild Turkey – a double. As she drew a bath, she sat on the toilet and obsessed about the Marken Case. She was disgusted with herself, her job, and her life. She was falling into the same rut. Vu had made her look like an ass. He pegged Riley. That had made a pasty out of her. *Fuckin' slant-eyed bastard.* Well, the little shit wasn't going to get the best of her. She may not have balls, but she certainly had a big cunt. If a woman had guts then she was a bitch or a dike. No option. What about strong women? Powerful women. The labels society drew... Vu had assumed she was the weaker sex. Hell, maybe Vietnamese women were subservient but she sure as hell wasn't, damnit. And he'd fucked her over in front of her own crew.

She slipped out of her work clothes and felt the water. Hot. A little pain was good. She pulled out a fresh bar of perfumed soap and dipped her toe in the soapy water. She held her foot under the water though it burned her skin. Then the doorbell rang.

Fuck!

She slipped on a terrycloth robe and left the room.

Facing the door she shouted, "Who the hell is it!"

There was a moment of silence. Then a women's voice replied: "Ms. Gates? I'm with the Bush Agency."

Gates glanced at her watch. "You're early."

"Our appointment was for nine."

It was 8:57. *Fuck*, she had lost track of time again. The booze.

Embarrassed, Gates unlocked the deadbolt and opened the door.

Standing before her was a seductive Asian woman, dressed in a sheer black dress, revealing a taut gymnast's body. The bright hall-light revealed her erect nipples, big as gumballs. A faint halo of the women's dark pubic hair shined through the see-through material.

"Where's Jill?"

"She has the flu. The agency sent me instead."

Gates felt a knot in her stomach. She looked the woman over. She was her physical preference. But she wasn't white, and she wasn't Jill.

"What's the password?"

"Sunny."

Gates hesitated.

"Something wrong, Ms. Gates?"

"No." Gates snapped out of it. "I was drawing a bath."

Gates showed her in.

She watched her cross the room. She strode with confidence to the front of her aquarium. She ran a delicate hand over the glass.

"You're into fish?"

"They're harder to kill than plants," Dorene said. "What's your name?"

The Asian girl smiled. "Bamboo."

"Great."

Gates went to the refrigerator and pulled out a beer. She held it up. "Would you like a drink, Bambi?"

"I'd prefer Scotch," Bamboo said. "Single Malt, if you have it."

Gates felt chided. She pointed to the liquor cabinet. "Knock yourself out, honey. I'll be right back."

Her bath had steamed up the mirror. When she dropped her robe, a slim hand touched the small of her back. Bamboo had followed her into the room. Gates seemed surprised at the sudden intrusion.

"I need to bathe first," Gates told her.

Bamboo put her drink down on the counter. "I don't think so." On tip-toes she kissed Dorene. Dorene stepped back.

"Take it easy, sweetheart."

"What's wrong?"

"I was expecting a six-foot dike, not a Lil' Kabuki. I need a minute to regroup."

"I can piss on you just as well as Jill."

Dorene swallowed hard. She felt a burning sensation crawl through her groin.

Bamboo hiked up her dress and grabbed a handful of Gates' hair and pulled her down between her legs.

"After you're through with dinner, I'll give you a nice shower from my Golden Triangle."

CHAPTER 25

Vu spent the morning driving across Alabama, sipping green tea from his thermos and listening to Cajun music on the crackling radio. Every so often his thoughts drifted with a smile to the surprising Ms. Caan. It was noon when he pulled up to the front gate at Maxwell Air Force Base, showed the SP his ID card, and requested a temporary vehicle permit.

"How do I get to the Air War College Building?" Vu asked.

"Who are you looking for?"

"My old boss, Colonel Morgan."

"Just head down this road, turn left at the second intersection. That'll be Franklin Street, follow it to the end. You'll see a gymnasium-style building to your immediate right. Colonel Morgan has an office on the second floor."

"Thank you," Vu said, and started to roll up his window. The SP stopped him, pointed at Vu's temple.

"You might want to check that out before meeting the colonel."

Vu turned his face toward the rearview mirror. Saw the smear of red lipstick, smiled proudly at the SP, and drove on through the main gate.

The War College Building was exactly where the airman had indicated. A two-tone, five-story, brick building with ornate trim, surrounded by lush green grass. Several large Aspen trees swayed like stick soldiers in the warm breeze. Vu walked up the main sidewalk, passing several students wearing Navy uniforms and entered the lobby. Inside, the walls were done in pine and decorated with photos, war memorabilia and flags from all over the world. The halls were freshly waxed and the area smelled like bleach. The acrid smell reminded him of his tenure in a similar building years earlier when he was with the Security Police. Such a strange journey from the killing fields, to the Security Police and a four-year degree in Administrative Justice. It was because of the colonel that he even transferred to OSI. Locating the colonel's photo on the wall, he mused quietly before turning his attention toward finding the stairs leading to the second floor.

Colonel Morgan's office was at the end of the hall. His office door was closed. Vu knocked, waited, and after no reply, knocked again. A female recruit struggled up lugging an armload of hardbound books and old journals.

She stopped to catch her breath.

"I think he's lecturing upstairs," she panted.

"May I assist you?"

Shaking her head no, the girl seemed obliged to turn him down. "If you hurry you can catch him between classes. He breaks around 12:30."

"What's the room number?"

"412 – I think."

"Thank you," Vu said graciously.

The recruit nodded, hitched up her books again, and walked off.

Colonel Morgan was erasing the chalkboard when Vu entered. It was your standard classroom that held about thirty-five students, some of whom were milling about in the back.

Vu cleared his throat. "Hello, Colonel."

Morgan set his chalk down and turned. "Why, Sergeant Vu, I didn't expect to see you again so soon." There was a false tone of enthusiasm in his voice.

"How'd the game of golf go, sir?"

Morgan frowned. "What? Oh – it went fine. The major has a surprising back swing. I assume this is a social visit. How long are you in the area?"

"With your permission sir, I need a word alone with you."

Morgan glanced at his watch. "That could be difficult. Can it wait?"

"No, sir."

"Then how long will this take?"

"That depends on you, sir."

"I see." Morgan paused. "Well, you've caught me at very inconvenient time. I've got a two o'clock and a another lecture at four-thirty. Then I have ..."

Vu interrupted with a force that surprised even him. "Sir, this has to do with the State Department. And a few of your Special Ops guys." Across the room, several of the students stopped talking and zeroed in on Vu's comment.

Morgan frowned. "Not here, Sergeant. Let's move to my office."

"Very well, sir."

Down in his office, Morgan cleared off a chair and tossed a stack of folders onto the floor. "Sit down, Sergeant." Morgan instructed, then glanced out his small window. The window looked down on the back of the building where a group of female recruits in sweats performed calisthenics. Their excited cadence echoed up through the window.

"They're making 'em tougher these days," Morgan told him and turned toward his desk. Vu was impressed with the walls lined floor-to-ceiling with books. Even if Morgan read only half the books in the office, it was years of work.

"Yes, sir," Vu replied.

"You married, Sergeant?"

"No, sir." Vu smiled inwardly at this banter. The colonel was well aware of Vu's status on all levels. Another game had begun with his old teacher.

"I've been married for thirty-five years. Three boys and a girl. Girl's the toughest of the bunch. Heart of stone. Runs five miles a day, works out regularly, tutors mathematics to the new recruits, and is top in her class at the Academy."

"That's nice, sir."

"This is about Lyman, isn't it?"

"Yes, sir."

"I told the major you were the right man for the job. That you'd do the right thing and provide the right evaluation."

Vu ignored the comment. "Sir, Lyman's alive and well and somewhere in the U.S. But that's not the only reason I came here today."

Morgan pointed at his phone. "Let's continue this downstairs, shall we?"

Vu looked with surprise at the innocent looking phone.

Outside the building, Morgan and Vu walked along the sidewalk down the north side of the building. They passed the recruits exercising in the grass. Once they were out of earshot, Morgan said, "I've found it's better to discuss sensitive matters away from the office. It's saved my ass on many occasions."

"You believe your office is compromised, sir?"

"I won't take the chance. You understand?"

"Yes, sir."

"Good." Vu waited as the colonel's mind worked the angles. "How's that scooter of yours..."

"I've been on assignment since I last saw you, sir."

"Too bad. Man should never be too far from his golf clubs or his bike. Not healthy for the soul. This last stint in Turkey about did me in."

"Sir, I won't take any more of your valuable time. If you could just answer a few questions for me. Will you please clarify why Lyman's squadron was assigned to the embassy in Lebanon?"

"Routine security detail. State Department was experiencing aggravated levels of terrorist threats. Wanted our boys to watch their backs. Keep the camel dung out of their eyes so to speak."

"Sir. I have reason to believe that is not entirely true." Vu quickly added, "Security details do not involve just a handful of men and large shipments of gold."

Colonel Morgan physically deflated as if someone had punched him. He turned to Vu and said quietly, "Who told you about the gold?"

"A former colleague at the Treasury Department. I wanted information about a gold coin."

Morgan took a deep breath and studied his small companion. "It was just a matter of time..."

"Sir?"

"You've learned well, Sergeant."

Vu remained focused. "Lyman was not in Southeast Asia when he was captured – was he?"

"No, Sergeant. That was fabricated to keep the fire burning over there."

A trail of joggers strolled by singing in cadence. The men waited to resume speaking.

"What I'm about to tell you shall not leave this area, understand, Sergeant?" Vu nodded. "Wheylicke should have briefed you. I presume he doesn't know the whole of it. There were four of them, not counting two men in the State Department. Jim Lyman, Ray Kano, and two brothers from Oregon, Alex and Case Flenner. Gerry Marken and Bob Leach were liaison officers inside the embassy in Lebanon. What really happened we don't know for certain. What we do know is that a large cache of gold bars, bullion, and a number of counterfeit coins, specifically rare British Sovereigns, were stolen from a renowned counterfeiter in Lebanon. These counterfeit coins may have some collector value – even if discovered to be counterfeit. Bullion is the market value of the gold. In any case, today bullion was traded at $323.60 an ounce. It doesn't take a heavy bundle to add up."

Morgan paused, and glanced toward the street.

"His ties to various terrorist and criminal organizations has been well documented for a number of years. And we wanted to simply redistribute the wealth to more charitable causes. But the operation failed. Lyman and his troops were to go in, steal the gold, and get out. Quick, easy, no fuss. The money would be turned over to the State Department and everyone would get a royal pat on the fanny for a good job done." Morgan frowned. "Unfortunately, it didn't turn out that way. The gold and Lyman disappeared."

"You think Lyman took the gold?"

"Well, that's where it gets messy, Sergeant. State Department claims the military kept it – in other words – Lyman and his men. Military says the State Department and Marken kept it. Treasury and the FBI threw up their hands. What little information we do have came from Marken about thirty minutes prior to his plane plunging nose first into the Red Sea. According to him, the operation failed. There was no gold. Lyman and the others shot their way into the safe house where the gold was supposedly hidden and it was gone. Lyman was left behind and later was taken prisoner by a group of pro-Islamic fundamentalists who were after the gold themselves. Fortunately, it appears Lyman escaped. We expected him to follow normal RE-UNITIZING procedures. But as you know, he didn't."

"Did the other men confirm the story?"

"To the nail."

"So who's lying?"

"Good question. Maybe no one. What do you think?"

"I don't at this point, sir." Vu scratched his head. "Let me rephrase that. I don't have a formed opinion at this time, sir."

"Look. One way or the other skeptics will say the State Department utilized the military, for shall we say, inappropriate activities. Lyman and a handful of others know it. The press would love to latch onto a hot story like that. It'd be Iran Contra affair all over again. You know what I mean, Sergeant?"

"The major made it clear, sir."

"We need to make this go away quietly. And at this stage of the game, we're not interested in knowing where the gold went or if there was gold in the first place. Marken is dead. Lyman's probably a section-eight case by now. Kano's retired to the swamp land to wrestle alligators. Alex and Case operate a small commercial fishing boat out of Oregon. We've kept an eye on this group for the last two years. None of the gold has surfaced. If you ask me, and I'm reaching here, I'd speculate that if there was any gold it disappeared when Marken's plane crashed into the Red Sea. If Lyman had not resurfaced, this thing could have gotten swept under the proverbial rug like so many other governmental conspiracies."

Vu looked down at his feet. "What is it, Sergeant?"

"Lyman, sir. If we knew all along where he was being held, how could we let one of our own remain prisoner? Two years is a long time, sir."

"Have you forgotten your own history so soon?"

"No Colonel. It is because of it, I am inquiring."

"Bitter sweetness of war, son. Fact is, we thought he was dead."

Vu believed his old mentor was lying.

"Locate Lyman and bring him back to the fold before this thing expands beyond our ability to control the result. Otherwise, it could be detrimental to all involved."

Vu got the message loud and clear.

CHAPTER 26

Gates sat with her hands behind her head staring at the wall. Across the room her office door opened. She looked up and frowned.

"I figured you'd be by."

Vu stepped up to the desk and opened his briefcase. "I will be leaving in the morning," he said. "I wanted to leave this with you first."

As Vu pulled a file out of his briefcase, Sergeant Hill marched in carrying a steaming coffee mug.

"Hello, Vu," Hill said cheerfully. "How goes the war?"

"Very well, thank you," Vu replied. He placed a large file on the detective's desk. Hill sat his cup down beside it.

Gates sat forward and sniffed the steaming coffee cup. "What is that?"

Hill smiled. "Green tea."

Gates flopped back in her chair. "You're drinking tea, now?"

Vu laughed. "How do you like it, Sergeant?"

"Tastes a little weak at first. But it kind of grows on you."

Gates took the file off her desk and opened it. "Better late than never, huh Sergeant?"

"Our government works slow."

"That it does..." Gates closed the Lyman file and slid it across her desk into Vu's open hand. "I have no use for it now."

"Lyman is no longer a suspect?" Vu asked, surprised.

"As it stands, I have an old thumbprint. I also have a member of the Air Force Reserves that states Lyman and Marken were once engaged to be married. That Lyman presented Ms. Marken with a necklace several years ago. And I suspect that the thumbprint dates back to that time period. As far as I'm concerned, Lyman is still MIA. Unless you're here to tell me different?"

Vu appeared relieved. "I am pleased to hear that, Detective."

Gates shuffled papers around on her desk. "By the way, Ms. Caan..." But before the words were out of Gates mouth, Betty walked into the office wearing a black kimono-style lab coat. Gates sighed. "Not you too?" she said to Betty.

Sergeant Vu gleamed. He realized he had left a small impression on the precinct. Hill was drinking tea. Betty was wearing Asian clothing. But it would be a stretch to see Gates trading in her cowboy boots for wooden sandals.

"Ms. Caan what?" Betty inquired curiously, blowing a secret kiss across the room to Vu.

"I was telling the sergeant that we've ruled out the possibility that Lyman killed Marken."

"You have?" Betty asked. "So who killed her?"

Vu picked up the file off the desk. "Well, if there is nothing else. It has been a pleasure working with you Detective Gates and Detective Hill. My only concern with this matter was if Sergeant Lyman was involved with Ms. Marken's death. Since we have concluded that Lyman was not in the area, then that will be sufficient information for my CO," he paused, then looked at Betty. "Ms. Caan, would it be possible to speak with you alone outside?"

Gates studied the little man. "You won't mind if we hold on to Ray Kano's hand for a little while, do you, Sergeant?" Vu stopped in his tracks.

Before Vu had time to reply, Riley entered. He wore a rumpled suit and a wide bandage around his head. Swollen black orbs gazed out of a twisted face. "Not so fast hotshot." He shakily pointed at Vu. "We have a few things to settle."

Riley stepped forward and swung his fist. Vu quickly sidestepped around it, locked onto Riley's wrist, and led him down to the ground effortlessly, where Riley dropped to his knees and smacked his forehead on the floor. Riley, stunned, breathless, gasped.

"...fuckin' bastard..." Riley squeezed out. "Someone arrest the Gook for assault."

Gates stood. "Riley, get up off my floor. And kindly tell me what the hell you're doing?"

Riley slowly climbed to his feet. Vu remained calm but posed to defend himself at any time. Hill took a long sip of tea and appeared amused by the whole incident.

Betty said, "Riley, your head is bleeding."

A tiny trickle of blood dribbled down the man's sweaty forehead. Riley found a mirror across the room and examined himself. "I'm going to sue everybody," he uttered, and grumbled out of the room.

"That man is not well," Vu said aloud.

Gates piped in, "So, Vu, what's going to happen now? You leave for Baltimore tomorrow, huh? Submit your findings in writing to your commanding officer?"

"That's correct."

"I bet your CO is going to be relieved to know that we didn't find any solid evidence that your man Lyman actually set foot in New Orleans. But now we have another problem. Since Lyman didn't kill her, then I have to assume Ray Kano did. Our friendly sperm donor, John Long, confirmed that Ray Kano knew Ms. Marken. The two were more than mere acquaintances. Once we were able to confirm the identity of the fingerprints from Ray Kano's hand, we obtained a DNA match on the sperm we found in Ms. Marken's rectal area. All thanks to the little gift you left downstairs."

Betty blushed and hung her head.

"I have not spoken with Mr. Long," Vu acknowledged with surprise.

"Of course you haven't," Gates said. "Because your contacts in Washington provided you with your information. I suspect you believed Ray Kano was guilty all along. You had your boys back East provide you with Kano's whereabouts and you went hunting." Gates glanced at her desk. She picked up a notepad and glanced at some writing, put it back down. "According to a kid named Dunkin, you paid him to boat you out to the Kano residence two days ago. He said you acted strange. Like maybe you wanted to do more than just talk to the man. Later, he stated it was possible you could have visited the residence beforehand. He said he found a boat in the trees that hadn't been there before when he checked on Kano's place. And that Ray Kano's jetboat was missing from its usual mooring. We went to the location and saw the boat. It's not too far a stretch to believe that you made up the story to Dunkin to cover your dirty works. And that you took Kano's boat and ditched it somewhere in the area. You then hired the Dunkin kid to make it appear that you had not been to the area before. That would have given you plenty of time to kill Ray Kano and dispose of his body in the water. It doesn't take a genius to figure out that alligators would devour the evidence before long. But then Dunkin found a boat in the trees and an object floating in the water. And it got him thinking."

"I had nothing to do with Ray Kano's disappearance," Vu stated.

"That's not what the Dunkin boy said."

"Then he's lying..."

"He may be." Gates swallowed. "But there is a waitress who places you in the vicinity."

"Then she also must have told you I was. . ." Vu bit his tongue. He didn't want to reveal what he knew about Lyman now.

"What, Sergeant?"

"Nothing. This is all speculation and lies."

"Not all of it," Gates said. "Ms. Caan was kind enough to show me where she was keeping Kano's remains. She needed a little prodding. Probably because she has taken a liking to you. But once a print confirmation verified that the hand belonged to Ray Kano, we had enough information to go to the D.A." Gates stood up. "Sergeant Hill, please read Sergeant Vu his rights and escort him downstairs to a holding cell."

Hill looked surprised. "Dorene? Have you lost your mind?"

"Are you disobeying a direct order?"

Hill stuttered. "Eh... no, ma'am."

"Well, then do your fuckin' job!"

Hill sadly faced Vu. "C'mon, Vu. Let's go."

Ms. Caan was unable to move. "You can't! Jack! What charges are you arresting him on?"

"We're holding him on suspicion of murder."

Betty turned pale. Vu remained calm. "I will need to make a call."

CHAPTER 27

The hard cold cement floor of the holding cell reeked of disinfected urine. Vu sat in the corner with his back against the wall and stared at the steel bars, his mind slipping into the past. To another time when he was a prisoner accused of crimes he didn't commit.

His family had been forced to vacate their home by the North Vietnamese soldiers. His father, a former member of the South Vietnamese military, was a target now that the U.S. had pulled out all of its troops. Vu was only a teenager at the time.

At first, the communists were too slow for the former military man and his family. They escaped into the country to live off the land like their predecessors had for centuries. However, one day the soldiers captured Vu and sent him to a labor camp. There, he was forced to work from dusk till dawn seven days a week. After the night terrors sunk into him, he escaped into the jungle but was recaptured. For punishment he was required to remain on his knees hands bound and gagged fourteen hours a day. After two months, he was returned to the labor camp. The next time he ran it was literally for his life. From the jungle, he made a raft of trees he had felled and floated across the ocean to Malaysia where he declared political asylum. Vu was a free man again. But now he was back where he started, and the jungle he needed to escape from this time, was filled with lies instead of trees.

"Jack!" Betty pressed her face against the cold steel.

Vu opened his eyes and looked out.

"What are you doing here?"

"That's no way to talk to your girl."

Vu slowly unwrapped his legs and joined Betty at the cell door. She reached in through the bars and took hold of his hand. "Were you able to call your CO?"

"Yes. A man from the Judge Advocate's office will be here as soon as he can."

"Jack? I know you didn't kill that man."

Betty pulled Vu up close to the bars and pressed her lips against his. The warmth softened the hard expression on his face momentarily and then it was lost. Deep lines of thought burrowed into his forehead.

"This is all my fault. The burrito bandit turned us in to Gates, but I could have lied or made up a story or something."

"I am only sorry you are involved in this intrigue. It wasn't your fault, Betty. And I don't want you implicated any further. You need to stay away from me now."

"No, Jack, I want to help. Tell me what to do."

"Go home."

Vu watched as his sexy pathologist sadly walked away.

CHAPTER 28

The Lucky Lady idled into the Warrenton harbor and killed its engines. Bobby jumped from the bow and secured her mooring lines to the dock while the Prescotts gathered up their belongings and stepped out of the main cabin.

The couple were unsteady on their feet. They stepped off the stern and lost their footing on the slippery dock. Bobby had his hand under Mrs. Prescott's arm and was able to keep her on her feet. Mr. Prescott flopped down on his fanny like a fat basset hound embarrassed and squinting into the setting sun.

"First step's a doozy."

"You okay, Mr. Prescott?" Bobby asked, and stepped around to help him to his feet.

"I'd be better if I was packing home a fifty pound halibut."

"Some days are a bust."

"Don't suppose you could refund part of our money?"

Smiling, Bobby wagged his head no.

Case stepped out of the pilot house and gazed down upon his weary passengers. "Have a safe drive back," Case shouted. The Prescotts hobbled off down the dock like two sad penguins.

After they were gone, Bobby coiled up the extra line and said to his brother Case. "Did you hear that guy? He asked for a refund."

"Let it go, Bobby," Case said. "Hand me the gaffing hook. Then toss me one of the jerry cans."

"Yeah, yeah..." he grumbled. "When's AJ coming back?"

Case glanced up at the parking lot. AJ's old GMC pickup pulled into the lot and parked. "He's here now."

Bobby looked up. His oldest brother unloaded scuba equipment out of the back end of the truck. He loaded the equipment into a dockcart and wheeled it down the gangplank.

Bobby jumped off the boat and jogged up the ramp. "What the hell's that?" he exclaimed.

"Help me get it aboard."

Bobby and AJ hefted the tanks onto the bow. Case climbed out of the rear hatch. “Case!” AJ shouted. “Give us a hand.”

The three brothers lowered the bulk of the equipment down through the rear hatch and strapped it against a foot locker used to store tackle.

“What’s that for?” Bobby asked.

“Stow the regulators in the locker,” AJ ordered and then pulled Case aside and whispered to him.

Bobby looked dejected, and haphazardly shoveled the gear into the metal cabinet.

“Bobby, take it easy,” AJ snapped.

“What the hell’s up?”

Case and AJ just stared at each other. “How much diesel is left?” AJ asked Case.

Case said, “80, maybe 90 gallons. There’s enough.”

“Enough for what?” Bobby inquired, squirming like he was going to piss his pants. “C’mon, ass holes, what’s with all the secrets?”

“Take off, Bobby,” AJ ordered. “This doesn’t concern you.”

“Fuck you guys...”

CHAPTER 29

A blinding flash went off in Vu's eyes. A reporter for the *New Orleans Tribute* shouted out:

"Sergeant Vu? What was your reason for killing Ray Kano?"

"Sergeant! How is the military taking the news of your arrest?" a reporter cried out at his back.

Another reporter shouted: "Are you a paid assassin?"

Then another... "Sergeant! Tell us about the Marken Murder? What was your role in that?"

Vu ignored them, kept his head down, and continued walking down the crowded steps of the courthouse into the sudden downpour. More reporters dogged his trail and snapped pictures at his back. Vu stopped and looked up and down the unfriendly streets. Storm clouds rolled into the city. A heavy rain pounded the pavement. Traffic stalled and horns blared. As he waited for a light to change, the reporters caught up once again.

"Sergeant! Did your Commanding Officer know of your actions..." Then another... "What will you do now, Jack?"

Vu continued walking.

Where would he go now? Certainly, his government credit card had been suspended. He had little cash. No rental car. No hotel room. Did he still have a personal line of credit?

Out of the shadows came an excited face. Betty Caan grabbed his hand and dragged him through traffic. Cars skidded to a stop. Horns blared. Vu stumbled along, his mind numb. They stopped at bright red Buick – an old one, with a dented hood. Betty pulled open the driver's door.

"Get in the back and play dead," she ordered.

As Vu climbed in, several reporters frantically crossed the street, and Betty sped away.

Several blocks later, Betty looked in her rearview mirror and said softly, "You can get up now, Jack. They're gone."

Vu sat up, rubbing his bloodshot eyes. He let the tape of the last few days play back in his head. Why had Dunkin lied? Had Lyman set him up? With Kano dead – if he was dead – where would Lyman go next? He needed his files.

"You can stay at my place for a few days," Betty said. "I've got your things in my trunk. And I have something for you."

Betty did the one arm scramble in her purse, dodging traffic. She eventually extracted a cell phone, which she triumphantly tossed over her shoulder to Vu.

"Use this if you need to make calls. It will trace back to the police station . . . it belongs to Gates . . . that should even the score." Betty chortled to herself. She snapped out of the laughter and turned backwards in her seat to face Vu, alarming him at her increasingly erratic behavior.

"Thank you for the phone, Betty. I do have a few calls I need to make."

"Forget it. You'd do the same for me if I was in a jam. Wouldn't you, Jack? I mean, if I was charged with murder and there were all these pesky reporters dogging my tail I'd expect you ... Jack, did you say you were hungry? We can stop. I don't think I have a thing in the house. Maybe there's some peanut butter. I wonder if Jerry got my message. . . the Stanley case. . . I could always cook pasta. You eat spaghetti, Jack?"

Vu had difficulty keeping up with Betty's thoughts. Her mind seemed to be spinning out of control. "Betty?"

"Yes, Jack?"

"Slow down."

Betty looked at the dash, slapped the speedometer.

"Am I going too fast? It doesn't feel like I'm going that fast. Did you know that my insurance doubled last month after that last speeding ticket?"

"Betty?"

"Yes, Jack?"

"How many Bennies?"

"Just a few, Jack. I've haven't slept well these past few days. I've been worrying about you."

"Betty." Vu cut her off.

"Yes, Jack?"

Vu laid his hand on her shoulder and it seemed to have a calming affect on the jabbering pathologist. "Let me drive."

"Okay, Jack. Whatever you say. See, I'm slowing down now."

Betty pulled over to the curb. Vu climbed behind the wheel.

Vu waited patiently. He looked Betty in the eye. "Oh, I'm sorry, Jack. Continue up this street for a few more blocks and then turn right. I'll tell you where..."

Betty lived in a two-story wooden house built at the turn of the century. The Asian furniture reminded Vu of his childhood, before the war destroyed everything. The wind and water feng shui he found calming. He assumed Betty had at one time explored Buddhism. That intrigued him.

Her bedroom was on the second floor facing east. She said she liked to watch the sun come up in the morning. As she climbed in bed she explained that the sun warming her face each morning made her feel alive.

Vu came out of her bath carrying a bottle of sleeping pills. He set the bottle on the night stand, picked up a glass of water and handed them to Betty.

"You need to sleep now, Betty," Vu instructed.

Betty sat up meekly and took the pills and chased them down with a drink of water. Jack took the water glass and placed it on the night stand.

"Gates has really fucked up this time," Betty uttered. She reached up and ran her hand through his thick dark hair.

"She's doing her job. And I must continue to do mine. I must find Lyman."

Sighing, Betty searched his eyes.

"Jack?"

"Yes."

"Not now. Stay here. You'll be safe with me. It's the least I can do. I think I'm going to close my eyes now."

"I'll be right here."

Vu sat in the chair opposite the bed for an hour keeping an eye on her. He felt at odds with himself. The arrest had not helped his state of mind. However, the confinement had given him time to think about Lyman. Now as he watched Betty's chest slowly rise and fall, his thoughts turned to more personal matters. He wasn't accustomed to such kindness and he wasn't exactly certain how to respond to the affection he felt for this soft woman with a spine of steel.

Spying her lipstick on the night stand, he tenderly picked up the slick tube and opened it and smiled as the sun glinted off the sparkly surface sending light rocketing around the room. Twirling the little wand, he tip-toed downstairs.

CHAPTER 30

The Lucky Lady floated under a full moon in calm seas. Case sat on the stern looking out over the ocean occasionally glancing down at his watch, then checking the winch cable. He paced and re-checked the rigging twice and waited some more. Finally, the signal from below came.

Case flipped the winch switch and coils of heavy steel rapped around a large drum. The steel gears groaned, hauling the bulky object closer to the surface.

Out over the stern, a diver emerged out of the dark water. AJ peeled off his mask and tossed it into the boat. AJ's excited and exhausted eyes sparkled in the moonlight as he climbed aboard and began removing his wet suit.

AJ sighed. "Sand's shifted. We'll need bigger shovels and extra air tanks for the rest. We'll have to come back tomorrow."

Suddenly, the winch bound. Case stopped the cable, backed it down a turn, and then tried it again. "Remind me to lube the piss out of the rear pinion shaft."

"See any boats?"

"Nah."

"Good."

"Is it all there?"

"It's all there."

"I'm glad we didn't wait for JD. Wonder where he was?"

"Beats the shit out of me," AJ said." "Probably got hung up in town."

"Just as well," Case said. "Something about him rubs me the wrong way..."

"He's a friggin' officer, Case."

Case grinned. "How the fuck could I forget that?"

The old rusted chest broke the water's surface and swung from side to side streaming glistening seaweed. AJ hooked onto the metal chest with a gaffing hook and swung the chest over the deck and signaled to lower the winch. The chest thudded onto the wood floor.

Case grabbed a rusted crowbar from the wheelhouse and stood over the chest, looking at his brother.

"Just in case," he said. AJ tried to open the lock but it was rusted tight.

Case held out the crowbar.

AJ grabbed it and forced the bar under the crate's lid.

"Step back in case this thing snaps," he said and pried back on the bar. The metal lid creaked and snapped opened. Case ripped off one of the loose bands. AJ continued prying. The lid broke open. Case stepped closer. AJ reached his hand into the crate. His hand struck something solid and stopped.

Both brothers stared down mesmerized as thousands of gold coins glistened up. Case dipped his sweaty hands through the heap of sparkling coins.

"Look at all this fuckin' gold!"

CHAPTER 31

"OSI Commander's Office, Airman Betas speaking."

"This is Sergeant Vu." He waited for a response. Nothing. He continued. "You once told me if I ever needed a favor – well, that you owed me one." Still dead air.

"Julie, I need one now."

"The Commander has no comment at this time."

"Wheylicke is standing right there, isn't he?"

"We will be issuing a statement on this matter later today."

"Can I call back?"

"Yes. You will have your statement in time for the evening news."

"I'll call back. And Julie, thank you." The line went dead.

Vu held the small phone in his hand and listened to the drone of the line. How bad was this? Would Julie help even if she could? Could he continue to put others in jeopardy just because he didn't trust his own commanders to protect him? He'd known Colonel Morgan for over ten years. Morgan had literally saved his life by plucking him from his sinking escape raft. Waterlogged, starved and beaten, Vu had responded to Morgan's stern fatherly guidance and help over the years. It had culminated in Vu pursuing his career at OSI with Morgan's encouragement and blessing.

Had it all been a setup? He knew that he had been a tool for OSI's purposes many times in the past, but he had always justified it because he thought it was for a "greater good." It had never dawned on him that they would ever turn against him. But Lyman probably thought the same thing.

Vu worked the angles while the sun set through Betty's lace curtains. As the sun slanted almost directly into his eyes on its march to the horizon, Vu redialed the phone. Betas answered on the first ring.

"Julie, thank you for taking the call. Are you free to talk?"

"Where are you?"

"I'm in New Orleans. Have you been specifically instructed to render no assistance to me and report any telephone calls made by me?"

"No. Of course, they never considered you might call directly to the commander's office or to me for that matter. I got the impression, despite a press statement claiming support, they think you are on the run."

"I said earlier I needed a favor. I need you to research Lyman's outfit. I'll need specifics. Get the names of any men assigned to his unit in Lebanon. I'll need their DOR's, SSAN's, DOB's, HOR's, and current DA's. If discharged, provide me with current addresses."

"This is a mighty big favor."

"I know it's a lot to ask, but you're the only one I trust." Vu was unused to asking favors and disliked the way his voice sounded. "If you say no, I will understand," he added.

"This will take some time. How do I contact you?"

"I'll call back in four hours."

"Then you'll have to call me at home."

"I wouldn't ask if it wasn't critical."

"Vu, you're on the up and up about this, right?"

"I assure you, I am."

Betas laughed nervously. "OK, Felon Vu, I will take my black and blue arm and begin hunting and pecking for the greater good."

CHAPTER 32

Bobby pulled off his helmet and slung it over the handlebars. He glanced out over the vacant lot and headed down toward the Lucky Lady. Moonlight glistened off her cedar planking.

Bobby slipped below deck and pawed around in the dark until he found the overhead halogen light and flipped it on. The harsh light flooded the cabin. He pulled open the locker where he had stowed the scuba gear earlier and reached down behind a stack of old clean rags. He fetched out a hidden bottle of whiskey and held it up to the light and took several long drinks. He noticed some water droplets on the scuba equipment and it caught his eye. He started thinking.

He checked the air tank in the corner and saw the gauge down in the red area which meant the tank was low on compressed air. Then he saw a canvas tarp draped over a large object stowed in the corner. He went over and pulled back the canvas and revealed a large metal chest. The lid had been pried open and then pounded back into shape. He tried the latch but it was frozen. He found a rusted crowbar in the tool drawer and pried back the lid.

He almost wet his pants as he peered into the old chest.

CHAPTER 33

Vu picked up the car keys from the kitchen counter, went into the garage and opened the trunk. He removed his luggage, briefcase and laptop. Inside the house, he inspected his laptop case. It had not been tampered with. That was good. His files were intact too and no one had searched his luggage. *Thank you, Betty*, he chanted to himself. He pulled out Lyman's file and studied it, made some notes from the SGLV-8286 Form and closed the file. Noting the darkness enveloping the yard, he checked his watch, shaking his head at the elasticity of time. He tiptoed upstairs and checked on Betty who was still sleeping soundly, and then returned and telephoned Airman Betas again. She needed more time, another day at least, in order to not arouse suspicion. Arrangements were made for the following day.

As darkness stole in through the windows, he entered a small office off the main room and sat down in front of a computer terminal. Something in the mirror caught his attention. He stood up and walked toward an open closet. Inside among some winter clothing was a black garment. Upon closer inspection it was a "gi" – a martial art's uniform. Beside the uniform was a long staff, used in weapons training for Jujitsu and Aikido.

Inside a photo album were pictures of Betty in a "dojo" with a group of other students and martial arts awards – certificates of accomplishment in Aikido, a soft martial art from Japan. Vu was intrigued. Both he and Betty had studied the form during the same time period. Aikido was more than just a non-combative, gentle fighting technique. Its practice was designed to turn the enemy's force back on him or herself. Vu smiled at this new connection as he carefully closed the album.

It took him six minutes to bypass Betty's password and enter her system. He went online and conducted various transactions. He was logging off when Betty padded into the room.

Vu asked, "How do you feel?"

"Groggy, but better." She yawned. She glanced at the screen, scratched her head. "What are you doing?"

He stood up, stretched, and retrieved two documents from the computer printer tray.

"Getting credit card statements."

"Mine?"

Shaking his head and smiling at his sleepy savior, he answered, "No."

Betty glanced at the other document. "What else do you have?" Betty snooped through the material. Vu stopped her.

"Lyman stole a rental car and charged gas on a stolen credit card. The charges stop in Houma."

"Who lives in Houma?"

"A former colleague of his, Ray Kano."

"Interesting," Betty mused. "So Lyman's real and he killed Kano? Do you think he's still in the area?"

"My gut feelings say no," Vu said. "I found a document in his military file indicating he has a sister in Salt Lake City."

"Lyman wouldn't visit his sister. It'd be the first place I'd look."

"He's been MIA for two years. They were close and he'd want to let her know he was okay."

"I wonder," Betty's voice wandered off.

Vu noticed the change in tone and looked at Betty with a wider scope. "I know so little about you. Do you have family?"

"None I'd risk my life for."

"I am truly sorry to hear that." Vu paused a moment. "You risked your life for me."

"Yes... People are sentimental creatures, aren't they Jack?"

Vu's stomach did a soft flutter as he leaned back into Betty's warm arms and kissed her lips.

Vu pulled back. "I'll be leaving in a few hours..."

Betty's eyes darkened like a cloud obscuring the moon.

CHAPTER 34

Sina was working the counter at the Astoria 7-11. She occasionally checked her reflection in the window. She rang up the price of a frozen t.v. dinner and took the elderly gentleman's cash, extending her jewelry laden, brown arm. Out in the parking lot the sound of a dirt bike engine revved up, then died. A moment later the front window boomed under a pounding fist, startling the girl and causing her to drop the customer's change on the floor.

"I'm sorry," Sina said to the startled old man as she stooped down to retrieve the coins.

"Who acts like that?" he asked, pointing toward the window.

Bobby Flenner had his face pressed against the glass, waving like a lunatic. Sina glared. "My boyfriend," she said. "He thinks he's cute."

Snorting and shaking his head, the customer quickly picked up his groceries and left the store. Bobby slipped in the door behind him, jumped up on the counter, and kissed Sina on the lips.

"Bobby!" Sina snapped. "You gotta stop this." Sina pushed Bobby off the counter. "What do you want?"

"Close your eyes."

"What for?"

"Just close 'em", his voice sounding half excited and half agitated.

"We're on camera, Bobby," Sina said in a warning tone, but closed her eyes and smiled expectantly.

Bobby jumped up on the window sill and placed a Kleenex over the lens of the remote video camera by the door. "Keep your eyes closed," he said playfully, hopping down.

Bobby faced the counter and removed a handful of gold sovereigns from his pants pocket. "Now keep your eyes closed and hold out your hand."

Sina reluctantly obeyed. Bobby dropped the coins into her small hand.

"Okay, you can open them."

Sina glanced down and frowned and picked through the strange coins. "What are these? Sunken treasure? They're fake aren't they?"

"No."

"Yeah, right... whatever." Sina rolled her eyes.

Angry, Bobby snatched the coins back and dumped them into his pocket.

"Bobby – I gotta pee. Watch the front, okay?"

"That's it?"

"I'm not into coins..."

"You might be if I told you how many there are."

"I gotta pee, Bobby."

While Sina was in the back room, Bobby took another appraisal of the coins. Then he hurried over to the cooler, pulled out a quart bottle of beer, and slipped it inside his jacket just as he heard Sina return.

Sina turned around and faced him. "Oh, let me see them again."

"Forget it." Bobby frowned. "So when do you get off?"

Sina spotted the bulge in Bobby's jacket. "Bobby!" She flashed a pair of angry eyes and pointed to the cooler across the store. "Go put it back. I'm not going to jail."

"What are you talking about?"

"C'mon, Bobby put the beer back."

"When do you get off?"

Sina stepped around the counter and put her arms around him. On tiptoes she kissed his cheek. She reached up under his jacket and snatched back the bottle of beer and dutifully returned it to the cooler.

"Eleven," she said calmly. "But I've gotta study tonight. I've got an English lit final tomorrow."

Behind her back, Bobby eyed a bag of peanuts from a rack by the door. Returning to the front counter, Sina spotted the Kleenex on the camera lens. Sighing, she climbed up on the window sill. Bobby stuffed the peanuts inside his pocket while her back was turned.

"Can't you sneak out for an hour? I'll have you in by midnight, promise."

Sina jumped down. "Yeah, and what about last night? My dad nearly killed me."

"C'mon, Sina. Just an hour."

"Can't." She shook her head firmly.

"Your loss," Bobby said with false bravado, and made for the door.

Through the glass window, she watched Bobby kick start the motorcycle. Bobby removed the bag of peanuts from his jacket and poured a handful into his mouth, smiling back at Sina.

"Bobby!" Sina started after him, then stopped.

Whatever was on her mind changed. She took her hand off the door and just watched Bobby ride off into the night.

CHAPTER 35

Lyman's small plane landed at a private airfield in McMinnville, Oregon. He paid the pilot in cash and hitched a ride downtown. The chain smoking driver of the Crystal Clear Water Truck chugged from a quart jug of cola perched between his legs.

Lyman grabbed some lunch at the Comstock Tavern and then walked two blocks to the nearest used car lot. After a brief negotiation with a salesman sporting spaghetti sauce on his tie, he paid cash for a two-door Ford.

He found a small pawnshop on Main Street and bought a used 12 gauge. At a sporting goods store, Lyman purchased three boxes of 12 gauge shells and four boxes of .38s. He locked the shells in the trunk alongside his shotgun and duffel bag.

Leaving town, he stopped at a convenience store and purchased a six pack of Heineken, beef jerky, some stamps and envelopes, and a map of the Oregon Coast. In the store's lot, Lyman drank his beer, absently chewing his cud, and studied the map. He figured the drive would take him less than two hours.

He drove west out of McMinnville on Highway 26, stopping at a cluster of buildings just as the sun dipped toward the horizon. He rented a room at the small weathered motel with a restaurant/bar attached. After stowing his gear, he made his way to the bar. He had three shots of Rye and listened to the jukebox while customers joked with the bartender. Eventually, he ordered a cheeseburger and fries to go just as the kitchen was closing up. Lyman returned to his room and ate his dinner alone, staring at the cassette tape he had removed from a large pillowcase, along with a large amount of cash and Kano's Smith & Wesson.

Lyman sat back attempting to recall the image of Leslie Ann Marken once again from his weary mind. He could see her walking across the plush carpet of their London hotel room. The youthful, sexy glow of her tan skin glistened from the hot shower. Water droplets of silver rolled down her shapely curves like warm rain cascading over a marble statuette. She approached him wearing an innocent gaze only lovers can share. He had taken her in his arms and bedded her with a passion he had never before felt.

It had happened spontaneously. The passionate exchange had grown into love. A moment in time that could never be repeated but was etched in his mind forever. Neither would ever be this happy again.

He attributed the relationship to the times and how they met – the heightened living conditions of the Middle East, and the secret mission they were privy to. That had been their last weekend together before the Beirut incident.

The image of her body so vital and loving now twisted in his mind's eye to a scorched and tormented hunk of burnt flesh.

He chugged down a beer and waited for the pain to subside. Eventually, he pulled out three hundred dollars, paused a moment and tripled it. Wrapping the cash inside a letter, he deposited it inside an envelope and addressed it to Emily Douchet. That piece of heartwarming business accomplished he reached for the cassette and after scanning a newspaper article about the death of Ray Kano and the noted arrest of staff sergeant Jack Vu, addressed the second envelope to Detective Dorene Gates.

He polished off a second Heineken and went to bed around midnight; the same time, Sergeant Vu nervously kissed Betty goodbye and boarded a plane for Salt Lake City.

CHAPTER 36

Water was heating in the tea kettle on the electric stove in Pam Flenner's kitchen. She rocked her newborn son in her arms, looking out the kitchen window, when the basement door opened and Bobby strolled out rubbing his bloodshot eyes.

Pam paced back and forth in front of the window. "You overslept again, Bobby."

Bobby glanced at the clock on the stove. "Shit!" he exclaimed. "Is AJ pissed?"

"Yes." She patted the baby's back.

Bobby scratched his bare chest then hitched up his flannel long johns. He opened the refrigerator and scanned its contents. He reached in and shoved items aside. "What happened to the milk?"

"Your brothers are upset with you."

"So what else is new...? There's no fuckin' milk?"

"When they get back, AJ will buy some."

"Case go along?"

"They had an extra charter sign on at the last minute. AJ's service buddy went with 'em."

"The fucking alarm didn't go off."

"Case said he smelled beer on your breath. If your parole officer finds out..."

"My parole officer can bite me."

The tea kettle whistled on the stove. Pam placed her infant in the highchair and made some instant soup. Bobby sneered at the infant behind her back.

"Was Sina with you last night?"

"No."

"Her dad called here looking for her."

"What'd you say?"

"What was I supposed to say? That she's out getting drunk and having sex?"

"When did the other charter come aboard?"

"Called last night at the last minute."

Out in the drive a mail truck pulled up to the Flenner's box and dropped off a handful of letters. Pam open the curtain and looked out the window.

"Bobby, go get dressed, and get the mail."

Bobby skipped dressing and paraded outside in his underwear and retrieved the mail. A neighbor across the street stood at her mailbox gawking. Bobby blew the neighbor a kiss and pranced back inside the house. Dropping the mail on the table, he headed toward the basement, slamming the door behind him.

Ignoring his drama, Pam sipped her soup and rifled through the mail on the table. Another sweepstakes offer. That made three this week. She picked up a stack of newspapers and started clipping coupons. She looked up as an old GMC pickup pulled into the driveway. John Long and the two older Flenner brothers piled out and entered the house. Case dropped a twenty-eight pound silver salmon into the sink. AJ kissed his wife on the cheek. "Can you cook us some lunch, hon?" he asked.

Pam put the newspapers down. "How'd you boys do?"

"Six plus the one in the sink."

Case said, "John caught the silver."

"With coaching from AJ, Mrs. Flenner," John admitted, winning her over with his smile.

Pam pulled a fillet knife out of the drawer. "AJ. We gotta talk about Bobby," Pam said in a worried tone. "He's out of control."

John perked up.

"Where is the brat?" Case asked.

"I heard him leave a few minutes ago. He's with Sina."

"She's in school."

"That doesn't stop him."

Case looked at AJ and frowned. AJ patted his wife's bottom and said, "We'll be right back. John wants to see the shop."

The shop was detached from the house. The sky was clear and the air crisp. John and the two brothers walked across the grassy path that led to the shop. The door was padlocked. AJ reached into his pocket and pulled out a set of keys.

John looked back over his shoulder. "She's right, you know."

"What?" AJ asked.

"I don't trust the kid. We should keep him out of it. It's for his own protection. We gotta lot of work ahead of us..."

AJ flipped on an overhead. A small outboard hung on the wall by the door. The other walls were filled with tackle which rattled when Case pushed the swollen wood door closed. Case followed behind John who snagged a cobweb in the face, crossing to the opposite side of the garage. The three men stopped in front of a sun bleached tarpaulin. AJ removed the cloth covering, revealing for the first time, three large metal antique chests. Chests recovered from a sunken vessel off the Pacific Coast.

John inspected the metal and then looked for something to wipe the rust from his hands.

"They'll do," he said. "Local purchase?"

"Yeah. Bought them a few years back from Luke Baxter," AJ said. "Local sea hound. They're authentic. Late eighteenth century. They fit our purpose fine. If you're interested, they're from the wreck of the St. Clair. Luke recovered them sixty years ago, twenty-six miles off the Oregon Coast. Little has been written about the St. Clair after it sank, which makes our job easier. We transferred the coins into some of these chests."

"So how much does the kid know?"

"His name is Bobby," AJ reminded sternly. "And he doesn't know dick."

"Has he seen the chests?"

"I told him they were for the wife. Fuckin' living room decorations. You're awful paranoid."

"I'm careful." His tone implied AJ wasn't.

"So am I." AJ smiled. "To a degree, Bobby can be trusted. And – Luke, the guy who sold us the trunks, has Alzheimer's. So don't get your shorts in a bind."

"I don't want the kid involved."

"He's our problem, John." AJ's face reddened.

"He's a liability. And he's not our only one." John's voice grew concerned. "Lyman's surfaced."

"Fuck me!" Case barked. "No way."

AJ swallowed hard. "What's your source?"

"A couple cops from New Orleans."

"He talk?"

"No."

"Then what's the problem?" AJ asked. "Some of this is his."

"The cops are investigating a homicide." Long swallowed hard. "Leslie's dead..."

"Shit!" Case shook his head mournfully. "Not Leslie?"

"There's something else." Long's voice cracked with anger. "Kano's dead too."

AJ and Case stared at each other with steely cold eyes.

Case snapped, "Is that fucking all?"

"Nigel found me. But I ditched 'em at the airport."

"Which airport?" AJ quickly asked.

"Relax – they're fifteen hundred miles from here."

Case barked, "So now the fuckin' Sand Monkeys are after us too?..."

CHAPTER 37

The dirt road seemed to go on forever. Vu followed it to the end like the guy at the Chevron had instructed. "Look for a brown house with white shingles." Vu saw a white house with brown shingles in the distance and decided it was probably the right house. He thought maybe the mailbox would have a name painted on it, but he looked and it didn't. Nothing around for miles. Just a small old house in the country among endless open fields.

He walked up to the front door and rang the doorbell. He didn't hear a ring. So he knocked twice, good hard knocks. Still no answer. He waited and tried again. Still no answer. His heart started to race a little. He walked around the side of the house.

Hanging laundry up to dry on a ratty clothes line strung across the backyard was a middle-aged woman who fit Millie Lyman's description. She wore a faded pink dress and rubber boots. Her hair was tied in a bun and pinned in place. Around her neck hung a long necklace, which kept getting tangled in one of her brassieres as she tried to fasten it to the clothes line.

"Hello, ma'am!" Vu called out. "Would you be Millie Lyman Brown? My name's Jack Vu. I'm with the Air Force."

Millie stood up straight and gazed across the yard. "Hello? Hey, could you give me a hand with this?" she asked.

Vu approached Millie as he took in the place. There were no signs of life inside the house. And the fields were as quiet as a prairie at dusk. Lyman didn't seem to be around.

"Easy does it, ma'am," Vu said, inspecting the problem. The metal clasp of the brassiere had fastened itself to the necklace. Vu realized that he had never seen a brassiere so large in all his life. The cups were large enough to hold small pumpkins. Its enormous size was intimidating. Vu's hands became clumsy and useless.

Vu repeated, "I'll have you out of this in a jiffy."

"Wouldn't it be easier to remove the necklace first?" Millie offered.

Vu scratched his head, thinking. "Perhaps it would."

Millie reached behind her back but the clasp of the necklace was bound up. "Mr. Vu, could you?"

Vu stood on his tiptoes. He too could not see how the clasp had jammed itself so neatly into a puzzle.

"The necklace is stuck, ma'am. I'm going to try to work it loose."

He grabbed hold of the brassiere and pulled. The clasp held fast. Millie's neck reddened. Suddenly the brassier broke free. The large elastic article of clothing was like a slingshot around his neck. Vu stood draped in the tangled brassiere. He thought he was pathetic.

Vu said, "Are you all right ma'am?"

Millie rubbed her neck. "Yes, thank you. Do you have my brassiere?"

"Yes. Would you like me to hang it back up?"

"Did it hit the ground?"

"No ma'am."

"Is it dry?"

"No, ma'am."

"Then by all means, hang it up, young man. Now if you'd also be so kind as to carry that basket for me to the back porch, I would be forever grateful."

Vu carried the basket at his side. He could feel the cold steel of his 9mm in his shoulder harness press against his rib cage and his sense of manhood slowly returned. It would be his rotten luck to have to draw down on someone while carrying a load of undies. The boys back in Baltimore would get a good laugh over that. Then it dawned on him, that unless he found Lyman, and got this whole mess ironed out, he may not ever see the Baltimore office again.

Millie invited Vu inside for a glass of iced tea. While Millie clattered around in the kitchen, Vu looked around the living room at some old family pictures of Millie and her brother Jim. There was one picture where Millie was behind the wheel of an old pickup truck.

"As I was saying, Mr. Vu," Millie shouted from the kitchen. "The man said he was a friend of Jimmy's. Said he served with him overseas. He seemed like a nice upstanding fella."

As Vu put the picture frame down on the mantle, he inhaled a whiff of rose air freshener and felt like he was going to sneeze. He pulled his handkerchief out of his pocket and returned to the photographs.

So this is what Lyman looked like as a kid? he thought to himself. A ruddy faced boy with a love of horses. Raised on a farm in the Midwest. And sharing second fiddle to a blinded younger sister.

"He brought me a package from Jimmy. Would you like to see it?"

"Yes, I would," Vu said.

Millie returned with a soiled envelope. Vu lifted it up to his face, searching for clues like a bloodhound as Millie went back inside the kitchen.

"You're certain he called himself Ray Kano?"

"Absolutely."

Millie entered carrying a tray of fresh drinks. She set it down on a small table and placed a glass before him. She pointed to a dish with sliced lemons and a sterling silver bowl of sugar and told Vu to help himself.

Vu waited until Millie sat down before he spoke. "Ms. Lyman, the man that visited you ... how shall I say it ... well, did you notice ... did he have two hands?"

Millie's face hardened. "I may be sightless, Sergeant, but I'm not an idiot. Yes, he had hands. Why?"

"Ma'am, we believe Jim is alive and back in the United States. We also believe the man who visited might have been your brother. If you would like an attorney present at any time, please stop me. You're under no legal obligation to answer any of my questions."

"Mr. Vu, are you telling me that I don't know my own flesh and blood? If Jimmy was here I'd know it."

"If you were to withhold information that might prevent us from locating him, it is possible charges could be filed against you." Vu took a sip of tea. "For aiding and abetting a fugitive."

"My brother's a criminal now?"

"He failed to report to proper authorities upon re-entering the United States. He is still a member of the Armed Forces and falls under the Uniform Code of Military Justice. That code makes it an unlawful act to be absent from your assigned duty station without authorized leave. In other words, AWOL. That is punishable by court martial. There are also some unanswered legal matters that the police in New Orleans want cleared up."

"You've made your point, Mr Vu." Millie sat back and sighed. Her eyes clouded up into moist buds. "I love my brother. I'd do anything to protect him. I don't think he ever got over my accident. I certainly hated him for a while. But I found a way through my dark period.

"We were just kids. Jimmy loved to hunt. He took me with him one morning to bag a pheasant. He rested Dad's old 12 gauge against a stump and was helping me over a barbed wire fence when the wind knocked the shotgun over. Jimmy must have seen it coming because he dove toward me and pushed me aside. The gun went off. It's amazing we both weren't killed. Neither one of us were hit by buckshot. But the fence post next to me exploded and shards of wood penetrated both my corneas. I had several operations but the damage was permanent. Jimmy took it pretty hard. I believe I created his demons. I hated him for his pity. For his sight." Millie gazed toward Vu. "I now view it as God's way of leading me down a different path. But Jimmy wouldn't see it quite the same. He's not a religious man."

"He probably felt responsible."

"Perhaps. But regret is life's way of holding us back, Sergeant. Jimmy moved forward with his military life, but I think his personal life suffered. I believe his heart is filled with darkness."

Vu nodded and watched Millie sip her drink. "So you're certain he didn't contact you?"

Millie said nothing. He studied her hands. They were large, hardworking hands. Vu wanted to calm her; but he refrained. He thought of laying a comforting hand on her shoulder, but didn't. "Millie, I have to find your brother. It's my job."

Millie stared at the wall. "I'll pray for you."

"You should pray for him."

"Why wouldn't he tell me?"

"To protect you."

"But it's been so long."

"Ma'am, did he say where he was going when he left here?"

"...let me think."

"Time is running out. We believe he may do something the Government would regret."

Millie's face hardened. A decision was made. "Time is running out for all of us, Sergeant."

CHAPTER 38

The sea water lashed against the hull of the Lucky Lady. The sky was grey and overcast. The two older Flenner brothers stepped out of the pilot house wiping their sweaty brows. Up in the parking lot of the marina, John Long shut the tailgate of the GMC and headed back down to the dock.

AJ stepped back inside the pilot house and turned the key in the ignition. The big twin engines cranked over and over. Engine number one sputtered, and fired. Engine two spit puffs of black smoke out the stern but failed to start.

Case frowned.

"Go down and bleed the line again," AJ said. "Make sure the secondary isn't plugged."

Case dropped down below deck as AJ stepped out of the pilot house and looked for storm clouds. The sky promised rain soon. Hints of moisture out of the north. John waited on the deck by the mooring lines. "I'll release the bow line."

"Hold up, John," AJ said. "Got a problem with number two engine. Case is checking it out now."

"Think it's going to rain?"

"In another hour or so."

"I prefer the sky over the sea any day," Long said, making conversation.

AJ swallowed. "Where do you think Lyman is?"

"It's anyone's guess."

"We owe him some of it, you know."

"The hell we do!" Long snapped. "No one told him to go back for the girl."

"He was doing his job."

"That's a matter of opinion. She was a civilian."

"You weren't there. Case fucked up."

"We've hashed this out a thousand times."

AJ looked Long hard in the eye. "He killed Leslie and Kano. We're next."

"Maybe not. Could be a love revenge thing. Kano was sleeping with her. Cops think it was Lyman. Makes sense. Lyman kills Leslie. Then he kills

Kano out of revenge."

"If it is a love revenge thing, he ain't got no love for us, and a big reason for revenge."

"Fuck Kano. Fuck Lyman. Fuck the cops. And fuck the Arab assholes. Who's risking a commission and 20-year pension here?"

"We all risked something," AJ reminded him.

Case popped up out of the hatch; grease smears running down his cheeks. "Bobby fucked up again. Secondary is plugged solid. Sediment slipped by the primaries. It's gotta be coming from the fuel tanks. We gotta replace 'em soon, AJ. I keep tellin' you. Those tanks are in pretty bad shape."

"We have a spare below?"

"Nope."

"Great."

"Well, let's get the show on the road. How long is this going to take?"

Case pointed toward the highway. AJ looked up as the red dirt bike rode into the lot and skidded to a stop. "Now that our part's runner is here. Not as long as we thought."

Bobby parked the dirt bike beside the GMC and removed his helmet. He jogged down the dock and stopped beside Long. He shot an angry look at his brothers. "What-the-fuck, AJ!" he shouted. "I said I'd go."

Case shouted, "Hey, Bobby! What about the secondary on number two? Forget something?"

Bobby kicked his boot on the mooring cleat. "Son-of-a-bitch, goddammit! I ... I meant to."

"Forget it!" AJ said. "Go pick one up at Cooper's Marine. Shouldn't take more than a half hour. Just hurry your ass back. Our weather window won't last."

Bobby ran up the dock. John watched the kid hop on the bike, yank on his helmet, kick like a madman until the bike's engine fired. The bike's rear tire spun gravel and the front wheel came off the ground as he sped out of the lot.

"We should leave him behind, AJ," Long remarked.

AJ frowned. "We're through leaving people behind, Long."

CHAPTER 39

"Excuse me, sir!"

The man in greasy overalls shot up straight and smacked his bald head on the engine compartment door of the twin-engine Cessna. Rubbing the tender spot, he glared down from the top rung of a feeble ladder, snarling. "Yeah? What you want?"

Vu stepped forward and showed the man his credentials. "I'm looking for a man who goes by the name of either Jim Lyman or Ray Kano? Have either of those men rented a plane from you recently?"

"Did you check with Glynis in the office?"

"There's no one in the office, sir."

"Goddamn that girl," the mechanic barked. "Excuse my French, mister, but let me give you some advice. Don't marry a redhead. They're like fire in the wind. You turn your back on them and they're off burning the forest down."

"Yes, sir. Thank you for the advice. Now if I may..."

The mechanic interrupted. "Kano or Lyman, eh?"

"He's a man of about your height and weight. Brown hair, brown eyes. I believe he may speak with a Midwest accent." Vu showed him a picture of Jim Lyman.

"I'm lousy with names, Sergeant. Where was this fella headed?"

"That's what I'm trying to find out."

"Rentals around here are slim this time of year. If Glynis was around she could certainly look it up for you. I'd be like a rooster in a hen house if I tried to play with the computer. Let me think for a minute ... We had a Piper go out on Monday. Or was it Wednesday? No. It was Tuesday. I had to throw some air in one of her tires. And we had a twin-seater go out yesterday and a four-place in the afternoon, but those weren't rentals. Privately owned. You a pilot, Sergeant?"

"No, sir."

"That's going to be a problem if you want to rent a plane."

"I imagine it would if I intended on piloting."

"Like I said, Glynis does all the paperwork." He scratched his head with a screw driver. "But your man might have flown out of here on Thursday. Bob Barker's our local pilot for hire. He owns a twin-seater Cessna and rents his services out through our office. His Mustang is still in the lot. He'd be the one that could tell you the most. If he was around."

"When might Glynis return, sir?"

"Anyone's guess," he said. "She's either at lunch. She dines down at the local Dairy Queen, or ..." The mechanic pointed toward the sky. "She's a jumper. Either way, son, she'll be back eventually."

"Do you have a pay phone?" Vu would have preferred to use his cell phone, but they could be traced. And at the moment, he wasn't certain of his legal standing.

"There's one by the soda pop machine. Around back. You'll see it. Doesn't give back change, Sergeant. Just warning you."

At the back of the building Vu used the phone. Nothing but open fields and grazing land in the distance. As he dug in his trousers for change, a plane released a speck of color which happened to catch Vu's attention. He watched a chute open and gracefully float toward the airport runway, then plugged a quarter in the coin slot and received no dial tone and no return quarter. Vu studied the phone, slugged it and stepped back. The jumper landed, scooped up the chute, and walked toward him. As the helmet came off, long red hair spilled out.

"You see my jump?" she asked.

"Yes."

"How'd I look?"

"Like a person jumping out of a perfectly good aircraft."

"You a pilot?"

"No, ma'am. I'm an investigator. I'm with the Air Force. Would you be Glynis?"

"Oh, shit? Tell me you're not with the FAA."

"I'm not, ma'am."

"Whew! Barker's running a bit behind schedule and I was worried about him. Hey, can you show me your ID, I love those things." Vu reached for his wallet. Glynis squealed and squirmed and danced around like a fire ant had crawled up her leg. Vu took out his plastic identification card and held it up.

Glynis dropped her shoulders, looking disappointed. "That's it?"

"Yes."

"I wanted to see a shiny silver or gold badge. Not a flimsy piece of plastic."

Vu would never understand the mind of a woman. He closed his wallet and returned it to his pocket.

They walked together toward the office. Then, as if the weight of her equipment was becoming an irritation, she stopped.

"You speak with Harry already?"

She calmly stepped out of her harness and dropped it at her feet.

"Harry is the mechanic?" Vu asked, realizing he had not asked for his name.

"That's right. But computers are not his forte. If you want to know anything around this joint, you gotta come to me."

"He assured me my request fell on deaf ears."

"What do you want to know?"

"Did a man by the name of Jim Lyman or Ray Kano rent a plane recently?"

"Kano did. I set it up with Bob. Big guy. Rugged looking. Needed a shave. But he seemed okay."

"Where did Mr. Barker take him?"

"Beats me. But Barker's flight plan is in my office if you'd like to see it."

Vu smiled for the first time that day.

CHAPTER 40

Lyman's sedan sat outside the Flenners' house unnoticed since sunrise. Lyman was crouched down inside watching the front door through binoculars. At 6:05 AM two men who Lyman recognized as the Flenner brothers came out of the house and loaded fishing tackle in the back of an old GMC pickup and left. The newspaper was delivered at 6:35. At 7:30, a young woman in baggy jeans and over-sized sweatshirt concealing baby fat and fitting the description of Pam Flenner stepped outside onto the front porch and retrieved the newspaper. Lyman focused on the young woman. She held a young child in her arms which she carried back inside. Through the open blinds Lyman watched the woman enter the kitchen and prepare formula on the stove. At 7:45 she removed the bottle from a steaming pan and fed the baby. Afterwards, she disappeared upstairs, reappearing at 9:10 at which time she began to dust furniture in the main room of the residence.

Lyman figured it was time.

So this was AJ's trophy girl – the cheerleader from Oregon whose picture he had worn raw in his wallet – his highschool sweetheart. The girl he went nuts over and told everyone about during SIGNET training. The one he knocked up in the backseat of his 69' Camero. His true love. Now his wife and a mother.

This was the leverage he needed...

Lyman eased back into his seat and planned what he had to do next. He sipped from a thermos of coffee and waited. Kano's information had proven correct. The gold was inside or nearby. A boat perhaps. It was AJ's style. He was a hoarder. He kept a close eye on his family and his possessions. Case was the careless, indiscriminate one. The younger brother – Bobby – was unreliable and dangerous. Youth was always unpredictable. He'd watch him. AJ ran the show now. Long, who would have insisted on keeping it simple and discreet, was as good as dead. Long was personal.

Lyman realized that instead of busting his balls ferreting out the gold, he'd take a different approach. He'd make a little barter. Funny – Kano had been so easy. There was no bickering, no bartering. Lyman wondered if it had been the pain he inflicted that had caused him to confess or if it was out of some sick sense of loyalty to the old squadron. It didn't matter. Kano was history.

It was time for the brothers to cough up his share. Or else the pretty little pom-pom queen and infant would be the next casualty reported on the five o'clock news.

Pam Flenner was cleaning the wood stove when she heard the knock on the front door. She lay the cloth on the counter and peered through the peep hole and didn't recognize the visitor. She opened the door anyway.

Jim Lyman had on a pale grey blazer and faded jeans. He had not shaven for several days and his spiky whiskers gave his face a hollow, sunken look. In his back pocket was a page from the directory which he had torn out and used to locate their address.

"Yes?"

"Hello, ma'am. I'm looking for AJ or Case Flenner. They home?"

"No, they're gone for the day. What can I do for you?"

"I'm an old friend. When are they due back?"

"I don't really know." Suddenly the telephone rang in the kitchen. "Could you excuse me for a second? That might be them now."

Pam started to close the door and then changed her mind and left it cracked. There was just enough light shining in from the kitchen she felt she could keep an eye on the visitor.

She lifted the receiver. "Hello." It was Bobby on the other end of the line. "Oh, hi Bobby. No. Sina hasn't called. Okay – okay – oh, Bobby – tell ... Bobby?" She put the receiver down and looked distraught. She walked around the corner and was startled by Lyman's presence in the living room. He was looking at some old family photographs on the wall.

"Sorry about that," Pam said, keeping her distance. "Is there something I can do for you – Mr?"

"Jim Lyman," he said tersely. "You look so young in your wedding photo."

Pam blushed. "Well, Mr. Lyman, my husband isn't that much older than me. He just looks older 'cause he's going bald."

Lyman studied the layout and figured the guns were in a back office or bedroom, locked up, out of harm's way.

"Are you staying in the area? Or just passing through?"

"Passing through, I'm afraid."

"Oh, that's too bad. AJ and Case are going to be unhappy they missed you."

Lyman nodded and pointed at a small picture of Bobby Flenner riding his dirt bike over a sand dune. “AJ mentioned he had a little brother. That him?”

“That’s Bobby. All one-hundred fifty pounds of hell on wheels. If he doesn’t kill himself on that thing first, AJ and Case probably will. He just can’t seem to grow up.”

“The Navy helped me, ma’am.”

“You were in the Navy?”

“Lateral transfer. I finished out my tour with the Air Force, Special Ops division. That’s where I met your husband.”

Pam softened. “I was getting ready to put some coffee on. Do you have time?”

Lyman checked his watch, and cracked his knuckles. “I guess I do. Sure, that would be fine.”

Lyman followed Pam into the kitchen and watched as she filled the pot with tap water, she said, “Have you been to Warrenton before, Mr. Lyman?”

“I’ve been out of the country on assignment.”

“I see,” Pam said.

“This looks like a fair-sized place. You do all the upkeep yourself?”

“No. Bobby lives in the basement,” Pam said, as she opened the cupboard and pulled out a sugar bowl, set it down on the counter. “If I threaten him, he’ll vacuum from time to time. And of course there’s my husband AJ. He does the upkeep outside. Actually, Bobby’s a pretty good kid. Just wild. That was him on the phone earlier. Guess there’s a problem with one of the engines. You know, I bet you’d have time to drive down to the marina and catch them before they head out. Better yet, if you want, Bobby’s picking up some filters at Cooper’s Marine Supply. I could call and have him swing by on his way back and show you where the boat is moored.”

A worn map of the Oregon Coast was stapled to the back of the kitchen door. Lyman examined it. Pam explain the layout of the town.

Lyman clinched his fist and moved closer to Pam. He started to raise his arm and then stopped. A baby’s crying echoed down from upstairs. Pam faced him. “Excuse me again.” She sighed. “Looks like Jed woke up.”

CHAPTER 41

Bobby walked out of Cooper Marine Supply whistling and carrying a brown paper bag of parts. He slipped the sack into his backpack and climbed on his dirt bike. He leered back through the large plate glass window at the new receptionist with the big tits. Bobby was too busy ogling the young girl to notice the reflection of the Ford parked across the street with its engine running.

Bobby knew he shouldn't do it but the girl with the big tits made him hard and he knew Sina was working a split-shift at Mac's store. He sped off down Highway 101 heading south. Lyman's blue sedan followed at a distance.

The parking lot was deserted at Mac's store when Bobby whipped in and skidded up to the front door. He pounded his fist on the glass and flashed a smile. Sina was sitting on the counter painting her fingernails and didn't appreciate the interruption. She screwed the cap on the nail polish.

Bobby walked into the store with his helmet on and the visor flipped up.

"Bobby. What are you doing here?"

"Cruising."

Sina hopped down from the counter. Bobby pulled her into his arms. Sina pushed him away.

"My nails, you idiot," she said playfully, and jumped back. She glanced out the door. A blue sedan pulled off the highway and parked across the street. A highway patrol car turned into the parking lot.

"Bobby! Get down!"

Sina pushed Bobby back behind the aisle. She stepped up to the door and waved at the officer in the patrol car. The patrol car pulled out of the lot and continued on its way.

"What was that all about?" Bobby exclaimed.

"Dad asked them to check on me." She turned back to face Bobby. "You've got to knock off the stealing."

"Your dad owns the place. He's not going to fire you."

"No. But he sure would have you arrested. He took one of the tapes from last week and told me he was going to have your picture printed off and give it to the cops."

"Sina, it's all a scam. Those images won't reproduce."

"You don't know that."

"C'mere!" Bobby pulled her into his arms and Sina slowly melted into him. They kissed passionately.

"Are you taking me to the dance tomorrow night?" Sina asked.

"Maybe," Bobby replied and secretly fastened a gold necklace around her neck.

"What's this?"

Sina checked out the necklace in the mirror behind the counter. Bobby had taken a gold chain and fastened a shiny sovereign to it. It was quite elegant under the artificial light.

Sina studied it. "It's kinda heavy."

"It's solid gold."

"Oh," she said, and changed the subject. "Well, what about the dance?"

"Sina, I'd feel like a fuckin' freak going to that stupid high school dance." Bobby toyed with the shiny necklace.

"Bobby. It's my last year."

"I gotta run."

"Bobby?"

Bobby slapped his backpack. "Parts for the boat. AJ's waitin'. I'll call you later."

"If I don't hear from you by six I'm going with Howie."

* * *

The crew of the Lucky Lady grew impatient. Case had managed to locate the spare secondary filter and had installed it, bled the fuel line, and idled the engines for a good ten minutes, convinced the problem was over. AJ and Long were on the top deck arguing over time. Bobby was running late. The clouds were moving in fast. They had to go now or wait another day, and that was risky. Case agreed with Long, they should go while they had the opportunity. Bobby should be left behind.

"We'll give him five more minutes," AJ said obstinately. "Then we go..."

The three men stared up at the highway and waited. What was the point of talking. Five minutes and AJ shouted for Long to cast off the bow and stern lines. Long tossed them aboard and hopped up on the gunnel and watched as the big old boat chugged out toward the open sea.

* * *

Too late, the dirt bike pulled into the marina parking lot. Bobby pushed the engine stop switch and the engine sputtered and fell silent. He flipped up his visor and gazed down at the empty slip. He looked out over the ocean. Leaving the protection of the marina was the faint silhouette of the Lucky Lady. A seagull followed her out to sea.

He lowered his head and slapped the handlebars, unaware of the blue sedan that had pulled off onto the shoulder behind him and parked, keeping a close watch.

CHAPTER 42

Detective Gates and Ms. Caan stumbled into each other coming out of separate restaurants along S. Broad Street about a half-block from the precinct. Betty carried a doggy bag emanating the aroma of curry. Gates was packing a styrofoam cup of espresso. Betty stopped and glared at Gates.

"That was a shitty thing you did to Vu."

"It's my job."

"You take your job too fuckin' seriously."

"Have you heard from him?"

"Do you think I'd tell you?"

Betty stormed off toward the precinct, like a solemn soldier marching into battle. Gates stopped, sipped her coffee, and stared down the sidewalk. Outside the precinct, an old dented pickup creaked up to the curb and parked.

They were waiting for Gates in the reception area.

The door to the Medical Examiner's office closed and Betty placed her takeout in the portable refrigerator behind her desk. There was a time when Betty stored her food in the main lab refrigerator but an assistant had mistaken some of her cooking for a dissection of a large intestine and it had caused a travesty in the court room. Stored beside the refrigerator was Vu's ice cooler. Betty put her hand on the lid and her eyes teared up. Then something besides sentiment crept into her face. She jumped up and hustled across the room and removed the hand from the medical storage locker. Betty carried the hand over to a stainless steel table and unwrapped it. She took out a scalpel and gently scraped the contents from beneath the nails and placed the skin fragments on a slide and placed the slide under a microscope. After a few seconds of examining the tissue, she jotted down some notes and added a drop of dye to the mixture. She made more notes. Then she pulled out the Marken File. She rifled through the numerous photographs, crime scene documents and found what she was looking for. She pulled out several lab printouts and studied them closely. Then she picked up the phone on her desk and dialed Gates' office.

Detective Gates sat at her desk staring across the room at these two cartoon creatures. A little old lady as feisty as a rattler and a snot-nosed smart ass, dumb as a stump.

"Give it to her!" Annie ordered.

"I found it. I'm keepin' it," Dunkin replied harshly.

"Look. Dunkin is it?" Gates cut in. "Your aunt is right. If you found the ring at a crime scene, you need to turn it over. If you don't I'll have to arrest you for withholding evidence."

"Where's the pill poppin' assassin?"

Annie slapped the back of Dunkin's head.

"If you mean, Sergeant Vu, I have no idea. But you have brought up a good point. Did he know about the ring?"

Dunkin shook his head No. "Okay, let me see what you have?"

Dunkin dug in his heels and once again refused. Annie snarled aloud as she cuffed his ears. "Dunkin, so help me God I'll ..."

The phone on Gates' desk rang. Gates picked it up. "Gates."

There was a long pause. "Okay, okay. I'll call you back." Gates hung up. The room fell quiet.

Gates looked across her desk. "Dunkin, I want the ring. Now!" Dunkin pulled it off his finger and walked it over to the desk. He took one last look and dropped it into her hand.

Annie stuck out her pointy finger. "Tell her the rest." Dunkin sighed, and flopped back down in his chair.

"Tell me what?" Gates asked, stretching out a sore shoulder muscle.

Dunkin swallowed. "I ain't goin' to jail. No way am I goin' to jail. I ain't takin' it up the ass. No way am I takin' it up the ass."

* * *

The telephone rang again, but this time it was in Baltimore. It had nothing to do with Betty Caan's recent discovery, or the confession that detective Gates was receiving at that very moment. It had to do with Major Wheylicke's secretary. Airman Betas marched into the CO's office, looking concerned.

Airman Betas had on dress-blues that needed starching. The sleeves hung like over-cooked linguini. Major Wheylicke was examining a stack of military folders that had recently been delivered to his desk by courier. Ten minutes earlier he had been on the telephone with the D.A. in New Orleans, discussing Vu's charges. He looked up obstinately when Airman Betas entered the room.

"Betas!" Wheylicke snapped. "Has Sergeant Vu checked in with you recently?"

"Not recently, sir."

"I received these from Headquarters Personnel Division, indicating you have requested documents from Lyman's former squadron. Is this correct?"

"Sir, if I may, I was only addressing Sergeant Vu's order."

"Well, here they are. You were in the bathroom so I signed for them. Take them off my desk immediately."

"Yes, sir."

Airman Betas retrieved the folders from Wheylicke's desk, and faced the door. "Betas, where is Sergeant Vu?"

"Sir?"

"He was to report back to this office after incarceration. Has there been a hitch with his travel plans?"

"I wouldn't know, Major."

"You requested the files, did you not?"

"I did, sir."

"And the sergeant must have had a reason to request the files, did he not?"

"I believe he did, sir."

"Then how is the sergeant going to retrieve the documents if he doesn't contact you?"

"That is a very good point, sir."

"If Sergeant Vu calls or shows his face in this area. I want to be notified immediately. Is this clear?"

"Clear as crystal, Major."

"Good. And one other thing?"

"Sir?"

"Under no circumstance are you to provide Sergeant Vu with any military information. Is that clear? And that includes these files."

"Clear as—"

Wheylicke cut her off. "I know... crystal."

"Very well, sir."

At the door, Wheylicke called out, "And Betas?" Betas stopped and faced the Major. "Do something with the uniform."

"Right away, sir."

Airman Betas dropped the files on her desk and examined her profile in the mirror. The telephone on Betas's desk rang. She answered it.

"Major Wheylicke's Office, Airman Betas speaking."

"Betas? It's Sergeant Vu."
"Shit's hit the fan, Sergeant..."

CHAPTER 43

The telephone in Glynis' office smelled like sweet perfume. Vu had been on the line for ten minutes speaking with someone long distance when he reached across the desk and handed the receiver to Glynis.

"What's this?" Glynis asked curiously.

"Tell Airman Betas your name."

Glynis was not shy. "Hello Airman Betas this is Glynis Simms. How are you today?"

Vu said, "Tell her to give you the names and addresses."

Glynis put her hand over the receiver and looked up at Vu. "What addresses?"

"Just ask her please." Vu was getting impatient with this game. But Betas had her reasons, she said.

"Girl? What's your first name? It feels awkward as hell calling a chick airman?" She paused and smiled up at Vu. "Okay, Julie, now were gettin' somewhere. I'm to ask you about names and addresses..."

Glynis listened intently. She appeared to like this cloak and dagger thing. She took out a notepad and scribbled down some items on a sheet of paper. Then she handed the receiver back to Vu. Vu held it up to his ear and heard a loud dial tone and handed it back to Glynis, who placed it on its cradle.

Glynis ripped the piece of paper where she had jotted down the information and passed it across the counter. "Can you read it?"

Vu stared at it intently for a long time, turning the page this way and that. "Not a word."

All he saw were random lines and scrawls. Glynis took the paper back. "Just having some fun," she laughed. "It's shorthand." Glynis put a sheet of paper into an old Royal typewriter and began transcribing.

When she handed it back, Vu tried it again. This time what he read was "clear as crystal."

He folded the paper up into a neat square and shoved it into his pocket. Then he took out his wallet and removed a credit card.

"Here," Vu said. Glynis took the card. "I need to charter a plane and a pilot."

"Harry'll have to fly you."

"Harry?"

"Bob is our only other pilot."

"What about your skydiving pilot?"

"You have something against my Harry?"

"Not at all, ma'am."

"Well Ginger is booked with a rock and roll band for later this evening. I guess Harry could do it. But Ginger's pretty hot for musicians. You play?"

"I played the flute in high school."

"That might work," she said. "Give me about twenty minutes here. Go buy a Coke or something."

During the same twenty minutes Airman Betas paced her office and chewed off her pinky nail. She rapped on Major Wheylicke's office door.

"What is it?" Wheylicke shouted.

Airman Betas entered cautiously. The recent media attention and calls from various governmental offices had everyone on edge. "I spoke with Sergeant Vu, sir."

"Where is he?"

"I believe in Utah, sir," Betas said meekly.

"What's he doing in Utah, Betas?"

"He didn't say, sir."

"Why are you lying, Betas?"

"I didn't know I was, sir?"

"What did he want?"

"Information from the files he requested. I didn't give him the information, sir, like you said." That wasn't really a lie.

"Good." Wheylicke leaned back in his chair. Airman Betas remained standing before his desk. "Something else, Betas?"

"Here's the number where he placed the call, sir," she said hesitantly, placing a piece of paper on his desk. Wheylicke examined the paper.

"Good work, Betas. Due to your diligence I can wrap this matter up. I'm going to call the local military police and have Vu arrested."

"Yes, sir." Betas faced the door as Wheylicke continued.

"I'm declaring him officially AWOL."

"Yes, sir."

Betas quietly left the office.

The twin-engine Cessna touched down and rolled up the tarmac. Vu trotted out to meet the plane. The pilot, Ginger Rogers, a big boned girl with prankster eyes and curly brunette hair poking out from under a Yankee's baseball cap. She pulled off her headset, laid it over the throttle stick and killed the engines. After making a few notations in a log book, she climbed out of the cockpit. Vu was waiting for her by the rear of the aircraft.

"Hello, Ms. Rogers, I'm Sergeant Vu. I'm with the AFOSI out of Baltimore."

"Skip the formalities, Sergeant. My name's Ginger. If you gotta take a pee or smoke a cigarette, do it now. Got a long flight ahead of us. I'm gonna have Harry top off the fuel and check in with Glynis. Then we'll be on our merry way. That all right with you?"

Vu looked up at the oil-stained fuselage. He fumbled around in his pocket and pulled out his pill vial. "That is perfectly fine, ma'am. Excuse me for a moment." Vu popped a handful of green pills and choked them down.

Ginger frowned. "Don't fret. The aircraft is as solid as Fort Knox. I've been flying since I was twelve. I'm fifty-three now. Did my tour of duty in the Aleutian outback. Nothing to worry about. Now, excuse me while I visit the cowgirl's room and take care of business. If Harry shows up before I get back, make sure he tops off both tanks. Got it?"

Vu nodded and grasped his stomach. He took several slow deep breaths, let them out, and walked it off. Then, from over near the hanger, he heard a loud pop, like a backfire from an engine. A few minutes later an old fuel truck rolled out of the hanger and into view. Harry's big grumpy face leered out from behind a dirt-streaked windshield. The windshield wiper swiped a couple dry passes and stopped. The truck ground a few gears and came to a stop alongside the port side of the aircraft. Harry left the engine running, jumped out, approached the back-end of the truck, and opened the pump-house doors. He ran out a line of grounding cable and fastened it to the undercarriage of the aircraft.

"Ginger's a good ole' gal," Harry said, making conversation. "I knew her momma before she died. Real hellcat on wheels. WWII pilot. Bet you didn't know they had women pilots back then?"

"Ms. Rogers wanted me to remind you to fill both tanks."

Harry pulled out a ladder from the fuel truck and set it up next to the port wing. He uncoiled thirty feet of hose and carried it over to the ladder.

"You at all interested in hearing about WWII pilots?"

"No, sir," Vu said. "I have an upset stomach. I feel the topic might exacerbate my condition."

"Well, if you get sick while you're up there reach behind the passenger seat. There's a airsick bag in the seat flap. Make sure you use it. Ginger is not the most compassionate person when it comes to things like that."

"I don't plan on getting airsick."

"No one does."

"Sir, can we discuss something else?"

Harry nodded and pointed toward the truck. "I forgot to open the fuel valve, damnit," Harry said disgustedly. "Sergeant?"

Vu interrupted. "Open the fuel valve..."

"On the right side. The one painted green It might be a bit tight."

Vu walked to the rear of the truck and poked his head into the small stinky compartment. There were three small valves each painted a different color. He found the one painted green and twisted. It took a little effort, but it opened. "Go ahead, try it now!"

The truck's pump burped and grunted like a bull with constipation and eventually began pumping fuel through the two-inch hose. Gulping sounds reverberated through the piping system.

Vu stepped back and watched for Ginger's figure to stride onto the tarmac.

The refueling took less than ten minutes and just as Harry was recoiling the fuel hose, Ginger reappeared carrying a small brown paper bag and two cans of soda pop. She offered one to Vu, who turned it down.

She smiled at Harry. "Both tanks, Har'?"

"Second tank just needed toppin'."

"Better plan on a scheduled maintenance when I get back."

"Will do."

She looked at Vu. "Ready, Buckaroo?"

Vu looked at them both meekly, nodded, and faced the passenger door. In the far distance, Vu noticed a pair of military jeeps kicking up a trail of dust, leading toward the airport. He stood up straight. He saw a vision of Airman Betas smiling.

"Ms. Rogers, we need to go!"

Ginger pulled open her door. "Take it easy, tiger. Have to run through the preflight checks."

"No time, ma'am."

Vu pointed out the window. Ginger's eye widened with interest. "Unfriendlies?"

"Yes."

"I'm not going to lose my license over this?"

"No, ma'am."

"You're sure?"

"Certain."

Ginger closed her door and began flipping toggle switches. "In that case," she exclaimed. "Time to skedaddle!"

Vu fastened his seat belt and slipped down out of sight.

CHAPTER 44

The dinner table was set for three. Pam pulled a steaming pan of meatloaf out of the oven and set it down on a hotpad on the counter. "AJ! Dinner's ready!"

A pot of green beans sizzled on the stove. Pam removed the pan, dished out a helping on two of the three plates. Then she pulled a brown paper bag out of the broiler and set it down on the table.

AJ strolled in carrying Jed in his arms. He placed Jed in a highchair beside Pam's spot at the table. Then he took a seat.

"Where's Bobby?"

Pam frowned. "Haven't seen him all day."

Pam carried a jar of baby food from the stove and sat down at the table. She fastened a bib around little Jed and spoon fed him what looked like mash potatoes. "You had a visitor today."

AJ buttered his bread. "Who was it?" He reached across the table and grabbed the salt shaker.

"One of your Air Force buddies."

"John Long?"

"No." Jed spit up his food. "Aw, honey, you don't like momma's cookin'?" Jed slapped his fists on the table, whining.

"Who was it, Pam?" AJ picked up a fork and cut his meat.

"Said his name was Jim Lyman," she said calmly.

AJ kept a straight face and picked up his fork. His hand was trembling slightly. He got it under control. Pam wiped Jed's face off with a napkin. Then she sat down and looked at her own plate.

"Said he was passing through town, wanted to say hello."

"Say if he's coming back or not?"

"Pass me the pepper, honey."

AJ stared across the table. "Is he coming back?"

"Where do you know him from?"

"We served together in Lebanon."

"He seems like a nice enough guy."

AJ took a drink of milk. He set the glass down and stared at his food.

"What's wrong, honey? Did I overcook the meatloaf?"

AJ slid back his chair and stood up. "The meatloaf is fine."

"Where're you going?"

"To let Case know Lyman's in town."

"Honey, finish your dinner first."

AJ ignored his wife and used the phone in the living room to dial Case's number. He let it ring ten times and hung up after no answer. He returned to the kitchen, sat back down at the table.

Pam took a bite of bread. "Well?"

"He wasn't home."

"He's probably at Spike's Tavern. Connie's workin' tonight."

AJ stared at his son. "He didn't leave a number or anything, did he?"

"Nope."

"Too bad." His voice sounded distant. "Maybe he'll stop back by. It'd be good to see him."

Pam studied the dark expression on her husband's face. "Everything go all right today with the boat?"

"Yeah, I sent Bobby to Cooper's after some filters."

"He said that."

AJ stared at his food. "So he called you?"

"If you wanted something else for dinner, you should have asked."

"Pam, it's fine damnit!" Pam scowled, and fed Jed a spoonful of mush.

"You're in a fine mood tonight."

Jed picked up Pam's butter knife and threw it across the table. It slammed into a glass vase filled with Irises. AJ jumped, shot an angry look Jed's way.

Pam swatted Jed's hand. "No! No! No!" Jed began to cry. Pam pulled him out of his high chair and cradled him.

AJ stood up. "I'll be in the shop."

"Go ahead and finish," she said. "I'll get Jed ready for bed."

AJ left his uneaten meal on the table and headed toward the door.

AJ closed the door behind him and looked up at the dark, star-filled sky. The cool misty air smelled like the sea. He crossed the tall wet grass and went inside the cold dark shop and switched a light on. He stepped over a pile of rusted anchor chain in the center of the floor and approached a cluttered workbench. He flipped on the overhead flourescent. He squatted down and removed the bottom right bench drawer. He dug around in the dark hole where the drawer had been and pulled out a small package wrapped in an old oily t-shirt. He carefully unwrapped it. Inside was a SIG P-238. He held the gun up to the light and inspected it. He released the magazine and dropped it out into the palm of his hand. From an overhead cabinet he removed a box of shells. He counted the rounds into the magazine. He popped the full magazine into the pistol butt, racked back the slide, loading one into the chamber. With one in the pipe and the hammer back, he turned the decocker safety, dropping the hammer and releasing the trigger to the long double action pull mode. Then he stuck the gun inside his pocket.

He closed the box of shells and returned them to the cabinet, switched off the shop lights and locked the door behind him.

AJ went inside the house and kissed his son goodnight. Pam put the infant to bed and quietly closed the door. AJ sat down in the overstuffed chair in front of the t.v. and stared at the screen. He fished around on the remote for a few minutes and settled on a sports channel. Pam went into the kitchen and cleared off the table, storing the leftovers in the refrigerator. She was rinsing the dishes when AJ got up, put on his jacket, and went into the kitchen.

"I'll be back in an hour or so," he said.

"AJ, I don't like it when you keep things from me."

"I'm just going to find Case. Maybe he's seen, Bobby."

"It's not Bobby I'm worried about."

"If someone knocks on the door while I'm gone. Don't open it."

"Why? What's wrong?"

AJ wrapped his arms around his wife. "You know that I'd do anything for you and Jed, don't you?"

"Yes, but..."

AJ's voice cracked. "Remember the time you hooked that monster Halibut using a condom Case jerry rigged as a lure?"

"Honey, what's wrong?"

"Not a thing, sweetheart."

AJ kissed his wife on the cheek and left the house.

CHAPTER 45

Case lived in a single-wide trailer east of town along Shadow Creek. The area was run down and mostly barren wetland. The trailer sat on a ridge barely above the flood plain. The driveway was back off the main road, a plowed narrow path through scrub grass and fruitless trees. The lights to the trailer were on and a Willy's jeep was parked out front. Off to the side was a red Firebird. AJ didn't recognize the Firebird.

AJ did remember when Case bought the old jeep. Back then, it had a eight-cylinder flathead eight, which blew a head gasket after the first week Case owned it. He scrapped the engine, put in a V-8 with hooker headers and glass-pack mufflers. The increased horsepower took out the rear end. Case replaced that the following month with a Ford gear set. Then Case and he joined the Air Force and the jeep sat out-of-doors under a tarp for three years. Case never stopped worrying about it.

AJ could hear music playing when he approached the front of the trailer. The door was unlocked. AJ pulled the SIG out of his jeans, held it at low-ready, and went inside.

The front door opened into a small living room area with a second-hand sofa and end-table. Two brass lamps were lit and the t.v. was on. One of the lamps was overturned and lying on the floor. An over-stuffed pillow sat propped against the wall. AJ thought he could hear distressed voices at the end of the hall.

He crept toward the sound. Two figures were struggling in the darkened room. AJ switched on a light. Case jumped up from the bed. Surprised and naked. A young tattooed blonde lying on the bed with no clothes on pulled the sheets up around her throat, and screamed. AJ calmly tucked the SIG into the waist of his jeans. "Sorry," he said, looking away.

"What the fuck, AJ!" Case snapped, shoved him out the door and slammed it in his face. A few minutes later, Case reappeared looking disgusted. He had on faded jeans but no shirt or shoes. Fresh claw marks highlighted his otherwise thin, white chest. AJ sat on the sofa drinking a cold bottle of beer, staring at the t.v. screen.

"Kindly tell me what the fuck is going on?"

AJ didn't mince words. "Lyman's in town. He visited Pam while we were at the boat. I didn't know Connie had tattoos."

"Enough about Connie. What'd he want?"

"I suspect he wanted to show he could walk into my life and take away the most valuable thing I have."

Case said, "You tell John yet?"

"Nope."

"Well, don't tell Connie."

Down the hall a woman's voice said, "Don't tell Connie what?"

Connie had a slender athletic build. She had on one of Case's flannel shirts. Her hair was uncombed and her eyes were smeared black slashes.

"Connie, you remember AJ?"

"Hello," Connie said. "Thank's for screwing up a perfectly good orgasm."

"Case 'll make it up to you."

"Sure he will," Connie replied. "Now, what's going on? Why the gun?"

"Connie, baby," Case said. "This is between us. Why don't you go back to bed."

Connie sighed, grabbed AJ's beer, and disappeared into the bedroom. AJ stood up to go. "Just wanted to give you a head's up. Have you seen Bobby?"

"Not since yesterday morning."

"Yeah, so what's new?"

"I'll swing by the airport in the morning and let John know about Lyman."

Case took hold of his brother's arm and escorted him out the door. "We'll take care of Lyman tomorrow."

The trailer door closed. The sound of a deadbolt locked. AJ stood out in the cold and listened to the sounds of the night. After several minutes, he got into his car and left.

Later that night while AJ lay in bed, he thought about what Case had said earlier: "We'll take care of Lyman." It seemed like an odd thing to say, considering Lyman had saved Case's life.

CHAPTER 46

That last night in Lebanon.

His name was Rahjeh Laudeeze. Rahjeh owned a modest house in central Beirut built of brick and mortar where he conducted his counterfeiting operation. His specialty, rare coin replication, specifically the British Sovereign. There was a high market value for the coin in the United States, especially among rich private collectors. The counterfeiting was conducted in a basement shop. A small but efficient operation. Gold was melted down and poured into dies that had been meticulously and painstakingly altered. It would take the eye of a trained numismatist to spot the flaws. But some flaws held real value. Rahjeh was the best.

Rahjeh also collected gold bars and gold bullion. These too were altered to appear old. Dates stamped across the face of the bars to replicate famous periods of time when gold was sailed out of South America and Mexico, destined for the new world. Rahjeh had a fascination for the "Gold Rush" period in America's history. He studied famous eighteenth century wrecks at sea. Like the Lady Scarlet that went down off the coast of California, around the area now known as Carmel. Trunks of artwork, jewelry, tons of rare gold coins, gold bars and gold bullion were never recovered. Or the wreck of the Modessa, reportedly carrying a crew of wealthy immigrants of Spanish descent up the coast of Baja, carrying a cargo of ancient coins, gold bars, rubies, diamonds, and bronze sculptures.

Rahjeh himself, Marken had said, was not a terrorist, nor a madman, nor a thief. Just a skilled craftsman who people of an unsavory character came to trust with their gold. Marken used his connections at the State Department to learn more of the man. Marken became one of the "trusted ones" in Rahjeh's circle of men. And it was Marken that provided them with the intelligence necessary to bring the operation down – the same intelligence that almost lead to the death of Case.

The operation was known as "Golden Shower." Getting inside had been easy. They knew in advance that Rahjeh would be alone that night and that the odds were in favor of him admitting an unannounced and attractive guest at his front door.

Leslie strolled up to the heavy doors in a black knit, tight fitting, thigh-length dress, revealing enough cleavage to inspire a monk. Her breath smelled of alcohol, her eyes had a lustful wanton look and her lips glistened in the moonlight. Rahjeh never expected a thing.

Rahjeh's eyes widened with surprise when he saw the young American at his front door. Normally a cautious man, Rahjeh held back his immediate response. The men waiting around the corner knew his penchant for American girls, especially blondes. He stepped back from the peep hole and slid his 9mm inside the pocket of his silk smoking jacket and opened the door. "Can I help you?" he said, staring at Leslie's protruding breasts.

"This isn't my hotel is it?" Leslie giggled, hiccuped and covered her mouth coyly.

"No, miss," Rahjeh said. "Where are you staying? Perhaps I can be of assistance." It had all been so well rehearsed. The drop of the purse, the reaction that would follow.

"Allow me."

Rahjeh casually stooping down to retrieve the loose items spilling from the lady's purse all the while running a lustful eye over Leslie's firm legs, and thinking how it would be. "It is not safe for a woman of your beauty to be out at night," he said with inviting eyes. Leslie smiled and bent forward revealing more of herself. All so carefully planned.

The small baton thudded against Rahjeh's skull, knocking him down but not unconscious. The crew trailed behind.

These facts were known: Rahjeh's son was away at college in Lisbon; Rahjeh's wife was visiting family in West Berlin; Rahjeh's electronic security system had been compromised; Rahjeh's cousin, who occasionally acted as Rahjeh's bodyguard, was in the hospital with a broken back – a odd hit and run accident, occurring the previous day; but what they hadn't counted on was Rahjeh's twelve-year-old daughter descending down the stairs lugging a Kalashnikov AK-47.

The plan had been as follows: Neutralize Rahjeh, keep the daughter upstairs, bound and gagged if necessary, steal the gold stored in his hidden underground vaults, leave the country. The gold would be smuggled out of Lebanon via Marken's sister, Leslie and John D. Long. Long had been a perfect candidate: a trusted pilot for an American airline company where Leslie was also on the payroll; a member of the military reserves; a dedicated family man, with a compulsion for high stakes. According to Marken he had developed the perfect system for smuggling contraband out of the country.

All under the watchful eye of the U.S. Customs Bureau. What they needed was for the gold to be delivered to the airport by a certain time, on a certain date. They would handle the rest. Once the gold arrived in the United States, Case and he came into play.

The problem that plagued AJ for weeks was, once they had the gold secured in the U.S., how were they to spend it without attracting the attention of the IRS and the Treasury Department. It had come to him during a moment of reflection.

The Flenner Family had grown up on the Oregon Coast around the sea and the old sea legends for generations. Even at the young age, the three Flenner brothers, including young Bobby, had found a portion of a sunken ship off the coast of Astoria. The discovery had made the local headlines. Overnight, the three became celebrities. Reportedly, the ship believed to be from the wreck of the Ontario, incited interest from a local salvage company. The brothers along with the salvage company, retrieved a number of artifacts – their most prized possession being the remains of an old canon – which was hoisted to shore and restored to a sparkling glimmer of its former self, eventually donated to the local maritime museum in their name.

So who would question, AJ told the others, if the brothers discovered a second sunken ship? The gold could be smuggled to the Oregon Coast and carefully laid to rest on the sea bottom? Everyone knew they were the local sunken ship afficionados. So it would make perfect sense if they discovered another treasure. They could avoid the scrutiny of the IRS and the Treasury Department in one fell swoop. As long as they made sure the rare coins, gold bars, and gold bullion matched the shipments known to have been lost in that area of the sea, no one would be the wiser. And so the plan was hatched...

But no one had anticipated the little girl, the gun, and the bloodshed that followed. Even now, thinking back upon it, AJ wanted to believe they had done the right thing.

CHAPTER 47

Right before dawn the small airfield just north of Seaside opened its wet narrow runway and allowed the twin-engine Cessna to land. The plane taxied to an uncovered parking area and the pilot shut off its engine. The passenger door opened, Vu got out and stretched his legs. He reached into his pocket, pulled out a vial and popped the top. His eyes sadly fell to his hands as he flipped the vial on end and realized it was empty. Ginger jumped out of the plane and made a few scribbles into her logbook and slipped it into her worn leather briefcase.

"I'm whipped. And hungry," Ginger said, her voice sounding fatigued. "Think anyone's up around here?"

Vu was thinking it had been a very long flight. He opened the storage compartment and took out a laptop and a single suitcase. He glanced around. A dozen or so planes like the one they had flown on. Two out-buildings with dark windows. A small parking area flanked by a long narrow building for long-term plane storage. No tower, no restaurant, no taxi service.

They picked up their belongings and began walking. Vu thought he saw something dart into the trees near the road, next to the public parking area, but figured it was just fatigue playing tricks on him. He passed by a sedan giving off residual heat from its warm motor and followed Ginger out to the main highway. They stood on the side of the road with their thumbs out, attempting to hitch a ride in the misty grey light.

"This sucks," Ginger said.

"Yes, it is unpleasant." Over his shoulder, Vu thought he saw the faint outline of a man standing on the tarmac, but when he focused his eyes he was gone. He ignored the airfield focusing on the long, straight, dark highway, known as Highway 101.

A man's dark figure stepped out of the shadows and watched the two walk down the road. A street lamp flickered overhead revealing the shallow features of Jim Lyman in a dark stocking cap. He had on dark coveralls and dark boots and work gloves. There was a trace of hydraulic fluid visible on one of the gloves. Lyman brushed his hand against his leg and went back toward the dark airfield.

Lyman was unaware Nigel and his men were watching....

* * *

They walked a mile and stopped. Eventually, a pair of headlights appeared on the highway, heading their direction. Ginger perked up. Vu had never enjoyed hitchhiking. He had been forced to do it while he was stationed overseas where it was a more acceptable means of transportation. But he didn't like it. He missed his scooter. Maybe he could rent one in the area.

"Let me do this," Ginger said. "Step back. Guys always pick up chicks."

"What if it is a chick?"

"Don't matter."

The headlights grew brighter. A two-door Ford pulled off onto the shoulder. Ginger hustled up to the passenger door and opened it. She spoke with the driver and then waved for Vu to join her and the two piled in the front seat.

Vu sat next to the window and leaned his head against the glass and closed his eyes. Ginger, on the other hand, was thrilled to have a new person to talk with. She looked Lyman in the eye.

"Damn thoughtful of you to stop and pick up a couple beaten down dogs like us in the middle of the night."

Lyman glanced at Vu and then back at the highway. Lyman still wore a stocking cap and his face was mostly in shadows.

"It's no problem. I'm on my way to the marina. Goin' fishin'. What brings you out so early?"

"Hotshot over here is some highfalutin government agent on a manhunt. I'm the lucky girl who happened to score a little action by flying him here."

Vu shot Ginger a menacing look. Something about the driver caught Vu's attention out of the corner of his eye. But exhausted, Vu couldn't place the man in his memory. He decided to change the subject.

"Ms Rogers is an excellent pilot," Vu said. "If you are in need of a charter, I recommend her."

"Ain't much on traveling, but thanks. You two staying in town?"

Ginger smiled at Vu. "I don't think we've discussed that. Breakfast sounds mighty fine at the moment."

Up ahead the neon sign of a 24-hour restaurant came into view. Vu took another glance at the driver. Something stirred in his mind.

The car pulled into the parking lot of the restaurant and stopped. "Well, enjoy your visit," Lyman said cheerfully.

Ginger shook Lyman's hand and quickly shoved Vu out the passenger door. Vu stood outside and watched as the car drove away.

Ginger started toward the restaurant and stopped. "Hey, hotshot, aren't you coming?"

Vu made a note of the car and plate before he followed Ginger toward the front entrance.

* * *

John Long rolled over in his motel bed and hit the alarm snooze button. He focused his bloodshot eyes on the clock's dial and made out the red numbers – 5:30 a.m. Plenty of time to shit, shower, shave, and shoe shine before he called a taxi to drop him at the airfield. The plane was already fueled and checked out. His share of the gold stashed aboard. He had done that the day before. It'd be a short flight to Seattle, and then he'd be home free.

He closed his eyes and drifted in and out of sleep. At some point he drifted back to New Orleans, to Leslie's hotel room. She had been so beautiful. What was he going to do without her now?

It was almost like a living death. He could still visualize her standing under the hair dryer for what seem like hours, blowing her long thick hair, humming an unknown tune to herself in the steamy mirror, when he had come up from behind and kissed her soft neck for the last time. The feel of her warm flesh made him rock hard, as he carried her to the bed, spread her legs open, and put it in. It was as good as the first time. He had always demanded to know everything about her, everything. That night would be no different. She would spend the next few hours applying fresh polish to her nails and ironing her uniform. Always wearing just a silky negligee. And then she would douche – keeping the warm juices inside as long as she could. She had told him on several occasions that she preferred to keep his cum inside her. She loved it coming back out and trailing down her thighs. It reminded her of him during the whole day. And he had delivered a full dose, good and hard and deep. It would be a very long flight to Japan, before they could be together again.

He had made excellent time getting to the airport and checking in with the crew chief. The flight was being held back while a minor repair was made to the heating system. It gave him enough time to place one last call to her hotel. He never expected to hear Ray Kano's voice pick up.

He wondered if Ray Kano had died a painful death. He had snuffed out the girl of his dreams. It felt like a hydrogen bomb exploded inside his heart. No one was more deserving an ill fate than Kano. The thought of Kano suffering brought moments of joy to his weary mind. But did he suffer enough? Or did he simply seal his lips and breath no more?

He woke suddenly from that dreamy state and wiped a tear from his eye, sat up and turned on the night light. It was 5:36. It had taken God six days to create the world. It had taken him six minutes to relive the end of his world.

He absently reached for his insignia ring, but it was gone. That's right, he'd lost it. The mind has a way of forgetting insignificant things at moments of duress.

CHAPTER 48

The two detectives were standing in front of the private tennis courts with their hands in their pockets waiting for the match to end.

Gates turned to Hill and asked, "You ever play tennis?"

"A couple times in high school," Hill replied. "I sucked. You?"

"Nope."

"Really?" He seemed surprised.

"Really."

The tall, tanned opponent walked off the court with her Wilson racket and a small hand towel which she used to wipe perspiration from her brow. She was over forty, fit and built nicely in all the right places, which showed in her tight white tennis uniform. She stooped down and tied her shoelace as the detectives approached. It was Gates who spoke first. She introduced herself and detective Hill and added, "Mrs. Long, thank you for seeing us on such a short notice."

"You're welcome, Detective," she said in an educated, sibilant voice.

"This shouldn't take long," Gates told her.

"Before we begin, you're aware John and I are in the middle of divorce proceedings?"

"Divorces are never pleasant," Gates acknowledged. "You have my condolences." Mrs. Long's dark eyes disappeared into a stony face. Gates went on, "Earlier in the week when we spoke with your husband, he indicated not only he but also you and your daughter were friends with Leslie Marken?"

Jennifer picked at her cheek. "Her death came as a shock. Horrible thing. It was discreet of you to keep our family name out of it. What does this have to do with me?"

Gates removed a small evidence bag from her pocket. She handed it to Mrs. Long. "Do you recognize this, Mrs. Long?"

Jennifer held the bag up to the light. Inside was a man's ring. One of those class rings you get when you enter an elite group. The initials scribed on the back of the ring where: Lt. J.D. Long.

"It's John's," Mrs. Long confessed. "Up until a few years ago he went by the name JD. Short for John Dean. Where did you get it?"

"From a teenager in Houma."

"Has something happened to John?" Her tone held no remorse.

"That's a good question, Mrs. Long," Gates said. "We're curious how his ring ended up where it did. I'd prefer not to tell you specifics. We'd ask him ourselves if we could locate him."

"He hasn't spoken to me since Leslie's death," she said curtly. "Well, that's not entirely true. He said the police might pay a visit and ask some rather unpleasant questions."

Gates returned the bag to her pocket. "I'll try and keep the unpleasantness to a minimum, Mrs. Long," Gates said. "Let's start from the beginning, shall we? How well did you know Leslie?"

Jennifer reached into her gym bag at her feet and removed a fresh water bottle. She took a long drink.

"My daughter and she were close," she said tactfully. "They went to school together. Palled around occasionally."

"Your husband indicated that he helped Leslie get on with the airlines. Is this correct?"

"Yes, John provided a character reference. I believe it probably helped her get hired."

Hill stepped in. "Were you suspicious of his motives?"

"If you mean did I think at the time it would lead to something else, Detective, then no I didn't." The woman's voice was calm and controlled. "Leslie was young, vibrant, and attractive. What man wouldn't have found her desirable?"

"Did Mr. Long tell you he was having relations with Leslie?"

"Eventually."

"Were you surprised by the news?"

"No. I imagine there were others."

"Were his relations a contributing factor to your divorce?"

"Moderately. Along with the gambling."

Gates eyes lit up. "Gambling, ma'am?"

"I imagine he didn't discuss the subject with you."

"No."

"John was a binge gambler. Without contrition, really. He would go months without betting a dime. Then all of a sudden, out of the blue, he would lay down thousands on craps, horses, dogs. It didn't matter. John loved high stakes. Big risk taker. It's what attracted me in the beginning. As I was saying, we nearly filed for bankruptcy over John's gambling debts. John's CO got him into counseling. It seemed to help for a while. At least we were able to save the house."

"Was Leslie a gambler?"

"I don't believe so."

"When was the last time Leslie had contact with your daughter?" Gates glanced down at her book. "Angie."

Mrs. Long waved to a fellow club member crossing the court. "What was that?"

"Did your daughter and Leslie have contact recently?" Gates asked.

"No. That ended some time ago," she stated. "After Angie caught John and Leslie in a compromising situation. Actually, I should have listened to my daughter back then. She was certain they were having an affair. Of course Leslie tried to convince her otherwise. That the kissing was just Leslie's way of seeking solace during an emotional time. And I know my daughter wanted to believe her. Of course Leslie at the time had a good reason for her actions. She had just learned her brother had been killed in a plane crash. The news devastated her. It was much later before John actually sat down with me and said he was having an affair and wanted a divorce."

Hill stepped forward. "Would you know anyone that might have wanted Leslie dead?"

"You mean besides me?"

Gates frowned. "We don't consider you a suspect, Ms. Long. However, it would be helpful if we recorded your whereabouts on the night of the 15th."

"I believe I had dinner with Angie that evening. I was upset after a long visit with my attorney. We met at the Club. It's called the Green Room. I believe Angie made the reservations. You can check with the front desk man if you like. His name is Bill."

Gates jotted the name down in her book. "So you didn't hold any animosity toward Leslie?"

"Actually, I'm grateful to her," she explained. "I sought therapy. It helped show me how shallow and self-punishing my relationship with my husband had really become. And it pushed me to do something about it. Until then, I was unaware I was staying in a bad marriage because I thought I could fix it. I figured I could get John to stop being so distant and stop gambling and spending so much time away from home, if I'd just hang in there. I know that must sound odd to you. I am an educated woman. But these things don't have anything to do with being educated, do they Detective?"

Gates jaw looked strained. She changed the subject. "Did your husband ever discuss Jim Lyman or Ray Kano?"

"I remember Lyman's name coming up several times during the course of conversations with John. John was a reservist and he hated that Lyman was MIA. He said he knew him. What I believe now is that Lyman was John's nemesis."

Gates frowned. "Explain that, Mrs. Long?"

"Well, Angie got most of the story from Leslie. At one time, Lyman was her fiancée. And John never approved. John and Leslie met both Lyman and Kano while they were flying overseas."

"Your husband met Kano?" Gates interrupted.

"I don't know the details of their relationships. But from time to time their names would come up. Especially recently, before Leslie's murder. At least Kano's name came up. Kano contacted John, but I don't know the extent of the conversation. John moved out shortly thereafter."

"So you don't know if either of them saw each other?"

"No."

"You're certain?"

"Yes." Then as if she remembered something more, added, "Looking back I suppose John was infatuated with Leslie even then and he was probably jealous of Leslie's affections for Lyman. I don't think John and Leslie began sleeping together until after Leslie's brother died. I never asked John for the gruesome details. The deception itself was enough. It hit Angie hardest. I think she wanted to believe that despite his gambling and long absences, he was basically a decent man. And that he loved her."

"So he never discussed Lyman in the present?"

"No. Just in the past when it involved Leslie."

"Were you aware that Leslie had a miscarriage?"

"Yes."

"Did Leslie indicate who was responsible?"

"She confided to Angie," Mrs. Long said.

Hill asked, "What about Ray Kano? Was his name ever mentioned in relation to Leslie?"

"Leslie was convinced Kano had something to do with her brother's plane crash. I find that hard to believe. But stranger things have happened. John said he would speak with his superiors about it. I don't know if he ever did. It was never brought up around the dinner table. What I do know is that after the incident, Leslie was never quit the same. Odd isn't it – how things turn on a dime?"

Gates paused. "How did Leslie's behavior change?"

"She became despondent, moody, unpredictable, downright mean some times. Especially to Angie. John was worried she might commit suicide."

"Did she ever attempt it?" Hill asked.

"Not that I am aware of," she said tactfully.

"Where can we find John?"

"I'm sorry. I can't help you," she said firmly. "I imagine you've tried the airlines and the base?"

"We have."

"Well, you might try his lawyer."

Gates jotted the information down in her book and thanked Mrs. Long for her cooperation.

"Is there anything else you'd like to say on the subject?" Gates asked.

Mrs. Long smiled. "Don't get married, Detectives."

CHAPTER 49

The startling sound of gunfire woke Bobby. He jumped out of bed and looked out the port window. The sky was just starting to show signs of life. The sea was still, but deep dark rolling waves lurked below the calm surface. An angry seagull cried overhead. Somewhere out over the horizon a distant trawler carved its way in the rising sea. Bobby rubbed his tired eyes and checked the other side of the boat. He was certain he had heard gunfire. But only a misty silhouette of a deserted parking lot, a few cars, a dirtbike, and a Swan Ice Cream truck chugging by on the deserted highway. No guns, no bullets. Just lurking sounds in his mind.

He pulled open the small refrigerator and removed a cold beer. He drank it staring at the sea. It helped his headache go away. He lay down but he couldn't sleep. It was becoming a habit of his lately.

AJ wanted him to sleep on the boat now. He wasn't certain if it was because of the expensive equipment below or because AJ just wanted him out of his house. It left him feeling empty inside. An hour passed. Then two. Eventually he rose and put on his clothes. The sky had clouded over. The sea had come alive. He checked the cargo below. He opened the chest for the hell of it and noticed immediately that it was empty. All the gold coins were gone. At first he panicked. Then he reasoned that his brothers had probably moved it ashore. Probably the shed out back. Or maybe Long took it. He didn't give a shit anymore. They didn't want him in on it – so fuck 'em....

He pulled out a bucket and a sponge from a storage locker and went on deck. He filled the bucket with water from the dock tap and dragged a hose down to the boat and scrubbed down the deck and cabin and rinsed off everything.

Out in the parking lot a sedan pulled in and stopped. Bobby couldn't make out the man in the back seat but the guys looked like ragheads. *Probably fuckin' tourists on a lollygag around the harbor.* He felt old suddenly, longing for a time when the harbor was just a home for fishermen. Tourists irritated him. Nosey bastards. The men stared down at the boats for a few minutes and then drove off.

Bobby coiled up the hose and was carrying it aboard when to the south, just beyond the trees in the distant sky, he saw a plume of black smoke.

* * *

Long had the taxi pull alongside the plane and stop. His Cessna sat in the sun with dew steaming off its wings.

"How's this, sir?" the cab driver asked.

"It'll do."

The cab driver glanced down at his clipboard. There was no meter. He rattled off a price which Long thought sounded reasonable, then scribbled it down on paper. Long pulled out his wallet and paid the man.

The cab driver looked out the windshield toward the sky and shook his head. "The sky is not a safe place today."

Long climbed out and stood by the trunk, waiting. The cab driver moved like a snail. He popped the latch, and stooped forward. Long snagged the bag first and hefted it from the trunk. "Have a good day, sir."

Long stood by the plane until the taxi was out of sight and then loaded his overnight bag in the co-pilot seat.

He skipped the pre-flight checks, climbed into the pilot's seat, fastened the seatbelt and fired the engines. He made a note of the time in his logbook. He noticed the engine oil pressure and fuel level readings. Normal. He flipped the switch for the running gear lights and slipped on his headset, turned the dial on his radio back and forth and then took off the headset and set it down on his luggage.

He idled onto the runway, ran up his engines. Something didn't feel quite right, but he ignored it. Maybe it was just the runway, shorter than most, or the tall trees surrounding it on all four sides, that needed topping. The 10 knot wind was out of the south. He was suddenly desperate to be away.

He throttled up and rumbled down the runway, watching his speed indicator dial rise. He felt his heart thumping against his chest as the wheels lifted off. His hands felt clammy. Something was very wrong with one of the ailerons. *Damnit. Too late for brakes.* He was losing hydraulic pressure rapidly. *Turn, damnit, turn!*

He looked up and saw a bank of trees dead ahead.

The plane smashed into the trees and exploded into a ball of flaming fuel and twisted fuselage.

CHAPTER 50

"Did you hear that?" Ginger asked.

"What?" Vu replied. Vu had been studying a black and white photograph for several minutes while they waited for the waitress to clear off the dirty plates.

Ginger looked down and rubbed her belly. "I should have ordered the bacon well done."

Vu put down the photograph and opened a packet of tea. "Here. Chew this. It will settle your stomach."

Ginger gawked at the small pile of tea leaves in his open palm. "You first." She then glanced at the photograph. "So is this the guy?"

"Put it down, please."

Across the smoky cafe two loggers flopped down at the counter. A frizzy-haired waitress made her rounds serving up menus and steaming cups of coffee over the sounds of eggs crackling on a hot grill.

Vu raised the tea to his lips. The waitress stopped at their table. "Customers usually add water with their tea, mister," she said quizzically, and left, juggling an armload of dirty dishes.

Ginger ignored the request and scooped up the photograph. After turning it this way and that, she said, "You know, if I had to guess, I'd say this was the guy who gave us a ride into town. Is this the guy you're lookin' for?"

Vu choked on his tea.

Out the window, a fire truck and ambulance raced by with their sirens blaring.

"So what now, sweetcakes?" Ginger asked, sliding the check toward Vu. "I'm ready to rack it in for a few hours before I head east. What about you?"

Vu gazed up at his companion's bloodshot eyes.

"Unfortunately, I must work," he uttered, and pulled cash from his wallet.

"Okay, then. So long, Jack." Ruffling his hair good-naturedly, she rose and ambled away from the table. Jack, somewhat disconcerted by the physical familiarity, self consciously recombed his hair with his fingers. Paying the bill, he headed outside to plan his next step, whatever that was, still uncertain if the photograph of Lyman matched the description of the driver of the car.

With the stocking cap and the dark interior, Vu didn't get a good look at the guy.

Vu caught up with Ginger in the parking lot where she was gawking as a second fire truck passed with its siren blowing. Vu picked at the corner of his mouth, still a little shaken by the long flight. Ginger pointed down the road. A funnel of black smoke appeared over the highway.

"Hope to hell it's not the airport," Ginger pointed out. Vu calculated distances. Two volunteer firemen drove by in their POV's, chasing after the trail of smoke.

"No – I think it is further south."

"Well I'm too damn beat to give a shit. Happy trails, Jack."

Vu awkwardly waved goodbye, ducking ever so slightly to avoid a potential head pat.

* * *

The GMC skidded to a stop behind a police car parked on the shoulder of Highway 101. Both doors flung open as AJ and Case bailed out and jogged up the road toward the thick bellowing smoke. Several hundred feet away, firemen were hosing down the forest floor where the twin-engine Cessna had crashed and burst into flames. Bobby hopped over a coil of hose and waved frantically as two brothers came into view.

"It's Long's fuckin' plane!" Bobby uttered.

AJ and Case studied the area, soldiers back in combat. AJ said, "Bobby. Get out of here!"

AJ's harsh words stung. "What for?" Bobby asked.

Case grabbed hold of Bobby's shirt and spun him toward the highway. AJ scanned the faces in the crowd and then moved toward the smoldering metal. He studied the wreckage. The gold was gone...

AJ caught up with his brothers back at the truck.

"You need to keep your mouth shut about whose plane that was," Case told Bobby. Bobby angrily knocked Case's arm loose.

AJ said solemnly to Case. "It's Lyman."

"What about the Ragheads?"

"I'd lay money on Lyman."

"What about the..." Case cut his statement short realizing his younger brother was listening. He glared toward Bobby.

"What the fuck you guys talkin' about?" Bobby piped in. "This was an accident, right?"

Case pulled the passenger door open. "Get in, Bobby."

"What about my bike?"

AJ said, "Leave it. We'll pick it up later."

Later, they paced the kitchen rehashing what they had discussed on the drive over. Pam stood across the room feeding a bottle to the baby. Pam said, "Alex can we talk for a minute?"

AJ was in the middle of a conversation with his brother and didn't hear his wife's comment. "... or he'll visit the boat."

"He's a calculating son-of-a-bitch," Case said.

"Alex!" Pam shouted. "Can we talk please?" AJ and Case stopped talking and looked across the room.

"And by the way, Case!" Pam snapped. "Please don't swear in front of my son."

"Christ, Pam," Case retorted. "As if he could understand."

AJ interrupted the squabble. "Can we stay focused for a minute? Bobby, you locked the boat up when you left?"

"Yeah."

Pam frowned. "Alex, I'm not asking again."

AJ motioned he'd be right there. Then he lifted up his shirt and pulled out a handgun. "Until this thing with Lyman is over I want you to carry this." He handed the firearm to Bobby, and looked at Case. Case showed signs that he disapproved of his brother's decision. Bobby was like a kid with a new toy. He twirled the gun around, pretending to be a cop.

AJ joined his wife in the living room, out of earshot of the two brothers in the kitchen. "Alex, you're freaking me out. What's this all about?"

"It's old business."

"You just gave your brother a gun," she said heatedly. "Alex, we have a son now. You are not in the military any longer. Why do you need to carry a gun?"

"You're going to have to trust me on this one."

Pam stared straight into her husband's eyes. "You love me?"

AJ's eyes brightened. "Of course."

"Then don't do this. Whatever this is about. Just let it go."

"I can't."

Pam studied his stern expression. "So help me God you better not get killed. Or I'll kick your ass."

AJ affectionately touched his wife's butt. Pam stepped back, and glared,

"Fuck you, Alex! Get out of the house. And take your brothers with you."

AJ faked a smile. "Don't open the door for anyone, okay, Baby?"

Pam blew him off. Chewing nervously on her lip, she rocked the infant in her arms and stared at the t.v.

Out in the garage, AJ broke into a tall cabinet and removed two shotguns. He handed one of them to Case. He shouldered the other.

CHAPTER 51

Police were keeping the small crowd of curious onlookers away from the crash area. Vu saw a sheriff's car parked alongside the road and tapped the driver's side window. Inside, a burly looking cop near retirement put his mic down and snarled Vu's direction. Vu pressed his government ID against the window.

The sheriff's tired eyes glanced over the credentials. The window came down. "Be with you in a minute, Agent Vu," the sheriff said. And then into his mic he said, "Sally, read them back to me. That's right. Yes, go ahead... niner, yes... 2856733 OGB. Yes, that's Orange, Grape, Banana. That's it. And tell 'em one of their agents just showed up."

Vu realized the sheriff probably had him confused with an FAA agent. He stepped back from the door and watched the sheriff uncoil his legs from behind the wheel.

Sheriff Griffin was his name. He stood better than six-five in flat feet. His pants were large enough to house three small children. Sheriff Griffin cinched up his belt and repositioned his broad hat on his square head. He'd been with the California State Patrol before transferring to Astoria, some thirteen years prior. Things were different in Oregon, he explained. Took him the better part of five years to figure that out. Vu just nodded and followed him across the grounds and through the police barricade.

Sheriff Griffin stopped about thirty feet from the crash site. The forest floor was still smoldering, but the fire was out. Most of the firemen were busy coiling up hoses. Still two stomped around in the woods with axes, prodding and poking around in the heavy moss and beneath broken limbs. The pilot's body had been removed and transported to the coroner's office. The plane itself was intact. Most of the front section was charred and smashed up. Glass was broken out and scattered around the open doors. The tail section was damaged but not burnt. An old man in dirty coveralls was examining the tail section.

"That's Donald," Sheriff Griffin pointed out. "He's the resident expert when it comes to aircraft, especially these twin-engine jobs. Retired Air Force. Been a pilot all his life. Worked for your agency for about five years. And, he also happens to be my brother. He does freelance work for some of the insurance companies in the area. Knows what he's doing."

"Have you identified the pilot yet?"

"Name's John Long. We've got a call in to the next of kin. Lives in Louisiana. Got it all from his logbook. Amazing it didn't burn up in the crash."

"Were there any passengers?"

"Not that we can tell. Unless they got thrown from the plane and are out in those woods somewhere. Rescue team didn't sniff out anything. I suspect he was flying alone."

Vu left Sheriff Griffin to watch over the area and joined the man in the coveralls. Vu introduced himself and shook hands with the man.

Harry pointed to the tail section. "Doesn't look right," he said with a heavy tone of concern. "See the hydraulic line going up to the tail section? It's got a clean break. Very odd. Pressure lines usually show signs of expansion or premature separation. Metal cores fail or fittings fail. This one looks different. Almost as if it was scored with a blade. My guess, when the pilot went to pull up, the increasing hydraulic pressure in the line caused a rupture to that area, resulting in a catastrophic pressure failure. Ascent would be next to impossible at that point. But even the best pilots get into trouble from time to time. This one probably couldn't clear the trees. Course I'm just speculating."

Vu rubbed his chin and stared at the damaged tail section. Behind them along the highway, a blue government sedan drove onto the site and parked. Two investigators from the FAA climbed out and walked toward the aircraft. Vu caught a glimpse of the men heading his direction. He quickly headed off a possible conflict.

He pulled out his credentials and flashed them at the FAA man in charge and explained that the pilot was a member of the Air Force Reserves. He had been in the area and was alerted to the site by his superiors. The two men seemed to accept the information but asked him to leave the area just the same.

Back at the police barricade, Vu approached Sheriff Griffin. He asked the sheriff where the plane had been parked prior to take off. The sheriff didn't know the answer to his question but quickly found a deputy that did. The deputy took Vu over to the location. Vu searched the ground and located a small area about the size of a golfball where hydraulic fluid had stained the pavement. He reached down and touched the fluid. It was fresh oil.

"See something, Sergeant?" the deputy asked. Vu shook his head and walked away. Sheriff Griffin sat inside his patrol car talking on the radio when Vu rapped on the window again. Sheriff Griffin motioned that he would be right with him. A few minutes later, the sheriff rolled down the window.

"Are you heading back into town soon, Sheriff?" Vu asked.

"Matter of fact I am, need a lift?" Vu nodded and climbed inside the car.

The patrol car pulled out onto Highway 101 and headed north. Vu spotted an off road bike parked along the shoulder and longed for his own scooter. He had to believe that things would come to a head soon. Had to. Lyman was in the immediate area. The plane crash was no accident. But why Long? It didn't make sense yet.

The patrol car pulled into a convenience store and stopped. Vu climbed out and waved to Sheriff Griffin as he drove away. Vu walked up to a pay phone and opened the telephone directory. He thumbed through the pages and stopped where the "Fl" section should have been. The page he needed was missing. Someone had torn it out of the directory. He located a car rental agency in Astoria willing to deliver a car to Warrenton for a small fee. Vu gave them the address and sat on the curb of the convenience store and watched cars drive by. Thirty minutes later his rental car arrived – a late model, full-size, American made, Cadillac. Things were looking up.

CHAPTER 52

The chilly night air seeped under the door and leaked into the Flenners' front room. Pam, alone, wrapped in a blanket, fixated on a Movie of the Week, nervously fondling her Saint Christopher's medal hung around her neck. On her lap was a fresh bowl of popcorn. She ate a fistful of buttery popcorn and washed it down with a can of Budweiser. She polished off the beer and went into the kitchen for another when a car pulled into the drive, its sweeping headlights startling her. She hurried back into the living room, muted the t.v. and switched the overhead light off.

The light outside her front porch was turned off. She peered out the door's peephole. The make and model of the car was as unrecognizable as was the driver. She started toward the phone, then changed her mind, instead pulling a small handgun from a side drawer in the kitchen. She waited by the door, listening.

A few minutes later, there was a soft knock. It was a Vietnamese man wearing a dark overcoat. She switched the interior and porch light on.

"Who is it please!" she called out.

"Sergeant Jack Vu, ma'am," Vu announced. "I work for the Air Force, ma'am. May I speak with you for a moment?"

Pam pressed her cheek up to the cold wood. She hesitated, and then eventually unlocked and opened the door. She held the gun pointed at his face.

"What do you want?"

"Ma'am, please put the gun down." Vu held up his official government credentials. Pam looked it over carefully.

Vu motioned for her to lower the gun. Pam stepped back from the door. "All right, come in."

Vu nodded gracefully and entered the house, closing the door behind him. Once inside, he loosened the top button of his overcoat. "It's brisk tonight," he said casually.

"What do you want?" Pam snapped.

"Alex Flenner, ma'am? Is he here?"

Vu knew from the worried look on her face that he wasn't. "Would you like to see my credentials again under the light, ma'am?"

Pam stepped back into the livingroom. "That won't be necessary."

* * *

Sina finished stocking the candy aisle in record time. Her boss called out from behind the counter, "Hey, Sina? I'm going to walk down to Mike's and grab a slice of pizza. You hungry?"

Sina looked up and shook her head. Her long black hair flowed down over her flannel shirt and got caught in her plastic nametag. "No thanks, Daddy," she said, and untangled her hair. She picked up the empty boxes and carried them over to the trash. Her father slipped out from behind the counter and left the store.

A car pulled into the parking lot and killed its engine. Sina glanced up as a tall man in dark clothing walked through the glass doors, ringing the automatic bell. The video camera mounted on the wall above the door clicked on. Sina unwrapped a stick of gum and stuck it into her mouth. The man approached the counter and checked out the hot food display and glanced at Sina's gold necklace.

"Where'd you get the necklace?" Lyman asked curiously.

"My boyfriend gave it to me," Sina said, and touched its sparkling coin.

Lyman stepped forward and smiled. "May I take a closer look?"

Sina hesitated. "Okay, but don't touch it." Sina leaned forward and allowed Lyman to examine the necklace.

"Nice boyfriend. What's his name?"

"Bobby Flenner," Sina rattled off. "You from around here?"

"No," Lyman said. "But I'd love to pick up something like that for my wife. Do you know where your boyfriend got it?"

"Nope. It's a big secret I guess."

"Well it's very beautiful on you."

"Thank you."

Lyman stepped back and couldn't take his eyes off the gold coin. Sina ran a hand through her hair nervously. "Can I help you find something?"

Lyman snapped out of it. "You carry Heineken?"

"It's in the cooler on the right. Second shelf down."

Lyman opened the cooler door. "I don't see it."

Sina frowned. "It should be on the right?" Lyman made no reply. "Still don't see it, huh?"

"No."

"Hang on, I'll be right there."

Sina stepped out from behind the counter. Her tiny feet padded across the hard floor. She stood beside Lyman staring at the frosted glass. She removed a six-pack of beer from the cooler and went to hand it to him. Lyman stopped her. His eyes were dark and menacing. Sina's cheerful smile disappeared.

Her hand slipped out the cardboard handle and the bottles shattered on the floor.

CHAPTER 53

The sounds of bowling pins crashing in the wood alley filtered out the door into the night air. Bobby stumbled across the parking lot and climbed on his dirtbike. A light mist was falling. Bobby started the engine, revved it up several times and dumped the clutch. The rear wheel spun out.

He veered onto the deserted street, stopping at a red light. He checked for cops then gassed it. Ran the red. The rain grew heavier on 101. His visor steamed over and he yanked it up off his face. Rain pounded his cheeks. He cussed at the clouds and pushed on, because from behind a pair of car lights barreled down fast. The car crowded his rear wheel. The driver flashed his lights on and off. Bobby tried to outrun the car but couldn't. The car dogged his tail. He grew concerned suddenly. Then a horn blared. Bobby reached over his shoulder and flipped off the driver. The vehicle flashed its high beams and drew down on him. Bobby sped up. *This is one crazy fuck*, Bobby was thinking. One crazy fuck all right. He zigzagged across the lane and twisted the throttle open wide. He was out of control, scared, and his tires were breaking traction on the slippery pavement. He lifted his jacket and pulled out his handgun. It was heavy and awkward against his bare hands. He wedged the gun between his seat and the fuel tank and waited. On-coming car lights approached ahead. Then a traffic signal blink red. Not much longer.

Then he heard, "Bobby! Damnit, stop!"

He skidded to a stop at the traffic signal and grabbed onto his handgun. The car from behind drove up beside him. He readied himself.

Case's angry face glared out the passenger window. "Pull over!"

Across town, Vu was trying to get the windshield wipers to operate properly on his rented Cadillac. The passenger blade would not swipe across the glass. He pulled onto the shoulder and climbed out. He couldn't get his mind into the job.

The Flenner house had been an unpleasant experience. The house had bad vibes. And Pam Flenner had been unwilling to disclose any information. The best he could worm out of her was that Bobby Flenner had a girlfriend named Sina Leechee. Sina worked at a 7-11 south of town. Sina kept tabs on

Bobby. And knowing the whereabouts of one Flenner brother was a step in the right direction if you wanted to find the other two. Because the Flenner clan stuck together. Just like soldiers. Then Pam broke down and cried and told Vu to get out.

He played with the wiper arm and grew agitated with his inefficiency. His hands were cold, he couldn't see what he was doing. And worse, he didn't know a thing about cars. Anything mechanical and he was all thumbs.

In the distance he heard a siren. He turned and watched as an ambulance pulled up to the 7-11 and two paramedics leapt out and hustled inside. A patrol car with its lights flashing drove in behind them and parked.

Vu gave up and climbed in behind the wheel. He turned into the convenience store parking lot. Sheriff Griffin's familiar face bobbed across the lobby.

A young Deputy Roberts stopped him at the front door. "What happened?" Vu asked curiously.

"What can I do for you?" Roberts said curtly.

"I'm looking for a girl by the name of Sina Leechee," Vu explained. "Pam Flenner said I might find her here?"

"What do you want with her?"

"I'm looking for the Flenner brothers."

"She's incapacitated."

"What's happened?"

"There's been an accident."

Vu tried to peer inside the brightly lit store. Roberts weighed in around two-fifty and did a fine job of blocking Vu's ability to see. Some movement seemed to be occurring around the coolers.

"She okay?"

Roberts said, "Why don't you be on your way."

"I'm on official business, Deputy." Vu pulled out his credentials. The deputy glanced at Vu's wallet.

"What kind of official business?"

"Ask Sheriff Griffin."

"I'm asking you."

The deputy had a chip on his shoulder. "When can I speak to him?"

"That depends on him."

The paramedics came bursting through the door carrying the girl on a stretcher. She was unconscious, and partially covered with a blanket. Her skin looked pale. So did her cheeks. As she was whisked by, Vu caught a glimpse of the girl's gold necklace. He'd seen the coin on that necklace before. In New Orleans? Yes, the Marken case photographs.

One of the paramedics asked the deputy for some help, getting the stretcher inside the vehicle. Vu waited until the time was right and entered the store.

Sheriff Griffin was standing by the coolers examining the floor. A small pool of blood was down by his feet, along with a pile of broken glass. The area reeked of beer.

"Hello, Vu," Griffin belted out. "We seem to be seeing a lot of each other lately."

"Hello, Sheriff," Vu said. "What happened to the girl?"

"As far as we can tell, just a little accident with a six pack of beer. A customer found the girl passed out on the floor bleeding from a nasty gash on the ankle. Paramedics revived her briefly but when she came to, she tried to stand and passed out again. So they sedated her. She'll need a few stitches but she'll be fine. What brings you here?"

"I was hoping to speak with the girl," Vu explained. "I'm looking for Bobby Flenner."

"Bobby Flenner, huh? Well, he's a live one. I've known the Flenners for years." Griffin looked toward the door. "Excuse me, Vu. This is the girl's father now."

A tall, nervous looking dark-skinned man entered the store carrying a small brown paper bag. He quickly called out, "Sheriff, where's Sina?"

Griffin crossed the store. "She's all right, Mr. Leechee," Griffin said reassuringly. "Nothin' to worry about. Just cut herself on a broken bottle. She needs a few stitches. She's out in the ambulance if you want to see her."

Mr. Leechee glanced at Vu. "Who's he?"

"He's with me."

"She's okay, huh?"

"Go see for yourself." Griffin pointed to the ambulance. The man seemed out of sorts with all the activity in his store. Mr. Leechee ran outside and disappeared around back of the ambulance. Deputy Roberts came bustling through the doors, looking like he was going to kick some royal butt. "Hey, you!" He shouted and pointed toward Vu. "What's the idea?"

"Cool your heels, Deputy," Griffin ordered. "It's okay. He's with me."

"Okay, Sheriff. If you say so."

Deputy Roberts bowed his head disappointed he could not take action against the trespasser. He moped toward his post.

Griffin poured himself a cup of coffee from the concession area. "Damn, this has been one heck of a day." He took out some change and laid it down on the counter by the register and waved for Vu to join him outdoors.

Under the protective awning, Griffin sipped his steaming cup of coffee and watched the ambulance drive away. Mr. Leechee spoke with the deputy at the door, watched him scribble something into a well-used notebook, and then went inside the store, turned off the night lights, and locked the front doors.

As he watched the activity in the parking lot, Vu couldn't get the image of the necklace out of his mind.

"What's your interest in the Flenner brothers, Vu?" Griffin finally asked.

"It's official military business, Sheriff."

"Well, I know they operate a charter service out of Warrenton. Things been a little bleak around here this year. Good men for the most part. Have you tried their boat?"

"No I haven't, sir."

"It's down at the Warrenton marina."

Griffin's radio squawked. "Hang on a second, Vu," Griffin said. "I gotta take this."

Griffin leaned inside his car and spoke on the radio. His face lit up with concern. He slammed the car door and hurried over to where Vu stood. "That was the ambulance driver. Said Sina woke up in a crazy fit. Blabbing about Bobby's safety. I don't know what the hell gibberish these kids are learning in school these days, but I wish they would learn how to speak English. You know what I mean, Vu? At times you can barely understand 'em."

Vu wasn't certain he understood a word of what Griffin just said, "Say that again, Sheriff?"

"Some nut case came into the store. Said he threatened her. Wanted to know about Bobby and her necklace. Said he tried to kidnap her, but she fought her way free. Best I go check in with Pam Flenner to see if things are okay with the family. You want a ride along, you're welcome."

CHAPTER 54

The sheriff's patrol car drove into the driveway and parked. The porch light was on and lights were on inside the Flenner house.

"Looks like they're home," Griffin said, and reached for the door handle.

Vu stared out the passenger window. Something didn't feel right to the AFOSI investigator. He climbed out of the car and joined Griffin at the front door. He patted down his pocket and remembered he was out of his green pills.

Griffin rapped on the door twice. Vu waited. When he didn't hear a response inside, he glanced down and noticed something wet by the door mat. He didn't remember seeing the spots earlier when he was there.

"What is it, Vu?"

Vu stooped down. "Blood."

"Christ almighty!" Griffin barked. He pulled out his revolver. Vu stepped back from the door. Griffin tried the door again. No response. Griffin tried the door knob. It was unlocked.

Inside, the room was trashed. Furniture on its side, a lampshade broken. Books on the floor. Griffin called out. "Alex? Pam? Sheriff Griffin here!"

Still nothing. Vu checked the kitchen while Griffin checked the adjoining bedrooms.

The kitchen was undisturbed. Pots on the stove were clean. No fresh cooked odors in the air. Vu climbed the stairs to the second floor. He checked the master bedroom first. Bed made, clothes hung up. He walked over to the baby's crib by the closet. Empty.

"Find anything?" Griffin shouted upstairs.

"No."

Vu rejoined Griffin downstairs. Vu followed the trail of blood. It began near the sofa, crossed the room, and lead out the door. Not a heavy trail of blood, just spots here and there. Maybe a small puncture wound or a nose bleed or even a non-vascular gunshot wound.

"I don't like this," Griffin said, looking around the room.

Vu had wanted to avoid this moment. And it was Wheylicke's last words that seemed to penetrate the heavy silence: "The whole matter could blow up in our face and be an embarrassment to the military."

Griffin put his revolver back in its holster. "I don't care what kind of official business you've got, I have to know what the hell's going on."

Vu stared at the broken lampshade. "There's a few things you ought to know, Sheriff."

CHAPTER 55

Fog rolled in over the sea. The Warrenton lighthouse could still be seen from shore. The rain had ceased. Just hints of mist and a chilly breeze out of the south blew in over the marina. The Lucky Lady glimmered like carved ice. Her heavy gunnel creaked under the taut pull of her mooring lines.

Case slid open the pilot house door and peered out into the dark night.

"See him?" Bobby asked from behind. Case ignored the comment and kept his eye on the parking lot. "Go down below with AJ, Bobby. Help him with the diving gear."

Case walked the deck. He knew Lyman's tactics. If he was coming, it would be now.

* * *

Rahjeh stowed the gold underground in locked vaults in the basement of his work shop. They blew the doors with plastic explosives. The dust was heavy and stuck to your lungs like melted rubber. Lyman and Kano made the first trek packing the heavy crates of gold up the stairs toward the door while he and Case prepared the second crate. Marken's sister was guarding the door. The truck was facing an alley that opened onto the main road leading north of Beirut. Get the gold to the truck. Then get the hell out of Dodge. Easy. But Rahjeh's daughter fucked it up.

Lyman had seen her packing the AK-47, her finger on the trigger, her eyes hollow slits of hatred. His own back to the stairs, Case hadn't seen her coming. Lyman jumped. The girl fired off one round, then dropped to her knees under Lyman's weight. The AK-47 slid across the floor. A trickle of blood leaked out of Lyman's shoulder. "Kano, go!" he ordered.

The front door flew open. Kano shouted, "We got company!"

Outside Rahjeh's house, thugs armed with automatic weapons opened fired. Lyman was the last man out. There was not enough time to make it to the truck. His eyes locked on Leslie. Then the girl wandered out into the street bleeding and crying. Shards of stone and wood exploded around her head. Lyman's impulse to protect the helpless girl was instinctive and oddly familiar. He pushed the girl back inside the house, used his body as a shield, and took a second bullet in the leg. The gunfire was coming at them from all directions. There was no time to go back. Lyman was on his own...

Leslie screamed, pleading. "No!"

She struggled to jump from the truck. They held her down. They had no choice but to leave him behind.

* * *

The air turned colder. Case zipped up his jacket and stuck his hands into his pockets to keep them warm. The area was calm as if a storm had raged through and was now gone.

The rattling of steel tanks seeped up through the wooden decking. Bobby appeared packing two SCUBA tanks. He strapped them down to the pilot house.

"What the fuck are those for?" Case snapped.

"AJ told me to bring 'em up. Ask him."

Case shoved aside his little brother and went below deck. AJ was inspecting an air regulator valve under the light. "What the fuck's up?"

AJ calmly faced him. "We're going out."

"It's too risky."

"Lyman deserves his cut," AJ said firmly. "I'm going to give it to him before something happens to you or Bobby or Pam or Jed. Understand? Christ, he visited my house. You think Long's plane just crashed on its own? He's here for the gold and I'm givin' it to him."

"He already got his share. Where was Long's gold? Did you see any at the crash site? I know I sure the fuck didn't."

AJ breathed a heavy sigh. "Let's just do this."

"What if it's not the gold he's after?"

"And what the hell's does that mean?"

"Think about it. We left his ass behind."

"It happens."

"Yeah. Then why didn't Kano show up? Because Long was right. He's dead. Lyman killed him. And he's going to try and kill us next."

"I won't let that happen. I told Pam to go stay at her mother's with Jed for a few days until this thing with Lyman blows over."

"Why don't we just sit on the gold and wait for him to show up?"

"Because he's not going to want to wait for his share. Trust me on this. If he's anything like he was when we served with him, he's not going to allow us out of his sight. He'll get his share."

"Fuck AJ! What'd you do, find Jesus or something?"

"It's the right thing to do. Leave Jesus out of it."

"Whatever."

Case climbed out of the hatch. Bobby stood on the bow, pissing over the side. AJ stood in the pilot house and hit the engine start switch. The twin diesels fired.

Case shouted, "Bobby, put your dick in your pants and cast off the bow line."

Bobby flipped him off and zipped up his pants. Case hopped down off the quarter deck to straighten an anchor rode then he cast off the stern line and took another long look along the dark dock.

Bobby stubbed his toe on a cleat and let out a cry. AJ stuck his head out of the pilot house. Bobby shouted, "We gotta move that fuckin' cleat."

"Bobby, get your PFD on."

"Christ, AJ, I'm not a kid."

AJ waited. Bobby grumbled and put on the floatation device. AJ nodded approvingly and turned his attention toward the helm.

Bobby stood on the bow listening. He thought he heard something move behind a stack of crab pots. He moved closer. From the stern Case shouted: "All clear?"

Bobby caught a glimpse of the blunt object just before it struck his head. Then his world turned black and fuzzy and he drifted into unconsciousness.

Lyman muffled his voice and replied: "Yeah!"

Lyman quickly released the bowline, wrapped the heavy rope around Bobby's limp body, and carefully lowered him down over the side and into the dark water.

The boat idled away from shore and headed out to sea.

* * *

Out in the parking lot a sedan killed its engine. Through the steamy windshield Nigel and his thugs watched the boat idle away from shore. Nigel leaned over the seat. This was working out just fine. With Lyman at sea it'd be a piece of cake getting the gold out of the trunk of his car.

He would have preferred to storm them all with AK-47's but this job took much patience if he was to see it through to the end.

"We will have a surprise for them when they return."

CHAPTER 56

Griffin had dropped Vu at his car and said he'd meet up with him down at the marina, once he paid a quick visit to the hospital to get a full statement from Sina Leechee.

Vu drove his Cadillac into the marina parking lot and parked beside an old GMC truck with a dirtbike strapped in back. A sedan pulled out of the lot about the same time and slowly drove away. Vu couldn't make out the driver or the passengers in the dark. There were a few other cars in the lot, but no people.

Vu stared out his windshield. Out over the water, he glimpsed a trawler crawling out to sea.

Vu slammed his car door. In the distance, he heard a faint cry. Sounded like a baby's cry, coming from inside one of the vehicles parked down near the docks.

Vu walked up to the an old pickup and glanced in the window. The cab was empty. He heard the noise again, louder this time, it was coming from the sedan behind him – a sedan he had seen parked at the Flenners' house on his first visit.

Pam Flenner was wedged down behind the driver's seat, her hands and feet tied with rope. She had an old sock stuffed in her mouth. Her nose was streaked with blood. Vu recalled the spots of blood on the carpet back at the Flenner house. Her infant son squirmed on her chest, crying. Vu tried the door but it was locked. He crossed to the passenger side of the car and found it locked too. Vu knew what he had to do. The Cadillac would have a lug wrench in the trunk. He popped open the trunk and dug around in the dark and found a bumper jack. That would do.

Pam's eyes were large dark quarters glaring up at the little man as he stood at the passenger side window and swung the heavy jack toward the glass, shattering it. Using his jacket sleeve to clear off the shards of glass around the lock, he released the mechanism and pulled open the door. He removed the sock from Pam's mouth and lifted the infant from her chest.

"Are you hurt?" he asked.

"I can't move," she uttered. "That son-of-a-bitch took my necklace and nearly strangled me getting it off," Pam uttered.

Vu realized that the woman was wedged in tight. She couldn't move from side to side which meant the only way to pull her out was by lifting her forward.

"This might hurt." Pam winced and pointed out the window toward the boats. "Hurry." Vu grabbed Pam's shirt and pulled her upright into a sitting position. He untied the ropes, freeing her hands and feet. As she struggled to her feet, she reached instinctively for her child to comfort it.

"What slip is Alex in?"

"C-4."

Sea water lapped against the empty slip. Vu saw something floating in the dark water.

From a crouched position, he pulled on the mooring line. A limp body floated toward the dock. Vu drug the body out of the water. He removed the life vest and placed it underneath the boy's feet, elevating his legs off the cold ground. Next, he checked the boy's neck for a pulse. Weak but alive. Vu removed the boy's wet jacket, removed his own, and wrapped it around boy's shoulders. Behind him, Pam Flenner appeared with her baby in her arms.

"Bobby!"

Vu stood up and retrieved his cell phone and dialed 911. The ambulance arrived shortly after that. The three were hauled away to the hospital. Sheriff Griffin pulled Vu aside.

"It is not over yet," Vu said. "I need a helicopter."

CHAPTER 57

Where the hell was Bobby? Case searched the boat from stern to bow. Maybe he went below deck. He searched the cabin area. As he pulled open the pilot house door, diesel fumes and stale warm defroster air smacked him in the face. The wood planking beneath his feet rumbled.

"AJ, have you seen..." Case stopped mid-sentence. AJ's worried eyes said it all. Lyman pressed a 9mm against his head. A wire noose was strung tightly around his neck and attached to the wheelhouse.

"Hello, Case." Lyman watched both men closely.

Case tensed. "Where's Bobby, you prick?"

"I hit him over the head and threw him over," Lyman said calmly.

"You fucker..." Case snapped.

Lyman lashed out, striking Case in the jaw with the butt-end of the gun. His lip split open. Blood leaked out of the deep gash. His head rocked back into the bulkhead. For several seconds, Case's consciousness was questionable. Then he seemed to shake off the blow.

AJ white-knuckled the steering wheel. "We don't have to do this," he reasoned.

"Sure we do." Lyman replied. "Case was always the dense one."

"It was your choice to go back."

"It was," Lyman acknowledged painfully. "And it was your choice to leave me behind."

"We did what we had to do."

"It cost me two years of my life, and it killed Leslie," Lyman said. "You're aware she's dead?"

"Long told us you killed her?"

"Why would I? I loved her."

Case rubbed his jaw. "What about Kano? And Long?"

Lyman's eyes filled with rage. "Call it karma."

Lyman shoved Case out of the pilot house. He wedged a long-handled gaffing hook across the pilot house door, trapping AJ inside the helm. He pressed Case's head against the glass. He reached into his pocket and pulled out Pam's Saint Christopher's necklace. Making his intentions clear, he waved it in front of the glass so AJ could see. “Get the gold!” he shouted.

AJ howled like a beaten child, the magnitude of his distress, reverberating through the thin cabin walls.

Lyman marched Case to the bow and ordered him down on his knees, fingers laced, hands behind his head. Several feet back, Lyman got down into in a lotus position and waited, watching the waves crash over the bow and splash water over his prisoner.

CHAPTER 58

Lyman's Ford was parked down the street from the Flenners' house. The neighborhood was quiet. The house directly across the street was dark inside. Down the street, heavy metal music spilled out of the bedroom window of a teenager's house. The street was deserted in every direction.

Nigel approached the car cautiously. He examined the interior. Nothing. Probably in the trunk, he figured. He looked at the trunk lock. No trip wires attached. One of his men walked up holding a crowbar. Nigel gave him the go ahead and stepped aside. He watched as the man wedged the jack handle from their own rental car under the lid and popped open the lock on the second try.

"Wait!" Nigel instructed.

Nigel examined inside the compartment. Beside the spare were two duffel bags, a small toolbox, and several empty beer bottles. The men reached for the bags but Nigel stopped them.

"The shithead was a Seal, remember?" Nigel pushed them out of the way. He scanned the trunk with his flashlight, looking for anything unusual. "Okay. Looks clear. Pull them out slowly. Don't jar them."

The men looked sheepishly at each other and then gently removed the heavy duffel bags, placing them carefully on the ground. Nigel backed up to a safer distance, and squatted down.

"Open them!"

The exposed men reluctantly followed the order.

Overhead, a Coast Guard helicopter soared by and headed out to sea. Blades whipped at the darkness.

Using knives, they slashed them open. Nigel suddenly appeared at the bundles and flashed his beam on the contents. After a deadly moment of silence, Nigel's anger raged. His eyes radiated fire.

He reached into one of the duffels and pulled out a handful of seashells, allowing the shells to spill through his fingers. Beneath the shells were softball size rocks. Lyman had succeeded in creating the illusion of gold.

"I kill the bastard slowly for this."

CHAPTER 59

"Poor visibility!" the pilot of the Coast Guard helicopter shouted to Vu. "It'll be hell finding 'em in this weather."

Vu covered his eyes. "We must try," he said, and climbed aboard the UH-1 Huey, A.K.A. "The Frosted Bird." Pararescueman Sgt. Nishimura pointed to a plastic seat and began strapping Vu in. Vu faced Sheriff Griffin, still standing on the tarmac, his feet planted firmly on the ground.

Vu shouted over the loud engine noise. "C'mon, Sheriff!"

"This isn't my war!"

Vu nodded vigorously that he understood the implications of Griffin's words. Sgt. Nishimura handed Vu a headset, and strapped himself in beside the sergeant. The co-pilot, Lt. White, signaled to the pilot.

The powerful blades sliced through the thick wet air and kicked up enough turbulence to blow Sheriff Griffin's hat from his head. Vu watched the ground disappear below and the big figure dance around chasing his feet.

The pilot's voice cracked in Vu's headset. "What were the last known coordinates?"

"Due west out of the Warrenton Marina," Vu responded.

"Could be anywhere, is what you're telling me?"

"Yes."

"Great."

* * *

The big twin diesels idled down to a gentle purr. The boat circled twice and found its mark – a small floating marker left after their last drop. The marker matched up with the correct GPS coordinates jotted down in the logbook in the pilothouse. AJ killed the engines and pounded on the glass that it was time to drop anchor.

Lyman unwrapped his legs and stood. Case was wet and shivering and very pissed off. Lyman ordered him to stand.

"If you fuck up, AJ's wife and child are dead. Understand?" Case reluctantly nodded. "Now go open the door."

From then on it went as planned. AJ put on a wet suit and Case assisted with the SCUBA. The pressure regulator worked properly and there was enough oxygen for thirty-five minutes of dive time with a five-minute reserve bottle. Case would operate the winch. AJ calculated it would require twenty-one minutes if everything went as scheduled. They were testing the limits of the winch, but two trips would require additional air supply which they didn't have. AJ understood that if he failed Case and his family would suffer the repercussions. AJ slipped on his flippers and sat facing the deck.

Lyman said to Case, "All right, you know the drill."

Case returned to the bow of the boat and resumed his position. Lyman kept his eye on AJ. "You've caused me great pain. I will not hesitate to reciprocate the feeling," he stated coldly.

"Take it easy, Lyman," AJ assured him. "In ten minutes lower down the cable to me."

Without further comment, AJ rocked backwards over the side and dropped into the sea. Lyman glanced over the gunnel, ensuring the diver was gone.

Lyman retook his position at the bow and stared out toward the misty night. Fog hung over the water reducing visibility to five hundred meters.

Resting the 9mm on his leg Lyman felt the phantom pain where a bullet had penetrated his flesh two years earlier.

The terrorists had been merciless. The armed thugs busted down Rahjeh's door and beat him to near death. One of the seven militants in the group, Nigel, was left with the final task of slicing his throat once they took his beaten body out into the desert just north of Beirut. Three of the six had taken their turns raping the little girl in the bed of the truck. Her limp and soulless body crouched in the corner like a broken doll. They kicked his wounded flesh out of the truck. Nigel jumped down and drug him along the desert on his belly. Hot sand and stones carved scarring imprints into his face. Nigel pulled out a large bowie knife and held it against his throat. The blade felt like molten iron on his soft skin. He tried to fight back but his body was unable to respond. He looked into the man's dark eyes and expected to take his last breath and instead used his last ounce of strength to spit in the man's eye.

Nigel swiped a stained sleeve across his face and laughed, dropping Lyman's face into the sand.

That image haunted and burned into his mind as he cooked in the hot desert under the scorching sun for days. A traveling band of Bedouins found what was left of him. He stayed with the gypsy clan until his body was mended and his spirit had returned.

For months he woke up in a cold sweat, feeling the sharp edge of steel pressed against his throat. Why had the man allowed him to live? Was it his last display of mercy? Or his final defying gesture?

The silence of the sea suddenly shattered. “Lyman!”

Lyman snapped straight. “What?”

“I never got a chance to thank you for saving my ass.”

“Don’t. I’m sorry I did it.”

Lyman rubbed saltwater from his eyes. “The girl was raped and killed. They broke my wrists, legs, ribs. Kicked me unconscious so many times I lost count. I pissed blood for weeks... Now it’s time to make it right.”

“We wouldn’t have fucked you out of your part of the gold. We thought you were dead.”

Lyman drug Case to the rail. They leaned over the side and spotted a trail of air bubbles in the water. AJ’s head popped up through the murky depths. He grabbed hold of the ladder draped over the side and pulled his mask back off his face. “I can’t find it!” he shouted. “Tides must have shifted. Bottom silt is worse than before.”

Lyman snapped. He picked up the gaffing hook and slammed it into Case’s meaty thigh. “Try again!”

Case bellowed out a cry and clutched his bleeding leg. AJ flashed fierce eyes and dropped below the surface once again. Ten minutes later there was a stout tug on the cable. Painfully, Case lowered the heavy steel cable into the deep water. The cable was hooked and the signal to “Lift” received. The big steel drum rotated like an enormous wheel and inch by inch the chests of gold neared the surface. Lyman’s eyes grew wild with anticipation. Case eyed the gaffing hook resting against the pilot house door and gave up the idea of reprisal, germinating below the surface of his strained face.

Silt and seaweed hung onto the chests as they broke the surface of the water. Lyman ordered AJ to stay in the water until the gold was safely aboard.

Carefully Case swung each chest one by one over the gunnel, clearing the planking by millimeters. Lyman guided the last chest down toward the deck. Case eyed him closely, figuring he had one chance.

Case released his hold on the lever and allowed the cable to drop suddenly. The chest crashed to the wooden deck. Planking sheered off and splintered like machetes. One hit Lyman, searing a four inch gashing hole in his thigh.

Blood spurted out of the wound as his 9mm slid across the wet deck. Lyman fought back the perforating pain as Case made his move. The two men struggled toward the pilot house where a gaffing hook lying on the deck glistened in the moonlight.

Lyman slammed Case against the pilot house door. The two men wrestled, exchanging blows.

AJ's muscular arm lashed onto the side rail and he pulled his body out of the frigid water. He peered over the rail, witnessing the bloody fight. But before he could climb aboard, Lyman knocked Case off balance. Stumbling backward Case lost his footing and tumbled over the rail into the dark sea.

AJ hesitated only a moment as he calculated the odds against Lyman, who was winded and bleeding heavily. He then turned seaward and dropped back down into the icy water swimming toward his helpless brother.

Lyman, wincing in pain, struggled to open the pilot house door. His weakened body was fighting to stay alert. He fumbled with the switches and eventually fired the engines. His vision blurred. He fell into the steering wheel, pressing a weak hand over his bleeding wound, and gazing out to the open sea. Eventually, he maneuvered the transmission in gear and sped away.

In the distance, the pleas of the Flenner brothers sank into darkness.

CHAPTER 60

"We're getting low on fuel."

Captain Chandler glanced at the gauge. "Sergeant, we're going to have to turn back soon."

Vu could barely hear over the loud engines. He continued to look through the binoculars at the choppy sea. Pararescueman Nishimura tapped his shoulder and pointed to the west. In the far distance a white light appeared.

The Huey made a banking turn and closed in on the light. Vu felt his heart pound. He wondered what he would say to the man after tracking him this far.

A ship came into view – a Frigate out of Korea. Vu discouraged, lowered the binoculars. The pilot shook his head at the co-pilot and made a slow sweeping u-turn back toward the Coast Guard Station.

* * *

The waves crashed around them. Gagging on saltwater and fighting back tears, AJ held on tight. Case was limp and hanging a inch from life in his arms. The prospects of getting to shore alive were slim. No one knew they were out there. The best he could hope for would be to signal a passing ship. But the likelihood that a frigate could see them in the thick fog and dark sea seemed impossible. AJ breathed in a deep breath, his mouth inches from Case's head. Keep him talking, he thought. He had to keep him conscious.

"Case! Case!" he shouted, jostling him as he spoke. Case's head rolled from side to side and garbled, undecipherable words fell out of his bluish lips. He gasped. Coughed. Gasped again. Life was leaving him quickly, AJ knew. "Hang on, Case. God damnit hang on."

A light appeared over the horizon. A bright light. AJ felt his heart explode with anticipation. "Case, look!"

His brother was still, unmoving; his breathing slow, shallow, and near extinct. Tears streamed down his distressed face.

AJ kicked his fins and swung them toward the light in the sky. There was no way they could get off a signal. There was no device, nothing. The light grew closer. He squeezed his brother tighter, praying.

* * *

From the rear of the Huey, Vu saw something. He turned and rapped the pararescueman's leg. Sergeant Nishimura snapped to attention and peered the glasses down toward Vu's pointing hand.

"Captain!" he shouted. "Bearing fifty-five degrees due east. Something in the water, sir? Have you received a distress call?"

"Negative, Sergeant. Let's go in for a look."

The co-pilot looked down and nodded to the pilot who made a steep banking turn and pointed the nose toward the sea.

"I see them!" Vu shouted. "Where's the boat?"

"Could've sunk," Sgt. Nishimura pointed out. "No guarantee these are your boys."

Sgt. Nishimura prepared the steel crib which would be lowered down to the men below. He explained its operation to Vu. "We're short a crew member tonight, Sergeant. When we get close enough, I'll go out. Watch for my signal. This lever here lowers the crib. This lever raises. This lever extends and retracts. Got it?"

Vu ran the directions through his head and nodded. Sgt. Nishimura pulled on his military-issued fins and mask. He leaned out the open door. The wind rushed in around the men. The co-pilot turned, keeping a close watch on the pararescueman. Sgt. Nishimura gave the "high-sign" and plunged into the dark stormy water. Vu leaned out nervously, swallowed back his nausea. His eyes stung from the burning salt water kicked up by the powerful blades. He steadied the crib out the Huey's door and waited, watching Sgt. Nishimura's signal.

Through the darkness he saw a hand raise out of the water. He moved the lever forward and watched the steel cable lower the crib toward the ocean. His heart pounded rapidly. His eyes watered. His hands were shaking. He saw the signal to bring them both home.

Vu recognized a resemblance to the kid he had found ashore. The Flenners. Sgt. Nishimura began CPR on the unconscious man. Then he pulled Vu aside and had him assist, while he read off vitals.

"He's at stage three hypothermia," Sgt. Nishimura announced to the co-pilot on the radio to the local hospital in Astoria. "Second victim is conscious but his breathing is irregular and slow. Hypothermia, possible mild cardiac tremors. I'm injecting 10 cc of adrenaline to each victim."

Vu was growing weary. The CPR was not reviving the man he knew as Case. The adrenaline hit AJ, who suddenly became lucid and violently threw Vu aside. AJ grabbed Case's shoulder and shook him hard, tears streaming from his bloodshot eyes.

Vu knew it was too late.

CHAPTER 61

The white Cadillac pulled up to the Royal Oaks Cemetery and parked. A parade of cars lined the narrow road leading to the plot site. Vu could see from the window the service was still going on. He straightened his tie and climbed out of the car.

There was a hint of sunshine bursting through the cloud-covered sky and the warm breeze was scented with the changing seasons. Autumn colors flickered in the oaks lining the cemetery. Vu quietly moved through the grass, soft underfoot, and breathed in the clear air. He felt remote and detached from life. His thoughts were on his past week, the days that lay ahead, and on the sorrow he was experiencing today. He remembered burying his own father years ago and recalled his mother's despairing eyes when the minister placed a wreath of flowers atop the casket and lowered it into the ground.

A year later he buried his mother. A cemetery in Baltimore, not Vietnam. What a blessing he was able to share their last years together. He would always be grateful to the Air Force, and his commander, for facilitating their reunion.

But it was time to move on. Death had always signaled a change inside him. Not always for the worse, though it sometimes felt that way.

Vu felt his losses as he retraced the timeless steps of man through this little coastal cemetery. Life was the only true bond any of us have other than death. This led his thoughts to Betty, his death maiden, who made him feel alive. The cell phone had been a vital lifeline to his old life and new love. He mused over Detective Gates, Hill, and Millie. He thought of all these things as he strode over to the Flenner party and paid his final respects.

After the service had concluded, and Vu had returned to his car he heard the gravel crunch and looked up as Sheriff Griffin pulled alongside.

"Found the boat!" Griffin shouted through the passenger window. "Interested?"

The two men drove along Highway 101 until they came to the Warrenton turn off and continued south for another six miles.

"Things don't always end like you thought," Griffin mused.

"Sometimes there are more questions than answers."

"It does keep changing. In this case it's hard to tell the good guys from the bad guys."

The narrow road off the main highway led them to the sea. The road dead ended into sand. On foot they followed the trail as it meandered down to the beach. The town of Seaside twinkled in the distance.

The Lucky Lady had busted in half, and was scattered on the rocks. Her stern was cracked open and seaweed strewn out of her planking. Only a portion of the boat had survived. The bow was caved in and destroyed. The pilot house gone. Just the stern and some loose tackle remained. An old winch and gallons of sea water filled her bilge.

Vu stared at the wreck. He thought of the Flenners and their dreams. Of Lyman and his schemes. He thought about all the ships lost at sea. His mind felt all the spirit of men with their dreams that lay dead and decaying on the ocean's floor.

"Was a body recovered?"

"Nope. No body, no gold, no proof that anything you or those other boys said was true. I noticed what I thought were traces of blood on the gunnels."

"Other boys?"

Griffin shrugged. "Your military pals are waiting for you. Look Vu, I don't know everything, but I believe you. Not those jarheads waiting to take you back to Baltimore."

Vu looked Griffin in the eye. An unspoken understanding was reached. Standing on the nearby knoll were two uniformed Air Force security police keeping close watch.

"What about the girl, Sina?"

"She said a man came into the store, complemented her on her necklace, wanted to buy a six pack of beer, and when she pulled it out of the cooler the bottom gave way and two bottles shattered on the floor. Her ankle got cut. The man told her to sit down and then he used the phone to call the police, and left. Since he didn't commit a crime, there's no reason to continue our search for that man."

"And the kidnaping?"

"Pam Flenner claims she hitched a ride to the marina because she was upset. She told us one of the locals drove up in the sedan. Offered to let her wait out of the weather for her husband to return. She fell asleep in the back seat with her child in her arms. You came along and panicked and busted the window. Deputy and I went back to the parking lot everything is gone. We got no evidence that she was actually tied up in the back seat. Just your word." Griffin leaned in. "The word of a wanted man."

"We work with first person testimony and visual evidence, not hearsay. And Alex Flenner says he and his brother Case snagged a crab-pot line. Alex went in to untangle the rope from the prop. Case somehow fell overboard and the boat got away from them."

"And Bobby?"

"AJ figures it was Case. They'd been quarreling earlier."

"And you believe 'em?"

"Sergeant, what I believe doesn't matter. Personally, I don't think their sworn statements are worth the paper to housebreak my dog on. But facts and evidence, remember?" Griffin squinted into the sun. "I don't even know for certain you're who you say you are."

Vu nodded and kicked a piece of driftwood into the water as he and the sheriff wandered toward shore.

"How about Long's plane?"

"FAA concluded a hydraulic line failure. The manufacturer conducted a recall on that specific part last year but the deceased's plane had not undergone the update. They ruled the crash accidental, component failure. It wasn't your man."

Vu stopped in his tracks. He realized his case was over. Without Lyman, without the hard evidence, without testimony of his efforts to do harm to the Flenners, to John D. Long, what did he have? Hearsay? Circumstantial evidence without hard proof. A fingerprint. A dead girl. Two dead former servicemen. A hand. But no evidence of the missing Special Ops man. That would be the official version. Unanswered questions, yes, but only on a personal level.

As Vu and Griffin walked away from the wreck of the Lucky Lady a flash of light in the sand caught his eye. He stooped over, picked up the shiny object and brushed it off. It was a gold coin. A British Sovereign. He studied the engraved images for several long minutes, then dropped it into his pocket and headed back toward Baltimore, escorted by two security policemen.

CHAPTER 62

Ms. Caan was examining a slide under the microscope when her office door opened and Gates walked in. Gates had on latex gloves and was carrying a cassette tape. She walked across the room and laid the tape down on the counter in front of the pathologist and cleared her throat. Ms. Caan ignored her and continued to stare into her own microbic world.

"Hello? Anyone in there?" Dorene asked.

Betty slowly looked up. "What's up, Dorene?"

Gates tapped the cassette tape with her finger. "See if you can get any prints off this."

Betty sighed and returned to her slide. "This is a priority?"

"It's about lover boy..."

Betty reeled around, staring hard at Gates. "Jack? What game are you playing now?"

Mockingly, Gates smiled. "Game? Why don't you tell me?"

Confused, Betty cocked her head at her challenger. "What are you talking about?"

"The next time you steal a cell phone, make sure it isn't mine. I know where your Bruce Lee is, who he's been talking to, and how much trouble the little bastard is in."

Dorene let the news settle on the pathologist as she watched Betty desperately try to control her facial reaction.

"You need to back off the steroids, Dorene. From what I hear upstairs, you're the one whose ass is in a sling."

Dorene's face tensed. Betty stood up and stretched out her tired muscles as she absently examined the cassette. She tried not to betray her keen interest in this new piece of the puzzle. What would it say? Whose prints were lurking? Her mind was moving at a frenetic pace as she slowly looked back at Gates.

"Sorry," Gates said. "This case has more twists than a tornado. I think we're all pretty edgy right now. What am I looking for?"

After the slightest hesitation, Dorene gave in. "Your lover boy's got a guardian angel. It's all on the tape. I want to know who sent it."

Excitedly, Betty held the tape as if it held the secrets of the universe.

"Who do you think sent it?"

Gates shrugged and headed toward the door. "Another fucking governmental mystery. You tell me. In the meantime, I've got a call in to Major Wheylicke. Good luck."

"Dorene wait!"

Gates ignored the request and stormed from the office.

Betty laid the tape down on a clean white towel and very carefully dusted its surface for prints. She seemed disappointed discovering the tape had been wiped clean. She scribbled the results on a chain of custody form and walked across the room and plugged the tape into a ghetto blaster and listened to the excited voices of Ray Kano and Leslie Ann Marken, recorded on the last day of Ms. Marken's life. She couldn't believe the horrid sounds emanating from the cassette. She stumbled toward the wall and braced herself and felt the pain crawl into her soul and explode into tears, running down her face.

Upstairs in Gate's office, Dorene sat down behind her desk. Her eyes canvassed her cluttered surroundings. It resembled, she thought, the state of her disordered and lately hostile mind. Maybe Betty had a point. The Marken case had been a royal fuckup on her part. She had not done her best work. Another death that once the headlines faded away from the morning tabloids would go unnoticed. A coverup – possibly. But doubtful. She could only conjecture at this point. There was always the slim chance that it was just another conundrum of the streets – a stewardess murdered in her hotel room – a former lover responsible and a jealous life-long friend seeking revenge. Neat. Digestible. Much more tacit than a government conspiracy. Just the same, facts she'd have to write up in her report and live by for now.

She held up the manilla envelop once containing the cassette and stared at the postage mark until her eyes couldn't focus any longer.

Surely, Ms. Caan would come up empty handed. She knew this already but played out the game. *And this fuckin' tape – who sent it? Was its sole purpose to vindicate Vu?*

Her mind needed clarity. She reached into her lower desk drawer and pulled out a pint of Bushmills Irish Whiskey. She stared at the bottle long and hard. She'd have to stop drinking her Dutch Courage sometime soon. But not today. She twisted off the top and took a long pull from the bottle. Then she dialed up Sergeant Vu's boss in Baltimore. Major Wheylicke answered on the third ring.

CHAPTER 63

Wheylicke hung up the receiver and leaned back in his overstuffed chair, staring out the window. Just a hint of a cynical smile played across his face. After a few minutes, a blue sedan pulled up in front of his office window and parked. Two uniformed guards climbed out and opened the rear door. One officer reached in, pulled out the prisoner from the back seat.

Wheylicke watched Sergeant Vu's small head turn toward the light, his dark dilated eyes squinting up at the bright sun, like a possum in the night caught in the path of a speeding car's headlights. An SP took his elbow and escorted him toward the AFOSI building.

Soon, there was a firm knock on his door.

"Enter."

The two Air Force SP's led Vu into the center of the room. The three men stood at attention awaiting direction. Wheylicke stepped out from behind his desk.

"Did he resist in any way, Sergeants?"

"No, sir," the larger of the two said.

"Then you're free to go," Wheylicke said to the security guards.

The guard on the left pulled out a Swiss Army knife and a bottle of pills and turned them over to the major. Vu rubbed his sore wrists where latent reddened cuff marks slowly dissolved into his brown skin. Finally, Vu said, "If I may sir, I need a glass of water."

"Help yourself, Sergeant."

Silently, Wheylicke watched as Vu walked over to a water cooler. Water in hand, Vu eyed his pills, before finally draining the cup. The major's face revealed nothing.

"You loused it up good, Sergeant," Wheylicke said. "I ought to throw you into the stockade."

"I don't think the Judge Advocate's Office would agree, sir."

"Leave JAG out of this," Wheylicke snapped. "I've spent the last week explaining this case to Headquarters and a number of asinine reporters. I'm not a very happy man at the moment."

"Nor am I, sir."

"It's just a goddamn good thing you located that tape and forwarded it to Detective Gates' office. You do a series of stupid ass things and then you pull a rabbit out of a hat. But as usual, you didn't go through proper channels."

Vu's eyes went vacant. "What tape, sir?"

"Don't fuck with me, Sergeant."

"I don't know of any tapes sent to New Orleans or anywhere else for that matter."

Wheylicke was having none of it. He stormed behind his desk. "I want your full report by noon tomorrow. Understand?"

Vu persisted, "I have been through enough to warrant an explanation, Major..."

"Vu, did you hear what I said?" Wheylicke's face reddened.

Vu could see the major come to some resolution. "According to Detective Gates, they received a tape which cleared your name. It was a recording of the Marken murder and the man responsible for the act. Ray Kano raped and killed Ms Marken. Captain Long in turn killed Kano. He was in love with the woman. Lyman's name stayed out of it. You know the rest of the story."

"Who sent the tape, sir?"

"Immaterial. It's over." Wheylicke's voice was final. Wheylicke turned and stared out the window. "The final report will show that the fingerprint found on the dead girl's body was historic in nature and of no current value in the Marken case. Further, Gates has indicated that her office deems no further inquiries into the Kano matter. The government will be left out of this. Your report should substantiate these results."

Vu looked at his superior and recognized the tone. A door had been firmly closed on the Lyman case. Vu's unanswered questions would have to wait.

The major handed Vu his knife and pill bottle. He was being dismissed.

Vu said formally, "Sir, I'm requesting two weeks leave effective immediately and following that, I'd like to be re-assigned."

Wheylicke looked Vu casually in the eye. "Okay, Sergeant." Vu remained calm and collected and met his heavy gaze. "I see. What base did you have in mind?"

"Keesler or Barksdale. Both bases have criminal investigations units, sir. There is also a detachment assigned to the US Coast Guard Station in New Orleans that would be satisfactory. I feel I can better serve the Air Force in any one of these locations."

"I see that all your choices are all within driving distance to New Orleans."

Vu broke the ice. "The operation – who's idea was it?"

"It's confidential, Sergeant."

"What about Lyman?"

"Lyman's name will not be discussed from this point on, understand?"

"Then I guess we have nothing further to discuss. Am I free to go now?"

Wheylicke studied the sergeant one last time. "Yes. Submit your two week leave request to Betas. We'll have to submit your reassignment papers to Headquarters. I want you to report by noon tomorrow."

Outside Wheylicke's office, Vu took a deep breath and let it out slowly. The color in his face started to return. Betas was behind her desk eating an eggroll.

She coughed and gagged on the mouthful of food. After she regained her composure she said, "I had no choice, Jack. I have my career to think about."

Vu remained professional, despite the turmoil simmering below the surface. "You're right, Betas, you do. You'll make a fine officer."

Vu left the AFOSI building solemnly and dialing his cell phone, wandered down the street. "Betty..."

Vu's voice faded in the breeze.

CHAPTER 64

The weather was cool in Kansas and the humidity low. Rain had not doused the area in six days. Emily Douchet was busy packing a suitcase when she heard the sound of a car pulled up outside her bedroom window. She peered out through the lacy curtains and saw a short man walking toward her front door.

Emily answered the doorbell on the second ring wearing casual, festive clothing. Standing on the step was a familiar face.

"Hello, Sergeant," Emily said cheerfully, hiding her surprise.

"I'm sorry I did not telephone first," Vu explained. "But there seems to be a problem with my cell phone."

"What brings you to Kansas?"

"You," Vu said. "I have some information about Jim Lyman that I thought you might like to know. Did I catch you at a bad time?"

Emily blushed at the mentioning of Lyman's name and pulled the collar of her light jacket closed. "Come in, Sergeant. I was just about to leave. I've got some business out of town..."

"This will not take long, I assure you."

Emily showed Vu inside and pointed to the fluffy sofa across the room. "Would you care for a drink?"

"No, ma'am," Vu said. "Where are you traveling to?"

Vu noticed the suitcases piled up at the door. "Oh, there's a cosmetic conference in Palm Beach. I always seem to be going somewhere. You just caught me actually. I thought you might be my cab."

"I won't keep you."

"Oh, nonsense. Tell me. What about Jim?"

Vu hesitated. "I was able to track your rental car to a place in Louisiana called Houma."

"Yes, I received a call from the police last week."

"I believe Jim used your car to visit a former colleague. He apparently obtained enough cash to fly to Utah where I believe he visited his sister."

Emily seemed genuinely surprised. "Jim has a sister?"

"She's blind. She lives alone in Salt Lake City. From there he flew to

Oregon where he connected up with some former members from his unit."

"Sergeant, you sound distressed. Has something happened to Jim?"

"I don't know."

"I'm confused," Emily said.

"Emily, has Mr Lyman attempted to contact you?"

"No," Emily said quickly. Vu studied her expression closely. Emily's eyes darted back and forth nervously.

"Well, this could be good news or bad news but the government has dropped its investigation into the whereabouts of Mr. Lyman. I'm afraid we're not going to be able to recover your stolen cash."

"So he's in Oregon?"

"Well, I don't know for certain. Let us say there was an incident that may have involved Mr. Lyman and a remote possibility that Mr. Lyman may have perished at sea."

Emily grasped her collar like the news choked her. "Jim's dead? That can't be..."

"I don't know for certain."

"Sergeant, I'm very confused. Why are you here?"

"I apologize. I had promised I would help if I could. But I ended up with more questions than answers. My case is closed. I can tell you that Mr. Lyman, if he's alive, is officially MIA – or put another way – a free man."

Emily allowed the information to sink in. "I'm sorry I can't bring you definitive news, Ms. Douchet. But it's all I have."

Emily showed Vu out. From the porch, in the hot afternoon sun, Vu squinted toward Emily's shadowed figure as she raised her arm to waive goodbye. Her jacket, parted at the front now, revealed around her neck an expensive and shiny gold sovereign necklace. Vu recognized the coin immediately even at a distance.

As he drove away he reached in his pocket to retrieve its twin.

CHAPTER 65

Nigel and his thugs walked out of the Lost Treasures Curio Shop in Warrenton carrying metal detectors. A little fat man in nickers and white tennis shoes came out of the shop behind them and shouted.

"Stay away from the oyster beds boys..."

Nigel shot the man a faint smile and nodded politely. The men loaded the equipment into their sedan and drove away.

The sedan followed highway 101 for several miles out of town and then came upon an attraction alongside the highway and parked. Rows of parked cars had sandwiched themselves into a small parking area that lead down to the beach.

Nigel got out of the passenger door and looked down at the miles of sandy beach. In the distance, you could still see the wrecked hull of the Lucky Lady poking up out of the water. Nearby, a number of curious fortune hunters combed the area for any signs of possible souvenirs.

There had been a small article in the yesterday's paper about the wreck of the Lucky Lady and it was hinted that the boat might have been hauling a shipment of gold. The residents speculated it was a ploy by the City Counsel to drum up another tourist attraction. But the little man at the curio shop denied that theory and was pleased to see that his selection of metal detectors had sold out.

Nigel descended down the small embankment slipping on the wet grass. He picked up his metal detector and headed toward the water. His thugs followed, keeping a few paces back.

Nigel flipped the switch on the device and held it out in front of him and paced back and forth along the shoreline and slowly grew agitated at the machine and at the whole idea of looking for his gold in such a ridiculous manner. A little kid wearing a baseball cap ran up with a shovel and plastic bucket started digging around where Nigel got a steady signal on his machine. Nigel glared down at the kid and kicked some sand his way. Crying, the kid scurried off. He then turned to his two thugs and pointed at the ground. One of the thugs, dropped to his knees and pawed in the sand and found something. He enthusiastically brushed the sand from the quarter-size object and passed it to Nigel who quickly recognized that it was a bottle cap and threw it wildly toward the sea, cursing Allah.

Nigel glared at the wreckage, the tourists, and the sea before slamming his machine into the sand. He stomped back to the car, several opportunists ran to claim the metal detector.

CHAPTER 66

The US Mail jeep idled up to the driveway and killed its engine. The lanky postman climbed out and walked the package up to the front door and rang the bell. Waited...

"Millie!" he shouted. "It's Elmore. Got a box for you!"

The door remained closed. The postman walked around the side of the house. In the back yard, Millie and a neighbor girl were stooped over a flower box. Millie was humming to herself and deeply involved in assisting with the planting of fall bulbs before the weather turned. Neither one of them heard the postman walk up.

"Hello, you two."

"Why Elmore," Millie replied cheerfully. "Why didn't you say something?"

"Got a delivery here."

Millie stood up straight and wiped the dirt from her hands on her flower-printed dress.

"Millie, I've gotta go now anyway. I've got homework to do."

Millie reached out and stroked the girl's hair. "Okay, honey. Thank you for your help."

"I'll stop by tomorrow and water 'em." The girl kissed Millie's cheek and scampered away. The postman watched her run across the grass. Millie's sun bonnet had tilted sideways on her head and the postman stepped forward and straightened it for her.

"So you have something for me, Elmore?" Millie reached out and touched the postman's hand.

"It's pretty heavy so I left it on the front porch. I'll walk you up so you can sign for it."

When they reached the porch, Millie examined the box.

"I'm sorry about the return address. It's garbled. Can't read it. Looks like the state is OK, or OR, or OH. Know anyone in Oklahoma?"

Millie thought it over carefully. "No, Elmore. Would you like a glass of ice tea?"

"That'd be fine, Millie."

"Then come on in. And would you be kind enough to bring the box inside for me?"

Later that night, after Millie had cleared her evening dishes, she sat down in front of the t.v. and examined the box. She took her time savoring the moment, unwrapping the brown wrapper and cutting the top open with a paring knife.

She opened the two flaps and reached inside and felt the hard cold objects. Coins, she figured. Hundreds of them. She searched through and beneath them until she found the letter. She pulled it out and unfolded it. It was in Braille. She read it over several times as her tears soaked the paper. Then squaring her shoulders, she walked resolutely toward the bathroom and flushed it away.

When she returned to her chair, she reached inside the box and removed one of the coins. She cradled it in her lap until she fell asleep.

That night, she dreamed about her brother...

CHAPTER 67

Vu put his road map down on the front seat and stared out the windshield. Beyond the haze of late afternoon dust was a majestic ocean stretching for miles until eventually dissipating into a horizon of glass. A shimmering lake of light. Vu stretched out his sore muscles and removed his glasses and secured them in the glovebox. He pulled out a weathered Powerbar and bit into the stale, thick chocolate dough.

He felt like a man of the road. Willy Nelson sang on the radio and he was calm inside. His Ford pickup was loaded to the hilt. All his worldly possessions in cardboard boxes sandwiched in between an Italian motorbike with a fresh coat of wax.

This would be as good as any spot. He reached behind the seat and pulled out a duffel bag. He removed two new vials of green pills and pulled out a small cooler from the bed of the truck.

Vu walked down onto the deserted beach. The sun was high and hot. Its bright splintering light stung Vu's eyes. He put on his sunglasses. He sat down in the sand and peeled off his shoes and socks. He opened the cooler and removed an iced Heineken and faced the sea. Its miles of open space gave him a sense of calmness he had not felt in a very long time. He popped the beer and drank deeply.

Somewhere out there he wanted to believe a lone soldier was enjoying the sunshine of Palm Beach with a lonely business woman from the Midwest. Two souls that matched up in the land of the Voodoo Queen. Not unlike he and his Betty. At some point during the investigation he had realized Lyman and he were alike. Two men with jaded pasts facing two different wars where neither was expected to survive. Yet they did. Who found unexpected happiness at the edge of despair.

It felt awkward but he was happy. Lyman was still officially MIA. The government had never known what to do with men like Lyman – soldiers who knew too much, possessed deadly skills and had the ability to survive in the asphalt jungle. How many men like Lyman had infiltrated society secretly, putting the screw in the bureaucratic bubble that smothers us all from time to time?

Vu drank his beer and stared out at the miles of ancient rock that lined the shore.

He hadn't coughed in two weeks. He felt the symbolism. Something was definitely off his chest.

Vu looked down at his vial of pills and he thought of Betty – the best medicine he had ever found for what ailed him. The human heart was always a mystery.

He closed his hand around them, gripped them tightly and raised them overhead. He paused. The pills meant more than just glass and chemicals. Then with a gleeful smile he heaved them into the sea and watched the tide float them away.

Vu polished off his beer, tossed the empty into the cooler and walked back up to his truck, spooking a stray rabbit. He watched as it scurried for shelter behind a strand of scrub grass.

All life struggles to survive, he mused, *But am I the rabbit or the grass? Who knows?* Then laughing to himself, he proclaimed out loud, "Who cares?"

Vu turned the truck toward New Orleans.

THE END

Printed in the United States
18592LVS00006B/172-201